W9-AXR-606

"Bill Dare's comedy credentials are impeccable . . .
This is classic romantic comedy in which the gags
come thick and fast."

—*Daily Mirror* (London)

"Painfully true, and totally hilarious."

—Hattie Hayridge

"Endearing."

—*The Guardian* (Manchester)

"Dare's debut novel has you in hysterics . . .
Extremely witty."

—*OK!*

"Funny and sad . . . I recommend that you buy this book."

—John O'Farrell, author of *This Is Your Life*

"Brilliantly funny."

—*Heat*

NATURAL SELECTION

Bill Dare

BERKLEY BOOKS, NEW YORK

THE BERKLEY PUBLISHING GROUP
Published by the Penguin Group
Penguin Group (USA) Inc.
375 Hudson Street, New York, New York 10014, USA
Penguin Group (Canada), 90 Eglinton Avenue East, Suite 700, Toronto, Ontario M4P 2Y3, Canada
(a division of Pearson Penguin Canada Inc.)
Penguin Books Ltd., 80 Strand, London WC2R 0RL, England
Penguin Group Ireland, 25 St. Stephen's Green, Dublin 2, Ireland (a division of Penguin Books Ltd.)
Penguin Group (Australia), 250 Camberwell Road, Camberwell, Victoria 3124, Australia
(a division of Pearson Australia Group Pty. Ltd.)
Penguin Books India Pvt. Ltd., 11 Community Centre, Panchsheel Park, New Delhi—110 017, India
Penguin Group (NZ), Cnr. Airborne and Rosedale Roads, Albany, Auckland 1310, New Zealand
(a division of Pearson New Zealand Ltd.)
Penguin Books (South Africa) (Pty.) Ltd., 24 Sturdee Avenue, Rosebank, Johannesburg 2196,
South Africa

Penguin Books Ltd., Registered Offices: 80 Strand, London WC2R 0RL, England

This is a work of fiction. Names, characters, places, and incidents either are the product of the author's imagination or are used fictitiously, and any resemblance to actual persons, living or dead, business establishments, events, or locales is entirely coincidental. The publisher does not have any control over and does not assume any responsibility for author or third-party websites or their content.

Copyright © 2003 by Bill Dare.
Cover design by Monica Benalcazar.
Cover photo: Red Brassiere © Tom Schierlitz / Getty Images.

All rights reserved.
No part of this book may be reproduced, scanned, or distributed in any printed or electronic form without permission. Please do not participate in or encourage piracy of copyrighted materials in violation of the author's rights. Purchase only authorized editions.
BERKLEY is a registered trademark of Penguin Group (USA) Inc.
The "B" design is a trademark belonging to Penguin Group (USA) Inc.

PRINTING HISTORY
First published in Great Britain by Judy Piatkus (Publishers) Ltd.
Berkley trade paperback edition / April 2006

Library of Congress Cataloging-in-Publication Data

Dare, Bill.
    Natural selection / Bill Dare.—Berkley trade pbk. ed.
      p.   cm.
    ISBN 0-425-20883-4 (trade pbk.)
      1. Best friends—England—London—Fiction. I. Title.

PR6104.A833N38 2006
813'.6—dc22
                                                              2005057129

PRINTED IN THE UNITED STATES OF AMERICA

10   9   8   7   6   5   4   3   2   1

To Lisa Whadcock, who opened the door and pushed me through it.

ACKNOWLEDGMENTS

Without the support of Gillian Green and everyone at Piat-kus, and especially the tireless feedback from my agent Lisa Whadcock, I would be one of the many people who are "going to write a novel one day." I'm also grateful to everyone at Jonathan Clowes Ltd., especially Chloe and Isobel for their encouragement in the early days.

After two hours of precious light, the sun begins to set on the Arctic seas. Wind blows surf onto the sharp granite rocks. Two walruses fight for the females they desire. There is blood on both beasts, but all of it comes from the same wound—a lesion four inches below a left tusk. The wounded walrus gives the signal of defeat, a repeated bow, and shuffles away, never to show his fangs on that patch of cold granite again. He is saved by an instinct for self-preservation. Somewhere in his dimly lit brain, the odds of winning and losing were weighed up.

It is rare in the animal kingdom for males to fight to the death for the female they desire. Indeed, it is usual for the lesser male to give way gracefully. He will mate with other females, ensuring his genes, though weaker, are passed on.

But first he must get out alive.

From *Darwin's Kiss* by William B. Habbard

ONE

This is the story of what happened when Victoria met Stefan. At least, that's what set things off. I have no idea whether the Victoria/Stefan story will be happy or sad because it isn't over yet. I suppose by the end, someone will get what they want or lose it forever. That's what an ending is, isn't it? Someone getting what they want or losing it forever. Maybe I can make an ending happen, I'll try. After all, I made the beginning happen. It was me who brought them together.

Stefan and Victoria.

Stefan I consider to be damn near perfect—mostly because he is pretty much the opposite of me. And Victoria . . . well, Victoria . . . how shall I put this? Victoria is a kind, interesting, attractive, funny, slightly nutty girl in a going-nowhere relationship. Fair? I think so.

I know Stefan is right for Victoria. Not just "right for" in the sense of being suitable, correct, someone her parents will be proud to show off to other parents in order to make them jealous.

I mean I know he'll excite and thrill her. He'll make her laugh, share thoughts that will set her mind racing, and they'll spend precious hours just walking on Primrose Hill telling each other how lucky they are. He will touch her, and she will say, "No one has touched me like that before," and it'll actually be true. She will say, "I love you," without thinking, *Do I mean that? Or am I just saying it because it's what I want to feel?* And he will say, "I love you," without thinking, *Am I good enough for her? Does she really love me? Is it just because she doesn't know me? When will she find me out?* No, Stefan will say, "I love you, Victoria," with a clear, full, beating heart, and none of those questions in his head. And he will hear her say, "I love you, Stefan," and believe it. I am certain of this. Sometimes you just know.

Take Tim and Barbara at college. I knew what made her laugh and I knew that he had that stuff in skips—and vice versa, come to think of it. They hardly notice each other the whole first term. But I watch and I wait. With names like *Timothy* and *Barbara* how could sparks *not* fly? I invite them both for a drink in a roundabout kind of way, nothing obvious. They meet. I watch from the bar with some mates. "See those two? Watch them for a minute. You see what's happening? They're falling in love. A story is about to begin." By the age of twenty-five, Timothy and Barbara were living in a leafy suburb with a bunch of kids.

I had the idea that Stefan and Victoria should get together while sitting at the Moon and Sixpence on Wardour Street. There I was, pouring a bottle of Newcastle Brown into a tall glass, and I just get the feeling that the time is right. Tonight, lives are going to change. (Well, I was right about *that*.)

I'm with Gerard, Charlotte, and Stefan.

Gerard, who's making a bivouac out of beer mats, is my gently psychopathic friend and colleague. Together we are going to be game-show millionaires.

Charlotte, an occupational therapist (unemployed), is trying to find her glasses in her handbag. I've known her since we shared bouts of depression together at college. She is one of the people who you know will be at your funeral if you don't go to theirs first. At least, that's what I thought then.

Stefan's over at the bar selecting a bottle of wine with the barmaid, who seems impressed by his choice. I haven't seen him for two years. He'd just landed some funding to direct his first proper low-budget film. He asked me if I wanted to get involved. I said I couldn't because I was just starting out in the game-show business. There were some other reasons I didn't go into. Like, I didn't want to end up being Stefan's sidekick. I didn't want to go back to that time when I compared myself to him—which was like comparing Syd Little to Lenny Bruce.

The other reason was that I'd just started going out with a wonderful, wonderful girl. I had the feeling that Stefan could click his slender fingers and any girl would come running. Even mine.

But now the boy is back. Lots of catching up, lots of being impressed by Stefan and lots of Stefan trying to seem interested and encouraging about us, yet not patronizing. It's a thin line, but he walks it well.

He asks Gerard and me how the game-show business is going. I tell him it isn't, we're on the outside, still haven't got that million-pound idea. In fact, we still haven't got *any* idea. Stefan thinks game shows "can be great" and we are "very creative" so we ought to be able to "crack it in no time." He then realizes he has made a small error. To suggest we can "crack it in no time," is to say that it's a simple thing, like a knack, or passing your driving test. That's belittling, and Stefan only belittles intentionally. So he starts building up game shows by saying something intellectual about them. "There's a universal need to see others in jeopardy, and game shows have a catharsis and a classical dramatic structure, and even a moral dimension." Sure, like we didn't know, but hey, the man has feigned interest really well. He even pretends to be jealous of Charlotte (which takes some doing) because she has a house and is getting married and planning a family. "I'm so jealous," he says. Like hell.

But he's good, the man is good. He makes people like him and, more importantly, he makes people like themselves.

But not me.

Especially not tonight.

"Are you feeling ok, James?" is what I've been getting all evening.

"Fine."

But I'm not feeling fine. I haven't been my own biggest fan for quite a while. Not since I gave up my job at a photocopy Internet place called Print Stop so I could devise hit TV game shows with Gerard there (who is now folding a chip packet into the smallest shape possible and is banging it to make it tinier, and people are beginning to stare). You see, I made the big gamble and I seem to be losing. I'm at that stage of roulette when you get so low you just think your luck *has* to change. It *has* to, it *must,* or there's no justice in the universe. Then you change your last tenner and lose it. And then it really hits you that *there is no justice in the universe.* And why should there be? In the words of Albert Einstein. God doesn't play dice. Why should there be any justice in the motion of a ball or the workings of the human heart?

While the others are being entertained by one of Stefan's brilliant anecdotes, I text Victoria:

drink? usual place

She's working as a production secretary just a block away. Let's make the sparks fly. Let's get Cupid shooting his bow and arrow.

Victoria won't be disappointed. She's always liked clever guys and Stefan is clever—and he's learned how to use his cleverness to make himself successful. (That is not a trick I've managed to pull off. My talent, such as it is, sits around on park benches smoking and throwing stones in the pond. It's doing me no good at all. I am the sort of bloke of whom people say, "He was a really clever bloke . . . what *happened?*") Stefan has harnessed his ability, given it some very good PR, a proper contract of employment and made it work for him. I swear the man *shines* with success, it precedes him into the room, it announces his arrival. And let's face it, success makes a man more attractive. Isn't that the point of it? Well, if there's another point, I'd like to know what it is.

Stefan has a great future ahead of him. There's nothing more attractive than potential. Alluring because it is mysterious, youthful. (Ever met an *old* bloke with potential?) It points to stuff that hasn't happened yet, stuff that's unspoiled by reality. (I was a Man With Potential once. But somewhere there's a line you cross in the dead of night, and you go from being a Man With Potential to that bloke-who-seemed-to-have-potential-but-I-wonder-what-happened? I can't see that line—maybe because I'm standing on it.) And people actually think Stefan is interesting, brave, innovative. Dangerous, even.

But is he sexy?

That's pretty key to the whole thing, isn't it? I mean it's pretty much The Thing when you choose one person over another.

Sexiness is where I come unstuck when it comes to men. I can't tell if a man is sexy, and I have tried, believe me. (Well, it helps with potential predators. If you don't know who's sexy you can't chase them away with the big stick.) Yes, through many years of practice, I have learned to sort out very good-looking blokes from the ones that look like Phil Mitchell out of *EastEnders*. I kept asking my first girlfriend, "Is he good-looking?" every time a bloke walked past. I got the answers: *yes, no, maybe, kind of, oh God no, please stop asking me*. Eventually I memorized the kind of shapes and facial structures needed for a man's looks to be called "good." But looks are only part of the story. I was twenty-five when I discovered, to my alarm, that ugly blokes can be sexy. Ugly blokes can be *sexy*? Say that again. *Ugly* blokes, the Phil Mitchells, the Andrew Lloyd Webbers, the Clive Jameses of this gender, can be sexy?

That was a humdinger. Not only should I chase away the beauties, but also the beasts.

But not even women agree about who's sexy and who isn't. The number of times a girl has told me that she finds so-and-so on the telly sexy and I have gone, "But he's not even good-looking," and she says, "I didn't say good-looking, I said sexy."

"What makes him sexy?"

"Well, he's got sweet eyes—but he's, I don't know, kind of melancholy—no—he's, well, got mmmm, you know, it's difficult, I think he's cheeky. That's it. But also strong. Yes—I think it's just his strength. I think he comes across as very strong. He's almost sort of ugly but there's something about...I mean, he's clearly clever. Really bright and somehow moral. Actually it's his hair."

There are no rules. No pattern, no way of predicting. As far as being sexy is concerned, men are in the lap of the gods.

But there's one man who I think...yeah. If I were a girl, I

reckon I'd fancy him all right. Yes, Stefan just seems to have it. The stuff with no name, no price. The stuff that, if you ever try to grasp it, will only make you look ridiculous. (Men trying to be sexy are inherently ridiculous, which is why male strippers are just funny.)

And I know this in my bones, not my head. I have spent years watching him. Watching, learning, being jealous, feeling uncomfortable but somehow needing it. Jealousy is useful. It's a great motivator. Without envy I would have accomplished even less than I have. Maybe that goes for the whole human race, too. (This book is written partly out of a jealous frenzy. It might turn out to be some kind of reckoning.)

My phone rings, I move toward the bar. The others don't notice. Maybe that's because I've hardly said a word all night—and why should I? We are in the presence of a master communicator; my voice would only bore.

"Not sure I can come—a lot of paperwork's piling up."

"Oh come on, Victoria—Gerard and Stefan are here."

"Your director friend?"

The same. Arty film directors are right up her alley. In fact, from everything I know about Victoria's previous record in the men department (and I know a lot), Stefan is going to be her idea of perfection.

"But I still feel a bit hung over. Do you mind if I give this a miss?"

"And miss meeting the sexiest man in the world?"

"Oh yes, so you said."

How could she forget?

"But it has to be an early night for me."

She says she'll finish typing a camera script, grab a low-fat sandwich from Pret, and see us there.

A gale of laughter blows from our table. Another successfully executed story. Stefan was the kind of kid who, when everyone had to read a bit of a book aloud, say, *Sons and Lovers*, would do it *with feeling*. But the weird thing is that no one beat him up afterward. But then, out of all of us, Stefan knew the most about being a lover.

That, I suppose, was the key to it. When Stefan arrived at Taunton School for Boys as a third-year, it became widely known that he had a Girlfriend. A Girlfriend who not only had the great advantage of *existing*—unlike most "girlfriends"—but who was pretty, willowy, a year older than us and who had been spotted snogging him at the school gates. Not so unusual you might think, but for form 3B in 1983, just having a Girlfriend of any age or type was unique. A Girlfriend as status symbol was worth ten goals, or three fights in the playground or any number of designer-label sports bags.

Stefan's now talking about a book, I think. I'm not sure, I haven't been listening, I'm too distracted. But it must be fascinating because even Gerard, normally enclosed in his own weird world, has abandoned his crisp packet and is paying attention.

I look up and there she is, coming through the door. The only girl who can be graceful and awkward at the same time. Oh, he'll like her, for sure. She hugs and kisses the assembled crew and there's an instant connection between Victoria and Stefan that would be too cute for Hollywood.

I knew it.

Everything is going to plan. Stefan says something to Victoria, I don't catch it, but it makes her laugh.

Inevitably.

She sits next to him.

Inevitably.

He conjures a glass from nowhere and is pouring wine from the bottle he ordered.

Inevitably.

They say, "Cheers."

Inevitably.

And so a story is about to begin. This story. Tonight two people will fall in love. (They don't know it yet, but they will.) Victoria will get out of that going-nowhere relationship.

And I will be alone again.

Sailing this ship along. Or will I try to find someone else? Or wait for my girl to come back? Or binge on other women? Or fight for her like a walrus? Or surprise myself by not missing her nearly as much as I think?

Or just cry forever.

TWO

This book is less of a whodunnit and more of a why-did-I-do-it. Why did I set up my own girl with another man? Obviously I'm not going to tell you. First, it would give things away a bit, and the only thing I'm prepared to say at this stage is that this story won't end with a wedding because I don't want it to be that kind of book. Second, I don't entirely know. Not knowing why you've done something is not unusual. Look at Hillary, the first man to climb Mount Everest. I'm sorry but "because it's there" isn't good enough. I like to imagine Hillary trekking along the Himalayas one day. He spots a mountain in the distance. He proclaims, "Gosh. What a wonderful sight. Please, gather round and bear witness, for I now declare that one day I shall conquer that mountain and put a flag upon its summit." Then someone whispers in his ear, "But Mr. Hillary, it's the highest, most dangerous mountain in the whole world."

"Really? Oh *shit*." Hillary throws his pick on the ground. "Bloody brilliant—I *would* have to pick the hard one."

But this is pretty much the opposite of what happened. Hillary chose Everest *because* it was the highest, most dangerous mountain, and the one *most likely to kill him*. And all he can think of saying is, "Because it's there." A more honest answer might have been, "Because it might kill me." Funnily enough, "Because it might kill me" is the exact same answer I always give to people who ask why I *haven't* climbed Mount Everest.

So where does that leave us?

It leaves us with the conclusion that a lot of people have no idea why they're doing what they're doing, even when what they're doing might kill them. Do you know why you're reading this? I rest my case. (By the way, it's not the biggest or most dangerous book in the world and it won't kill you unless you are already prone to depression.)

But let's try to discover what factors led to my strange behavior. Let's sift through the evidence, examine the clues and interrogate a few suspects.

I first meet the girl in question in 1992. A coffee bar at London University. I am sitting alone, pretending to read an interesting, arty kind of novel (it's the one that begins with someone's mother dying today—or was it yesterday?). I stub out my Silk Cut on a tiny ashtray made of tinfoil, and wonder, for the millionth time, how I ended up studying biology. Oh, I know why I ended up studying biology really, of course I do. It was basically Stefan's idea. He thought that we should both do science degrees, for although we might end up as artists of some kind one day it was important to have a "different discipline" under your belt, otherwise you would become "inward-looking." Also, my dad, being a beekeeper by trade, has always had a liking for the natural world that he has tried to instill in me, with mixed results.

I was genuinely interested in biology for a while. Especially the evolutionary stuff. What makes one species survive and another perish? What separates the winners from the losers? Why are certain individuals better at attracting a mate? I am fascinated by the fact that every species on earth has an equivalent to asking some-one in for a coffee. For the blowfly it's a persistent humming noise made with its leg, for the reindeer it's having a powerful pair of horns, and for the dung beetle it's, well, dung. These are all ways of turning the lights down low and shuffling up on the sofa. (Evolution could be the ultimate reality game show. Sex, violence, perma-nent extinction——it's the best show in the cosmos.)

Trouble is, biology may be fascinating but biologists are not. I stopped being fascinated by the mysterious world of biology as soon as I began meeting other people who were fascinated by the mysterious world of biology. It was during a sleepy afternoon lecture on reptilian respiratory systems that I realized that, 1) I would never fall in love with a girl who wanted to dissect lizards, 2) I would never fall for a girl who would fall for a boy who wanted to dissect lizards. I realized that the only mating ritual I cared about now was the human one, and I could pretty much narrow that down to one human in particular. I simply came to the conclusion, after looking round at the faces watching the diagram of an adder's lung, that the clichés are true (aren't they always?): all science students are dull, nerdish and im-mature. All art students are interesting, unpredictable, stylish, full of irony and knowingness. They don't laugh——they smile, stroke their chins, and let out the oc-casional snicker at the expense of someone or something crass or naive.

They swank.

They smoke and aren't bothered by the effect it has on those little things in your lungs that are too small to see, and that I'm glad I've forgotten the name of (those things are for scientists to care about). Art students don't "discover" drugs, they borrow them from their parents. They hug each other and sit around in unisex groups. They miss lectures and have sex all day long. They also have friends who are girls, who they don't try to sleep with because they really are "just friends." They have rich parents, which is why they can afford to study subjects for which there is no known point. They have albums by Iggy Pop and Velvet Underground——and my sources inform me that it's exactly the same now, and probably was a de-cade before I became a student. Any other band you care to mention is passé and uncool, whoever they are. Art students wear clothes that you can't buy at Next or

Gap. Where do their clothes come from? Somewhere obscure that has just closed down. They find obscure shops that are about to fold and buy up all the gear so no science students can get at it. They have nervous breakdowns and other cool psychological "problems." They are a pretentious bunch of time-wasters and freeloading poseurs.

And I want to join them.

Why?

Because they talk about interesting things such as Human Beings (rather than computers and cars and football teams and electronic organizers). Also, let's face it, arts faculties have better-looking girls. So I decide that I must become some kind of creative artist-type person. There is no course called "creative artist-type personology" but if there were, it would be oversubscribed. But at the moment I am an artist trapped in a scientist's body. I can't even wear a disguise because the obscure shop that sells the clothes has just closed down.

Take the Film Unit—which is a club for students who want to be Orson Welles. Everyone in the little Film Unit assumes, from the very first meeting, that I want to do something with lighting or special effects because I have "science student" written on my forehead. Anything truly artistic such as acting, writing or directing would be handled by a student with clothes from somewhere obscure that had just closed down. So this parochial, country-bumpkin Science Student is put in charge of Helping the Lighting Designer. Great. Lighting design seems like the dullest thing in the world. I know nothing about it, but how can moving some lights around be fun? If it was fun, people would do it at home. They would get some lamps, invite their friends round and have lamp-moving parties.

I didn't say this, of course, I just said that I would do my best to make time between lectures to help out any way I could. (The film, I gather, is a ten-minute subversive satire about a wounded soldier in the Gulf War and his relationship with a British nurse who helps him heal—but in an incredibly profound way: she heals him spiritually as well as physically. Get it? Apparently, it has been written by someone recently returned from the Gulf.)

Giles, the "executive producer," seems about ten years older than his twenty-two

*years and keeps bumming my supply of Silkies. He takes a shine to me when he dis-
covers I come from near Taunton in Somerset. "Taunton? As in the cider . . . ? Nice
one," were his words. I think he thinks I must be slightly working-class or "street,"
but Taunton is about as middle England as you can get. I am to meet the lighting
designer "in due course," says Giles.*

*Three days later and there is no word about the film. I am still an Outsider, an
awkward young man, a less good-looking version of Morrissey—if you can imagine
him wearing clothes from Gap, I'm coffee-barring my way through college, unwill-
ing to mix with the biologists who were beginning to bore me to the point of almost
joining the chess club.*

*Picture me in the coffee bar, pretending to drink from a cup that I'd drained
twenty minutes ago. How long can a man pretend to read a book and drink coffee,
hoping that some beautiful, arty type will talk to him for no reason at all? I normally stick to an hour. I close the book, and look around for someone to:*

> *think about smiling at*
> *wonder if I dare*
> *decide that I don't dare this time*
> *but definitely will next time I see her.*

*That's my usual routine. Just as I'm about to give up hope, Giles, "the execu-
tive producer," enters—nay, wafts and swanks—into the coffee bar with an entou-
rage of bohemians-in-rapture.*

*Giles and his disciples sit down while one of them goes to the self-service coun-
ter (arty types offer to buy a round of coffee for the group, Science students line up
together like kids for school dinners). I glance over at Giles, expecting a nod or a
wave back at the very most, but he beckons me over with great enthusiasm, like I'm
the person he most wants to see in the whole wide London-University-art-student-
film world. I can't quite believe it and I look behind me to check he isn't gesturing
to someone else. I can feel myself going all red, tongue-tied and foolish. It's as if
foolishness is a cloud that wafts around and descends upon me without warning.*

I get up and trundle over, trying not to bump into anything. I am being summoned to the Other Side and am about to be offered a place at the table. When I arrive I find that Giles is holding forth and does not greet me. Instead, he puts his hand on my arm. Of course something inside me thinks "poof," but I am now entering a different culture and I must change. I rest my hand on his shoulder as unhomophobically as I can. (I do this with all the ease of those coppers you see trying to look like they're having fun at the Gay Pride march.) But Giles is still holding forth and seems to want me to stand there until he has finished making his point. I feel like a lemon, but I can't leave unless I physically remove his hand from my arm. Eventually his point is made and the whole group nods in agreement. He releases his grip and addresses me.

"Sorry, James—I'm a real pain, but do you have a smoke?"

I fumble for my pack of Silkies, wondering if they're considered a trendy brand by these movers and shakers. Giles grabs the pack.

"I'm going to be extremely rude, my friend, and stow one for later. I'm quite impecunious these days." Huh?

He places a Silkie behind his ear like some milkman out of a seventies sitcom. He turns back to the group because he has another very, very important point.

Excuse me, is that it?

Am I to go now? Have I been summoned all the way from the far table to provide some smokes?

Oh no you don't, pal. I am taking a seat and joining in. So I take the empty chair and pretend to ignore the momentary flurry of unease among the Chosen Ones.

"This is James, everyone, from Devon." *I don't correct him.* "He's going to be the lighting designer. Aren't you?"

Christ, I thought I was just going to help with a bit of fetching and carrying. I smile my nervous half smile and everyone introduces themselves to me with their confident full smile. I sense they all think, science student, bless.

I make myself look interesting. I do this by narrowing my eyes slightly while people are talking—it makes them think I have a shrewd idea about something.

This can backfire when they ask what's on my mind because invariably nothing is, and I have to say that narrowing my eyes helps moisten my contact lenses. (This book is full of great tips.) Giles takes one of the Silkies and breaks the filter off. "It's like smoking fresh air otherwise." Then he puts the cigarette in his mouth and moves his head slightly toward me. Does he really expect me to light his cigarette with this merest of gestures? No "please"? No words at all? I worry about my hands shaking. (No, really, I was incredibly nervous in those days. I was not the cool, confident customer you see before you now.) The worry about my hands shaking is, of course, the cue for my hands to shake.

It's as if they said to each other, "He's worried we might shake."

"Better start shaking, then."

I pretend my lighter's not working to gather my nerves for a moment. Then I flick on the lighter and use both hands, which must look a little odd. Giles nods a thank-you as he continues on some detail about "the shoot." Pathetically enough, I actually feel in some way honored to have been of service. The executive producer is smoking one of my cigarettes, that I lit, and it's going well, it's still alight, he isn't complaining or snickering or muttering that it tastes parochial or crass. Result.

And then it happens.

Out of the blue—right in the middle of a cloud of foolishness—I have my one-and-only Mills & Boon moment. I say "moment" but I think it is really a period of six seconds that it took me to fall in love with her. (That may sound like romantic twaddle to you, but ten years later, nothing much has changed.) What strikes me is that she looks both beautiful and funny at the same time and I have never seen that before and it deserves pause.

You see, Victoria . . . she has a face that divides opinion (it's ok everyone, Victoria knows this is what I think, and she's fine about it). Some people say she is a "natural beauty," while others say she is "pretty in a quirky kind of way." Now, for my money, that's the best kind of beauty. An unalloyed beauty, devoid of character, is fine for the glossy magazines, but you wouldn't want it in real life. (Gosh, the number of times I have had to turn women down because they're too beautiful you wouldn't believe.) But there's another theory about Victoria's appearance that goes like this: she is a natural beauty in repose, but when she speaks, she is so ani-mated, so full of life and humor that her silent beauty, her glossy-magazine beauty, is sacrificed at the altar of being funny, interesting, and a little bit crazy.

Victoria, don't ever change.

I watch, riveted, as this beauty begins to speak. She's doing the faces, voices and gestures of tutors, lecturers and fellow students that they all know. Everyone laughs. The impressions are cruelly accurate—somehow I can tell that without ever having met the victims.

I'm mesmerized by her willingness to make herself look ridiculous for the sake of a laugh. At the end of her story, I say to myself that one day I will go out with her, we will fall in love, perhaps spend our lives together. I also say to myself that this is ludicrous, and that I shouldn't indulge in that kind of romantic twaddle, even in the privacy of my own head.

But hey, sometimes you just know.

"Have you done any lighting before?" she asks, after the attention of the clique has shifted back to Giles. Cue James Hole saying his first-ever words to the girl he has just fallen in love with. This is the moment: choose your words carefully, friend.

"No."

Not a bad word. No is quite a good word as far as it goes. It's concise, decisive, and no one could accuse it of pretension. But something is missing; what can it be? Oh yes—other words. I try to add something to this word, this naked syllable, but it simply lingers, frozen in the air between us. She nods and waits. Oh, come on! One bloody syllable—is that all you can manage? Look at her! She's waiting for more! But my self-flagellation only hinders the process of actually thinking of some-thing to say about lighting. Syllable, go forth and multiply!

"No. Not at all, actually. Nope. Never done it before." Come on, James! "But . . . it's something I've always been interested in. I always notice the lighting when I watch a film." And thus my entire conversation about lighting is exhausted. I have nothing to add. My head almost hurts with emptiness. She asks a question.

"What's up? Have you just had an idea?"

"Oh . . . no. I, um, I'm keeping my contact lenses moist."

She looks at me quizzically. Then I realize that on this particular day I am wearing glasses. I thought glasses might enhance my man-with-book image. Will she draw attention to this predicament or let it lie? Suddenly I'm rescued by my old pal Blatant Honesty. (A handy fellow when old pal Pretension lets you down.)

"Actually, I was narrowing my eyes to make myself look interesting."

She smiles approvingly.

"It's very, very convincing. I did find you fascinating for that brief moment. Do you do any other faces?"

"I do 'embarrassed' quite well. Sometimes without even trying. Do that face again—the one you were doing a minute ago."

"This one?" She puffs up her cheeks and crosses her eyes and, if you can imagine someone doing the splits using only their facial muscles, you'll get an idea. I laugh. (Trust me, it was funny.) She pulls a few more idiotic faces for me, which I try to copy. We start adding various equally stupid noises that get louder and louder and it's not long before we have a small audience of rather cool coffee-drinkers looking at two of the least cool people ever. But we carry on, partially to amuse ourselves and partially, I think, because it seems, in a very small way, subversive. All right, in a very, very, very small way, subversive. Some time goes by (I have no idea how much) and the coffee bar goes quiet. I close my eyes and do my Albert Steptoe. I get quite carried away. When I open my eyes, Victoria has stopped and looks more serious. I sense, without looking round, that I am being watched, and that I'm not exactly storming it. But if I stop now, I will be acknowledging my embarrassment so I carry on, but with greater gusto. There is no going back, I am in this thing too deep. I must make it as confident and large as possible. I try to drown out the terrifying silence with ever-louder Steptoe-isms. My only thoughts are about how this shameful performance will end. Will someone slap me? Will they call security? Should I suddenly run out of the coffee bar—and even out of London—or even the Western world—and never come back?

"What's going on, friend?" asks Giles. This comes as a relief. At last I have an excuse to stop.

"Just doing some impressions."

"As in, Steptoe?"

"Yes."

"How idiosyncratic of you."

"Thanks."

"It was an observation, not a compliment."

"Thanks for the observation."

And slowly the chattering classes resume doing what they do best. Victoria squeezes my arm briefly and the embarrassment almost seems worth it. I think this is the most fun and pain I've had since losing my virginity.

YOU: *So you ask her out.*

ME: *You'd have thought so, wouldn't you? No, we became best mates.*

YOU: *But eventually you get together.*

ME: *Eventually is the operative word.*

YOU: *Took you a month or two.*

ME: *Oh, sure.*

YOU: *A year?*

ME: *Much more.*

YOU: *Several years? This is beginning to look sad.*

ME: *Actually, seven. No, it's actually more like eight.*

YOU: *Eight years of being friends with someone you're in love with? That's tragic. I thought this was going to be a "light read."*

ME: *Look, do we have to go into this?*

YOU: *There's not much point in writing a book about something you'd rather not go into, is there? It wouldn't have got Hanif Kureishi very far, would it?*

ME: *I suppose I didn't feel ready for her and thought she didn't feel ready for me. Also various things happened at the start that got us off on all the wrong feet.*

YOU: *For example?*

ME: *For example . . .*

On the Wednesday after the coffee-bar performance I see Victoria at the "shoot." She is playing the blind nurse in the Red Cross helping Marines who've been wounded in their fight to liberate Kuwait. Now, how a nurse can do her job when she can't see where to put the needle is never explained—maybe it will appear in the program notes. And guess what? The blind nurse has a lot of wisdom—she can see things (like bigotry and hate) that other people are blind to. Do you get the irony? Brilliant. The Marines are brought in with severe injuries and what do they get, a nurse who can't see what she's doing who lectures them about how Operation Desert Storm is all about oil not justice, and how the women of Kuwait are enslaved. Not really what you need when you've got a lung full of depleted uranium.

Anyway, I am far more interested in watching the lovely Victoria than humping around bloody great lamps at the behest of a short-tempered little Welsh director (if Poland ever wants invading again I know just the chap).

Giles, who has been wafting around importantly all day, though not apparently doing anything, finally says, "That's a wrap" and I know this means it's the end of the shoot because I watched the same Blue Peter program about films that he did.

Almost immediately, Victoria comes up to me and says with a beaming smile, "I wanted to ask you something. You probably think this is . . ."

"What?"

Is that a flirtatious giggle I see before me?

"You probably think I'm . . ." Ah, she's all coy and embarrassed.

"Ask me."

"What are you doing tonight?"

Jesus. I thought she might fancy me a bit but this is ridiculous.

"I'm not doing anything."

"Come plate-spinning with me."

"Plate-spinning?"

The craft of plate-spinning is not one I ever thought I would master or indeed had any inclination to try. But love leads us to strange places, often by the nose.

At 7:30 that night I am sitting in a semicircle of chairs in a Bloomsbury Theatre rehearsal room watching a "performance arts teacher" demonstrate the "traditional turn" of plate-spinning, which dates back to blah, first developed by blah, and is now rarely performed because of blah.

"I'm really glad you can come—I don't like going to this kind of thing on my own, thanks a lot," Victoria had said to me when we met outside the bookshop.

"Not at all. I'm really interested in the circus, actually. I've always been meaning to learn . . . you know . . ."

"You mean you've always wanted to learn plate-spinning?"

"Well . . . kind of." Yeah, right. What an extraordinary coincidence that I just happen to be a frustrated plate-spinner.

The teacher is surprisingly serious for one who, we learn, also teaches the ancient crafts of prat-falling, custard-pie-throwing, and "slapstick for actors." He reprimands a latecomer, "You're not late for any of your other lectures, are you?"

"Sometimes."

"Well don't be late for this one or you won't know what's going on. You can't just buy a book on it and study up, ok?"

"Ok."

He knows that what he is teaching is of little relevance anymore, but feels that it has some integrity, some worth, that needs preserving. If he ever has to make a speech at a graduation ceremony I imagine he would say "science, the arts and plate-spinning—all vital for the lifeblood of a first-class university."

Now it's time for the exercises.

"Ok, we're going to start you off in pairs." Me and Victoria. "Don't rush it—this is not about beating the clock, it's just about getting one plate to spin properly before trying another. You won't get anywhere if you treat it like a game of catch-as-catch-can."

Huh?

"So why are you interested in plate-spinning?" I ask Victoria as I carry my plates to our spinning table.

"Oh, if I do a dissertation I want it to be about traditional entertainment—magic, circus acts, farting tunes and so on. Then I saw this subsidiary course in circus skills."

"Right."

We spin the plates and I have to say we make a good team at first. Victoria spins with total concentration and I load the plates with equal determination. But try as we might, they keep falling off. It's only when I say to her, "So can we do a farting tunes class next time?" that things begin to go right, or not, depending on your point of view. If your point of view is that of a very earnest performance arts teacher then it's where things start to go wrong. We get the giggles and there's no stopping them. We lose concentration, and balancing plates, hard at the best of times, becomes impossible. Plates fall and smash and we are incapable of preventing them. Then our tutor does exactly the wrong thing. He heavily and humorlessly reprimands us.

"You two, I know it's great fun and everything, but those plates do cost twenty pence a throw."

I really try to keep a straight face. I am not trying to take the piss.

"I'm sorry—just the giggles," is what I try to say, but the word giggles is more of a demonstration of the word's meaning than the word itself.

We try to regain control but the minute either of us has to speak the other can hear the laughter in the voice and immediately convulses. The plates go flying.

"Would you please stop clowning around."

This from a teacher of circus skills.

"Next he's going to tell us this isn't a circus."

Well now there was no turning back. Hysteria grips us, and try as we might, we just can't get ourselves free. I bend over in an effort to pick up some unbroken plates and accidentally fart and then we simply give up trying: there is no point, the hysteria has won the day. There is scorn from our fellow pupils and anger from our master, who simply loses it.

"This is willful damage of university property—I will demand that letters are sent to your parents. Now get out of my class."

We grab our things and leave, our heads bowed, looking as ashamed as we *possibly can. We say nothing till we reach the pavement outside, where we both burst out laughing again with relief, with embarrassment and joy all mixed together, and we hug each other—partly as a way of trying to stay upright.*

We begin walking home, and I hardly notice that I am going her way rather than mine.

And we find ourselves arm in arm. There was no premeditation—there was no "move" on my part, it just happened. She tells me this is her road. For once in my life there is no doubt: I know that this is the start of something, I know we will kiss tonight. I don't worry about whether she feels the same—of course she does. I can relax, choose my moment, any moment, I will have a pick of moments. She asks me in for coffee, naturally. That was a fait accompli *long ago. I am basking in the ease of it all.*

We're in her kitchen and she puts the kettle on and says she'll be back in a minute. Alone for a moment, I take the time to let out some of the euphoria that's bubbling up inside me. "You have done it, mate. You have done it. You have fucking well done it." I punch the air, then again rapidly like I am beating a punchbag—the energy just has to go somewhere and this is all I can think of doing. I must look slightly deranged.

"You all right?"

I turn round to find Giles standing in the doorway, wearing a collarless white shirt, his wavy dark hair swept back like some romantic poet. I like to think, I really do love *to think, he had only been standing there for a nanosecond.*

"I was just doing . . . exercises."

"How very idiosyncratic. Must be the water they drink over there in Cornwall. How was the . . ." He mimes plate-spinning.

"Fine. Good. Bit hysterical."

"Where's Vic?"

"Vic? Oh, in the loo I think. I didn't know you two shared a flat."

"Oh yes." As in, I thought everyone knew that.

And in walks Victoria. Can I detect a slight sign of disappointment on her face when she sees Giles?

"Hi, Giles."

"Hello, sweetheart."

They peck each other on the fucking, sodding, fucking lips. Giles's hands slide down her back onto her bottom and give it a good squeeze and he holds them there, just to make sure I've clocked them, and they break off.

I reckon I just stood, looking at Victoria's bottom, and where his hand had been, for a good few seconds, as I try to keep the plates spinning in my mind. The plate that Victoria fancies me looks wobbly. The plate that she's single looks very wobbly. The plate that I am going to make love tonight is about to fall—and—there it goes!

Smash.

"All right?" asks Giles, my rival male. If I were a walrus, a fight would be in the cards. But thousands of years of civilization have mostly put an end to such primitive means of securing a mate. (I say "mostly", but come to Taunton on a Saturday and you might be surprised by the effect a good fight can have on some of the "birds," as we called them. Winning a fight can get you laid. So can losing one.)

I sometimes regret things aren't that simple anymore, given that I could have Giles on the ground and bleeding in about three seconds. I think I want to fight both of them. Victoria was leading me on—she must have known what I was expecting. What was she thinking, walking with her hand round my waist for the last twenty minutes? Plates cascade around me and smash into smithereens.

"Young James here was doing a very strange thing with his fists just now, Vic. Looked like a circus act in itself. And James, you were saying something to the mirror—what was it?"

"Oh, Giles, you're a Peeping Tom."

"In my own kitchen? Impossible. James, you look a bit nervous."

"No." I say as calmly as I can, which is pretty calm, I think.

"A bit tensed up. Something wrong?"

"No, not at all." Still very calm.

"No need to get defensive."

"I'm not." Beginning to get annoyed now.

"Let's not argue, hey?"

"I am not arguing!" Not calm at all.

He taps me on the shoulder. "Cool it, friend."

"He's fine, Giles."

"Thought he seemed a bit hyper."

He moves to tap me on the shoulder again, but I move away. I wish for a moment it was midnight in Taunton town center and we were both sixteen. Giles's condescending little put-downs would do him no good at all. He wouldn't get so much as a chance to swing a punch. God. I could flatten him now. My heart's pumping, my stomach is ready for a blow, my reflexes are tuned to perfection, and I am involuntarily picking out targets on Giles's face.

I am physically and mentally ready for an activity that, far from impressing Victoria, she'd regard as anachronistic, immature, thuggish, pathetic. I have to be on the outside within sixty seconds or things could get ugly.

"I just remembered I'm supposed to meet my girlfriend for a drink."

The word girlfriend is so crudely crowbarred into that sentence it makes me cringe to recall it. But it seems the only way out of them both thinking I was fisting the air because I thought I'd pulled Victoria. Me, a country boy, a beekeeper's son, thought I had pulled Giles's girlfriend. Surely not. How very, very idiosyncratic of me. I'm opening the front door when, wouldn't you know it:

"Oh, just before you go . . . I am definitely going to buy some soon. Honest."

I hand him a couple of Silkies.

Life's a compromise, isn't it?

On the walk home it occurs to me that Giles reminds me of someone. He's a kind of low-grade, cheapo version of Stefan Catchiside. If Victoria fancies this Stefan Lite, then if she ever gets within sexual range of the real thing, her knickers will explode.

The next evening Charlotte comes over to my flat. Charlotte is often over at my flat. (It's a place I share with three miserable male science students with whom I've nothing in common, apart from being miserable, male, and a science student.) Charlotte is reading psychology and is a bit chubby, rather mousy and timid. Like an overweight pet gerbil. She doesn't do herself any favors in the looks department and doesn't have the personality to compensate. She is not totally ignored in social gatherings, but neither can she aspire to the higher level of being noticed by her absence. Few people in her lifetime will ask, "I heard a rumor Charlotte was coming—have you seen her?"

Charlotte seems to fancy one of us flatmates—either miserable Malik from Sri Lanka, or morbid Tu-chi from Singapore, or morose Patrick from Derry, or melancholy me from near Taunton, but none of us care much for Charlotte from Haywards Heath. We've even lost interest in the idle pastime of trying to guess which one of us she fancies. None of us boys knows whose friend she originally was, or how she first came to the flat. Did she follow us all home from the pub one day? No one knows. But she's around so often I once suggested to them that we put her on the inventory when we leave: "Mousy psychology student. Quantity: one. Condition: in need of repair." Maybe she visited this flat before we moved in and hasn't noticed that the people have changed, or doesn't care. It is usually left to me to chat to her in the kitchen because no one else can be bothered.

After a few weeks of this I guess that I'm the one she fancied all along. I notice that when we watch TV she is not watching the TV at all, but me. I have this face looming at me in the corner of my eye watching for my reactions. She laughs when I laugh (which is seldom) and tuts when I tut (which is often). The boys are slightly mystified as to why I spend time with her. But (and if this sounds callous then it probably is) Charlotte has her uses. She is always available, and therefore whenever I want to go to a bar, a gig, or a club, I am guaranteed company. Ok, I'm sometimes embarrassed by her but she's bright enough to chat to and I don't have to make much effort. The downside comes when I'm out trying to "get girls." For a start, girls think she and I are "together" and if I get past that obstacle ("no, she's a flatmate") then there's the problem of what to do with Charlotte while I go out to impress—which, when you're a biology student from Taunton, can take some time. But she's got such a pash for me that she waits around, playing on a game machine, *until I have either pulled, in which case she goes home alone, or not pulled (more likely) and we go home together and she probably hopes I'll "make do" with her.*

Oh, there have been times when I've been drunk enough to think about it. I mean, everyone feels much the same in the dark, but what would I do with her in the morning? No, that's never going to happen.

So I exploit my loveability. Those tender feelings she has, of warmth, lust, love, I use to my advantage. Not proud of it, wouldn't do it now, but I was younger then. And we've all done it.

But tonight this tolerable arrangement changes. I ask Charlotte out for a drink and of course she comes along. I want to tell her of my experience. She is a girl after all, and I can't talk about that kind of thing with my miserable flatmates, who have had one and a half girlfriends between them. I have fallen for someone for the first time since splitting up with my First.

I am in love.

"Second love is such a brilliant feeling, Charlotte. Because now I realize that Amy (my first) isn't unique. I can have those feelings again. Yesterday there was just one person on this planet I ever loved, now there is—or could be—another." Well, I said something like that and yes, it feels a bit over the top now, a little sickening, even, but I'm smitten. "But she seems to be in the thrall of some ponce from the film unit who thinks he's Orson Welles. What do you think—she has her arm round me on the way home but then her boyfriend appears. And what about this—next day there's a note in my mailbox saying thanks for a nice evening: 'Shame you had to run off.' What do you think? Does she want me? Does she want to give Giles the heave-ho? Is she a tease or what?"

Charlotte beams with pleasure but doesn't appear to be taking it in. "I'm really, really pleased for you."

Hel-lo? "But she has a boyfriend."

"It's wonderful news. Fantastic. Wonderful."

The euphoria is beginning to grate—she's more pleased than I am. It's only after her second red wine that she slaps her hands on her lap, takes a deep breath and says that I am a tactless little shit.

"You tactless little shit," she says again.

"Pardon?" I say.

"You tactless little shit," she says.

(Oddly enough, do you know which of her three words slightly offends me? Yup—little. I am six foot one in socks.)

"Why?"

And then comes the wine-over-the-shirt routine. You must have seen it; it was all the rage in the eighties, apparently. It seems to me that some men drink wine, some men throw wine, and some men get wine thrust upon them. I seem to be in the latter camp and I'm not entirely sure why. I am entirely sure about this though: I would rather be in my camp than the other ones. But I am not entirely sure why.

I rescue my packet of Silkies from the liquid that rains onto the table and I ask her what this is all about.

"You tactless little shit. I'm not telling you how I feel. I'm not giving you the satisfaction. You know the effect you have. You can't pretend you don't."

"Know what? I really don't understand what I've said!" Well, one doesn't like to presume.

"You want me to tell you?"

I know what's she's going to say. She is going to make what was tacit (her "love" for me) a declared fact. This fact is something I have been happy to ignore. But if it becomes a verbalized entity, I will have to "deal" with it, talk to it, give it tissues, listen to it, and possibly even hug it, and waste a whole lot of my valuable time.

"You know how I feel, don't you?"

Oh, why doesn't she go and fancy someone else? Someone in her own league? I mean, I may be a science student, a bundle of nerves and not very fashionable, but please, I have standards and as a sixth-former I was considered a pretty good catch. I have been out with one of the most desirable teenagers in Taunton— don't laugh. Charlotte is not very beautiful or very charming. There's no point in evading the issue: if I went out with her people would think I was selling myself short.

"Jamie, Jamie, Jamie, why does it have to be you?"

"You can't choose who to fall in love with. It just happens. And you can't choose who not *to fall for." I say, pulling my sagest face. Then I tell her in no uncertain terms that the feeling is not mutual. I tell her that I do not want to go out with her. (I do not tell her that it's bad enough that people might* think *I go out with her.)*

"I kept thinking you were just a bit too shy to tell me how you felt. But you keep giving me signals."

Oh, right. So I have been giving you subtle indications of my passion——such as, falling asleep while you are talking to me (twice) and going to my room (alone) five minutes after you pop round "for a chat" (a dozen times).

I want to get the conversation back to Victoria but she keeps on vacuuming it into her own emotional dust bag.

"We have such a lot in common, we both laugh at the same things."

No, Charlotte, you laugh at what I laugh at because you're in love with me.

"We share the same opinions about so much. I really thought we got on. You tell me everything."

Is this a sales pitch? I know it's tragic and mean, and a terrible shame, but falling in love (and out of it) isn't something you can talk *someone into doing. After a while Charlotte begins repeating herself, then repeating her repetitions. I begin examining the chips and snap each one before eating it.*

"Can't you see that I love you, have loved you, will always love you, and can never stop *loving you?"*

It's impossible to tell exactly where a chip will break just by looking at it.

"You're killing me."

That one snapped diagonally——the first chip to do so in this particular snapping session.

"And no one will ever love you as I do."

Oh God, that might actually be true. It strikes me that Charlotte knows me better than any other girl (and boys don't even get close). She knows me because I don't put on an act with her——I'm not trying to impress her or keep her keen. I reveal my faults, my bad habits, I pick my nose, I expound some of my less savory social theories, I allow a range of genuine bodily odors to waft in her direction without a care, I snap chips while she dissects her heart.

Over the months I've spent hours and hours with her, revealing stuff about my dad, the divorce, my childhood, hopes, fears, embarrassments, my former girlfriends, the fights, and my lurid evenings in Taunton nightclubs. I've told her about Stefan. She's the only person in the world who knows that a bloke my own age has inspired me, changed me, made me jealous.

God, she knows me better than Dad, better than anyone else on the planet. Because I don't fear her rejection, I have opened up like a Terry's Chocolate Orange. This girl knows me, and yet she loves me—surely there's a logical flaw there somewhere. But no, she loves me river deep and mountain high. Maybe no one will love me as she does. Charlotte's may, for all I know, be the most well-informed love I'll ever get. That has to be worth something, hasn't it?

Hasn't it?

"I do love you, I do, I do."

I feel sick. I mumble some words of surprise, flattery and sympathy in more or less that order. Then Charlotte says she's not going to cry any more and she doesn't want to ruin my "Mills & Boon" moment and I immediately wish I had never shared that corny phrase with her. I want miserable Patrick, or morose Malik or even that silent depressive Tu Chi to drop by and lighten the gloom. I go to the Gents just to get some toilet paper for her nose. I think about being sick but the nausea has subsided. I return to where we were sitting and Charlotte's not there and she's not at the bar. She's done the walking-out routine. This is aimed to hurt and humiliate, which it does. It's the social equivalent of suicide: shocking, irretrievable, mystifying, guilt-inducing. I down my pint in one and walk to the fry shop. Perhaps I'll find her tottering in the road trying to get hit by a truck.

THREE

INTERIOR, A PARTY, NIGHT.

ME: Oh, I devise TV game shows.

YOU: Anything I might have seen?

ME: Ummm, let's see . . . oh . . . ummm, no.

YOU: But I watch game shows.

ME: You wouldn't have seen any of mine.

YOU: How do you know I won't have seen any?

ME: Because I haven't devised any.

YOU: But—

ME: Any that have actually been made, I mean. I devise game
shows that people *want* to make, *say* they'll make, *promise*
they'll make. But don't make. I am a failure. You're talking
to a man on the edge, wondering whether to jump. That's
what comes of getting a third-class degree in Biology.

YOU: (LOOKING FOR A WAY TO ESCAPE) Oh. Well, it must be very
hard. You have to keep plugging away, I suppose.

(A NERDY MAN APPROACHES.)

NERDY MAN: Did you say you make game shows? Look at
   Millionaire. The Weakest Link, Pop Idol and *Big Brother.* The people
   who devised those are multimillionaires. Actually I've got
   a bit of an idea myself. It's a cross between *Big Brother* and
   Pets Win Prizes.

(YOU TAKE THIS OPPORTUNITY TO MAKE YOUR WAY TO THE BOWL OF
   CHICKEN WINGS.)

"The Weight Game," says Gerard, facing the wall, his nose about
three inches from it. This is a common position for him to take.
It helps him focus, apparently.

"Who can lose the most weight in a week? It has information,
competition and a good hook—can the fatty turn thin?"

I turn on the hot-water tap. The water heater *whoosh*es with
burning gas. It soon spews out water at near boiling point—enough
for a decent brew. I think the idea sounds quite promising.

"Any more thoughts on it?"

"I dunno," he says. "That's it."

Gerard often starts with a title and half an idea, and usually
gets no further. He's good at the spark, but very bad at using
the bellows, poking with the poker, fetching more coal.

"Go on," I say. In the twenty seconds that have passed I have
gone from thinking the idea was a tiny bit promising to being
certain that it's shit. But even though I know a game show about
diets is a total non-starter it is important to keep Gerard's mind
on something constructive.

One of our mottos is: "great ideas from total crap do grow."
We start with something that is hopelessly unsellable, then keep
improving it till eventually it's a goer. For in order to have a good
game-show idea you must, absolutely must, come up with many,

many, many crap ones. It's basic Darwinism, really. Loads of ideas, the unfit ones perish, the fittest survive. But you need someone who can sift through the crap to find the survivor, and to kill off the unfit. That's my job. Sorting winners from losers.

I scoop a hot tea bag from the mug and squeeze the juice out with my finger. I put a teaspoon of sugar from a bag of Tate & Lyle, which was once a nice bag of sugar, but now resembles a box of dirty-looking irregular lumps.

Like a lot of codevisers, we follow a simple pattern. Gerard is totally optimistic, unreliable, and has hardly any ideas or creative contributions to offer, apart from the odd million-dollar concept that'll make us both rich. He doesn't work at it, he doesn't beat himself up about his lack of success, about morals or money. He doesn't spend months trying to knock the idea into shape. He just *has ideas.* He doesn't know if these ideas are any good and, even if he did, he would not know how to articulate them, communicate them, or sell them.

Gerard is the window-starer, I am the typist. I am the selector and rejecter of the mad thoughts that emanate from Gerard's cauldron of a mind.

I am on time, Gerard is late. Gerard is rude to producers, I am polite. I arrange the meetings, Gerard forgets to turn up. I wash, Gerard smells. I shave, Gerard does not. Gerard is a mess, I pretend not to be.

But you see, the mind that comes up with this kind of stuff with passion and inspiration is a mind unfettered by doubt. Gerard is a fast river crashing down the mountains and I am a rather sensible little dam, harnessing the energy.

The tea is made, and even stirred. I take the biscuit tin lid we use as a tray into the bedroom we use as an office, and place it on a chair we use as a table. Everything, including the house, belongs to Gerard. He was "given" the house by his parents when they left London. (They do not see him now—the house was their way of saying: "We did all we could for you, we failed, now good-bye.") And they gave him the house because they knew that he could not support himself. Gerard just isn't the sort of person who can do proper paid employment. It's not lack of intelligence or lack of will, particularly, there's just an otherworldly quality about Gerard that means he doesn't connect with the ordinary details and trivia from which no man can escape.

Example: he once had a job in a library but refused to let people take books by Jeremy Bloom.

YOU: Who's Jeremy Bloom?
ME: Exactly. Just an author of little note to whom Gerard took a personal dislike.

"I am a librarian. Part of my job description is to advise customers. I advised customers that Jeremy Bloom is shit."

That was Gerard's defense at the meeting with the council's deputy head of personnel.

He wasn't fired. At the time, the council did not see total incompetence as a reason to fire anyone. In fact, it seemed to be something they actively encouraged. They just gave him lots of leave "to consider his behavior." He got paid for six months for not even turning up. Then one day he didn't get paid anymore and Gerard has never worked since. He survives (almost) by renting a room in the leaky, damp, smelly house to a Japanese student who spends all her time at her boyfriend's.

"Sir Tim Rice is writing another bloody musical."

Oh no, my heart sinks. Not Tim Rice. I stub out my Silkie on the sawn-off Coke can we use as an ashtray.

"No, you were saying about *The Weight Game*. It sounds promising." It doesn't, but I need to keep the machine going, the crap coming. There's gold in that there crap.

"Bastard is worth about fifty million."

"The Weight Game," I repeat. I need to keep Gerard's mind from going down pointless and destructive roads—like Tim Rice. Tim Rice is Gerard's number-one *bête noire*. "Tim Rice is a man who has made more money in proportion to his talent than any other living Englishman," he will tell you. More than once. Tim Rice is Gerard's number-one hate figure on the one hand, and role model on the other. As you may gather (and if you haven't, you will) Gerard is, and he won't mind me saying this, a man of contrasts. *Gerard, I feel the same way about Tim Rice but I have it under control. My feelings about him, intense though they are, don't stop me from getting on with my fucking life*—sorry, but this aspect of Gerard infuriates me.

"Fifty million. And now he's going to get even more. He's probably written another song while we've been talking about him. That's another million squids in his back pocket."

"Let's stick with the weight theme, though. Maybe something that involves makeovers. Maybe a show in which people have makeovers and the best makeover wins. No, it's crap. Now, what were we talking about earlier?"

"Tim Rice."

"No, it was the candid camera idea . . ."

"I heard him on *Quote, Unquote* the other day. He probably gets a hundred quid for that, too."

I give up. The Tim Rice drug has taken hold. It could be twenty minutes before the Gerard mind can be harnessed for the job in hand.

YOU: Why game shows?

ME: Well, it goes something like this: I left university wanting
to be in the movies. I don't know why now; maybe it just
seemed like a cool thing to do. I didn't have any skills or
experience or proven talent, so that left producing. But I
had no money, so I thought directing might be the thing
to go for. Obviously I couldn't pick and choose so I
decided that to direct *any* film would be a great start.
Then I lowered my sights to any job in the film industry
that might lead to directing. Then any job in the film
industry. Then any job in film or TV drama. Then any
job in film, TV drama or entertainment, drama, comedy/
drama, news, current affairs or children's. Then any job
in film, TV drama or entertainment, drama, news,
current affairs or children's, community programming
or national radio. Then any job in film, TV drama or
entertainment, drama, news, current affairs or children's,
community programming or national radio, local radio,
pirate radio, hospital radio, Internet, advertising, in-house
training videos, photography, newspapers, magazines,
publishing, children's comics or bubblegum cards. And
don't think the bubblegum cards are for comic effect.
That was a job I actually *got*. I came up with picture-and-
caption ideas for three series of science-fiction bubblegum
cards for a Dutch company. They went global and in over
three months I made a small fortune—about ten grand,
which is a small fortune in my book (and this is my
book).

What I'm saying is that trying to get a job has really
been my life's work. It's been a career of job-seeking. If
there was a job called job-seeker I would be great for it. If it

was job-*finder* then I'd be in trouble. But if it's just the seeking you want, I'm your man.

My approach has been to knock on a lot of different doors hoping one will open—rather than knocking on the one door and waiting forever. More doors, more chances. It makes lot of sense when you think about it.

But think about it all you like, it doesn't work.

Here I am. Twenty-nine, with not much in the way of skills or experience. Not a morning goes by when I don't wake up and think, Jesus Christ, I have really messed things up. What the hell has gone wrong? Why me? I'm not evil. Ok, I was a bit of a no-good teenager but I got myself together, eventually. At university I blossomed, eventually. Why oh why oh why can't I get a decent job? No one would believe that a chap with as much potential as I had could end up with so little. I have let down my parents, my friends, my talent. Whatever happened to the man most likely to succeed? The flamboyant and influential man on campus? The *enfant terrible* of London University Student Union coffee bars?

He's teetering on the edge of throwing himself off the nearest very high bridge, that's what. Unfit for cohabitation. I should e-mail all my college friends: *Do you want some* schadenfreude? *Come to Tavistock Bridge at midnight on Saturday. You'll be glad you did.*

"How does someone like Tim Rice persuade Andrew Lloyd Webber to work for him?"

"Look, if you want to be as rich as Tim Rice we have to create the game show of game shows. And we can't do that if you don't concentrate."

"Persuasion."

"*Persuasion*? A novel by Jane Austen."

"Persuasion. That's the idea. It's brilliant."

"What's the idea?" I grab the notebook. Gerard may be having a eureka moment.

"What's the idea? The idea is to make millions of pounds so we don't have to work in an office that smells of damp, drink lukewarm tea and—fuck me—these biscuit are stale! Why are we eating stale biscuits? We're better than that. We have brains, we have ideas, we have talent and we work hard. WHY CAN'T WE HAVE NICE BISCUITS THAT AREN'T STALE?"

"Persuasion. What's the idea?"

"Persuasion. How good are you at persuading people to do daft things? You know, like the punter goes up to someone and persuades them to take a picture of them naked. If they succeed, they win. Or going into a bank and persuading the teller to come outside because there really is a giant ape on the loose. Some people could probably do it, others couldn't."

"There might be something in it. Hidden camera?"

"I need a dump."

And so I wait while Gerard makes the half-mile trip to Kentish Town Library, his former place of employment, which he now uses as a toilet when his cistern breaks down, which it frequently does.

This is no life, it really isn't.

One of the reasons I stick with it is that we have been very close to getting a game show on. So close it breaks my heart. As with any form of human endeavor, getting close is what gets you. Whether it's a mountain you nearly climbed, or a business that's almost profitable or a woman who almost loves you, getting close is the drug. And it doesn't let go.

It grabs you by the short and curlies.

But *nearly* climbing a mountain is an achievement, a woman who *almost* loves you might end up as a great friend. But with game shows, getting close counts for nothing. It's no better than getting nowhere at all. It doesn't pay anything, it doesn't look good on your resume and it doesn't impress the ladies. In the game-show business, winners take all, and the losers go home with nothing.

Natural Selection is the closest we came to winning. It was a cross between *The Crystal Maze* and *Robot Wars.* Contestants are placed in a jungle set and presented with various threats and predators. They have preselected a number of attributes (such as the ability to run fast, fly, climb trees or see in the dark) and vulnerabilities (such as bulk, slowness) and the most effective creature wins.

We had meetings, plans, plans, meetings and plans. "This is the hottest idea since *Millionaire,*" to quote someone-or-other who wore a leather jacket. "It's virtually green-lit—but if Jack [Dee] gets on board we've clinched it."

Jack [Dee] gets on board. I remember these words like they were uttered this morning, uttered by our BBC producer, Charles Gretorex: "Jamie, it's a top priority. Everyone's jumping up and down with excitement. There's an offers meeting tomorrow and I'm sure we'll get the nod subject to a finance meeting on Thursday. We'll shoot in autumn and there's a second series penciled. Don't book a holiday. There'll be repeats too, and Elaine is clearing schedules just for us. Your arse isn't going to hit the ground."

A time slot is finalised. We are 99 percent sure that it's all going ahead and it'll be brilliant. One hit—serious hit—game show and you are made. Seriously made—millionaire. No, multi- multi- multimillionaire. You can sell it to fifty or a hundred countries. It gets shown five nights a week in fifty or a hundred countries plus repeats, books, T-shirts, board games, computer games, toys—all in fifty or a hundred countries. (Do you know how much the format owners get for *Blind Date*? Thirty-seven thousand pounds sterling for each show. That's just in Britain. It's shown in forty countries. It is shown somewhere on the planet every minute of every day. Now ask yourself this: how much did you earn today?)

Natural Selection was going to change me from a penniless nobody with no career to being the bloke who devised the show that the whole world watches. Instead of sending off my ideas to a production company I would be able to buy the production company.

But the best thing about selling *Natural Selection,* the best thing of all, would be that I could buy a bottle of champagne and share it with Victoria.

Aaaah. Sweet, but true.

I could thank her for standing by me in the hard times. I could thank her for sticking with me, for backing a man with potential, a man on the ground floor.

I could be a nice person again. (I was a nice person once, honest.) The nice person she met nearly ten years ago. I could enjoy making love because I'd feel like a proper man. I could take Victoria out to eat—yes, *take* her. Pay for the meal with my own money because I'm minting it.

The next day there is no call from Gretorex. Three days later it comes: "The meeting was delayed, that's all. It's still top priority. God, I am excited."

A week later and Charles Gretorex is as positive as ever.

"It's just a question of finding the right slot. You see, they're worried about the target audience. It might be more BBC Two. They think Jack is too risqué for prime-time."

"But Jack was their idea."

"But the research shows he's better post-watershed. What do you say we get a Bruce [Forsyth] or a Bob [Monkhouse]?"

"But they're not edgy. They're as edgy as blancmange. They wanted edgy!"

"Change of strategy. Edgy is seen as a bit too Anne Robinson now. The dark-edgy bandwagon has just left town."

And that is really what he said, true as I'm here.

Two weeks of no calling. I leave messages but they are not returned. Finally I catch him in.

"There's been a change of emphasis. It doesn't fit with the new schedule, but the controller is still very keen on Jack."

"I thought they didn't like Jack."

"They want a Jack vehicle."

"But Jack was the one thing they didn't like last time we spoke."

"Jack's back in the prewatershed mindset."

A month later we pay Gretorex a visit. He has a small office crammed to the ceiling with VHS cassettes, books, board games and paper. There's a water cooler in the corner but no water in the tank. Gerard must have looked at it oddly because Charles feels the need to explain.

"The MD has stopped the water fountain thing. Economies."

Gerard is off.

"But the man-hours wasted with people going off to get water from a tap or buying—"

"I know what you're saying but it's just PR. The BBC has to be seen to be stingy so the license payers think they're getting value for money. Small stories about cutbacks on croissants and water get in the papers, and makes it look like we're skinflints, which is what the public wants."

"But the BBC wants to keep its talent, doesn't it?"

"Yes."

"Well, I'm talent, and I refuse to work for a company that does not provide coffee, croissants and nice water. We'll take our ideas elsewhere, a place we feel pampered and appreciated. How about that? Oh, and my colleague would like to smoke a Silkie."

Charles looks hurt and embarrassed. Such is Gerard's confidence, that he can frighten a BBC producer of some reputation, despite the fact that Gerard has not sold a single idea to anyone, ever.

"I want you to stay in-house. If that means I have to buy the croissants myself, I will. But smoking is forbidden anywhere except the designated smoking rooms."

"That's ok. I don't want one," says Mr. Sensible. Anything to move things along.

"*Pain au chocolat* for me, please," says Gerard.

And so a top BBC producer gets up to fetch us each breakfast from the kiosk on the ground floor. He returns with baked goods, coffee and a bottle of mineral water which we consume like a couple of Dickensian waifs who have never seen such luxury. He comes straight out with it.

"After the success of Jack's new ITV show they decided they want more shows like that. Instead of your one."

"I thought they wanted something original, different."

"Jack's show is totally original and different, that's why they want one like it."

Short pause.

"But if we devise a show *like* his it won't be original and different, it'll be *like* his."

Another short pause. Charles looks like someone who'd just

been asked an impossible question on *Millionaire* and he's used up his lifelines.

Gerard continues with undisguised contempt, "Do you see? If it's *originality* you want, it can't be *like* something else."

"Yeah. Absolutely. We want something unlike any other show. Just like Jack's show. Give us something like that."

For the first time I begin to think that not all BBC producers are intelligent, clever, creative people. They had jobs I had been rejected for but intelligence can't have been the distinguishing factor.

Or maybe I'm just bitter.

Gerard continues. "Our idea is not *like* something else. It is *o*riginal." He pronounces the "o" as in "opal."

"But you see, it's been on the shelf a while. Look, I'll give it another push. It's still possible. We're going to put it into the autumn offers."

"Autumn? But we've been waiting for this for a whole year, you arse," is what we don't say. We spend the next half an hour slagging off other shows and trying to come up with some new "areas." Then Charles has to go to a "development coordination" meeting, which seems like a contradiction in terms.

"Will there be croissants at your meeting?" asks Gerard.

"No. Biscuits."

"Are biscuits cheaper than croissants?"

"Much. And the uneaten ones are reused. Uneaten croissants were thrown out."

"Blimey. There *is* a logic to it."

Two weeks later and no calls. No calls are returned.

With each week that goes by, our 99 percent certainty becomes a 90 percent probability, then an 80 percent chance, to a

50 percent hope, to a 10 percent pie-in-the-sky. There is never a moment when you give up all hope for an ailing TV idea. The life-support machine is never switched off. You never have closure or a chance to grieve. Program ideas never die—they just become infinitely improbable. *Natural Selection* is infinitely improbable.

Our winner turned into a loser.

So a few meetings with the BBC is all we have to show for ourselves. Neither of us earns any money. Neither of us is doing a course that will earn a qualification. Neither of us has private means. We're just dreaming our lives away and it's becoming quite terrifying. Each morning I think, this really has to end. I should go back to working at Print Stop. Victoria doesn't know this but I feel like an impostor in her bed. She is part of the world of work, money, getting on, owning property. I am sliding into the world of the Unemployable. That word—*unemployable*—is the first word that enters my head when the alarm clock goes. Unemployable. I am an Unemployable. A person who hasn't worked for so long no one trusts them. Out of the loop of civilized working men and women. I close my eyes and feel myself sliding. House prices are rising faster, faster, I'm getting older, older, and success is getting farther, farther out of reach. My heart feels like a great thumping enemy with giant footsteps. Could I really end up as a member of the underclass? Does that happen to beekeepers' sons who come to the city? And it'll be my own fault, too. I have been arrogant enough to think I could make it Big. And I couldn't make it at all. For how long will Victoria carry me? How long can I pretend to be good enough for her? I must run away before she sees me for what I am.

Gerard has stopped staring out the window, and is staring into space again. (His trip to the Kentish Town Library toilets proffered no inspiration; it seldom does. Records show that Shakespeare rarely relied upon going for a dump.)

Maybe Gerard's on the verge of a brilliant idea and he's just trying to formulate it in his head. Is it burgeoning in his subconscious, and about to walk through the invisible door into his conscious mind? Or is there no idea? Is he simply looking at the dust that swirls in the sunlight, wondering where it all comes from? Can it all be dead skin like they say? Why do we shed dead skin, anyway? It looks like a desert storm. Mmmm. I'd like to go to a desert. Deserts must be fascinating. I'd like to walk across the—

"Hel-lo?"

"Mmm?"

"We need a plan."

"Huh?"

"I can't take much more of this. I want a plan and a deadline. Let's give ourselves six months to sell a show. If we haven't done it, I'm out of here."

"You always say that."

"And I always mean it. Let's get a show on or I'm going do something . . . something, I don't know . . ."

"Something weird? Something shocking?"

"No. Be a nurse or a teacher or a chef full time. Or go back to Print Stop. Six months to hit the jackpot, to make a million or two, or we jack it in. Finish."

Silence. Gerard has finally grasped the urgency of the situation and is grappling, perhaps for the first time, with a thing called Reality. "Tim Rice never had to make that kind of decision. Right from the start, he shat money. Lucky bastard."

FOUR

I try to give good chuck I do, I always try to do it nicely. But it's not easy. I hate the way their lips quiver and tears well up in their eyes and they ask if you have a tissue. As if. "Yes, I have one tucked in my sleeve for just such an occasion." You want to hug them and kiss them and say that you can work things through, give it another go, sort things out. But you can't, you have to go through with it, you have to stick to your plan.

You have to plan. You can't just come out with it. (Do you want small popcorn or large? By the way, I want to finish with you.) You need to find a time and place for the axing, a patch of ground for the burial. Should it be the pub tonight or at home tomorrow night? Should you wait till after Dan and Kate's party? Or after that dinner with her parents? Or wait till after Christmas (you can't ruin her Christmas). Or after the holiday? You leave it a few days—there's no rush.

Or maybe a couple of weeks? Maybe you should wait till she passes her driving test so she can at least be happy about something. Maybe you should wait till after the wedding, after the kids have grown up, after your lives have been spent.

I had a girl like that once. She was going through a bad patch that turned out not to be a bad patch, but her life. Nothing went right for her. It's hard to leave someone when all they've got is you. How will they survive?

Months went by as I prayed something good would happen for her. Something good, so I could leave her with the good thing, whatever it was, instead of nothing. But nothing good happened— that's how some people live, with nothing good ever happening. She never got that new job, her mother never found somewhere else to live, her skin thing was never properly diagnosed, the roofer never did come back to finish the job, the money promised by the insurance company never did come through, she did not pass her driving test.

I must have stayed for nearly a year as I waited for the moment to leave. Holding her hand, wiping away tears, making love, all the time looking into her eyes and wishing she would disappear.

So I did it one night after seeing a film—*Betty Blue*. The place: Pizza Hut. The time: 10:40. The weapon: a hammer-blow to the solar plexus. Yes, I expected tears but there was no end to them. And the question—why? Why? Why? Why do you want to leave? I told her everything but it wasn't enough. I even told her about Victoria. In the end I had to say, "Because I don't want you." That was the hammer-blow. In the end you have to be *that* hard because every other reason leaves hope.

But the tears flowed on.

They went on and on and on, the only way of stopping the tears would have been to say, It's ok, everything's going to be all

right. Let's work something out. But baby, I had to go, didn't I?
I had to stick to my plan, even if you drowned yourself in tears.

And how do you begin the end? There are fifty ways, apparently.
You need to "talk" about "things," about "us."

You steer things ever so gently toward the end. Point her in the
right direction. Let her come up with the idea of parting so she
says, "Well, maybe if that's how you feel, we should part." That's it.
Make it *her* idea. She pulls the trigger. It's better for her (she doesn't
feel so rejected) and better for you (you don't feel so guilty).

Victoria is in the kitchen flattening out some aluminium foil that
had been wrapped round some cheese. She cuts off the hard bits of
cheese and shoves them off the breadboard onto the counter. A
year ago she would have thrown away the foil and the cheese, too.
But I have trained her in the ways of abstemiousness. She is careful
now, like me. She looks at me and smiles. There's no resentment.
She's doing it for me, but she doesn't mind. It's just one of those
compromises you make. I watch and, though I'm not a great remi-
niscer, sometimes she'll pull a face that reminds me of that Mills &
Boon moment ten years ago when I thought that one day I would
live with this girl. I thought it was a foolish dream. And now this
foolish dream is looking at me and is about to say, "What's up, blos-
som? Why are you standing there? Are you monitoring me?"

This is said with kindness. My faults, of which I have many,
amuse Victoria. What has irritated others makes her smile. She
has taken my annoying habits and, before my very eyes, turned
them into amusing quirks that we can both enjoy.

You are a wonderful magician, Victoria.

"It's a new dish. From this."

She folds back a cookbook that is open on the counter. *Easy*

Vegetarian Food For Busy Meat Eaters. Given to us by Alison, presumably so we can cook nice veggie food the next time she comes to dinner. Victoria reads the title and laughs.

"I don't think it's specific enough. I think it should be vegetarian food for busy meat eaters, on a small budget, one of whom is freelance, the other has an office job and they both live in Kentish Town."

"One of whom hates anchovies and the other marzipan," I add.

"One day everyone will be a famous chef for fifteen minutes."

"One day everyone will have their own famous quote."

She grabs me by the waist and kisses me. I hold her and we look, not into each other's eyes, but beyond them. She's thinking: How rare these moments have become. Where did they go? Will they ever return?

The feel of her back is different. My hands aren't at home on her anymore. They don't belong. She's someone else's girl (though I don't think she knows it yet). She senses something wrong. She hugs me harder, squeezing a little more goodness out. She has squeezed so much goodness out, there's not much left now, and she knows it. She grasps my jaw between fingers and thumb, like a mother grabbing a child's face before swiping the lips with a tissue. It's a firm grip—she thinks I will pull away. But she means business. A kiss on the lips is her intent. It is brief and achieves nothing except to remind us how rare they have become, and so token. A small reminder that we are lovers, or meant to be.

I could cut the throat of our love now. Precipitate a row, an argument. Let anger push grief aside, if only for a moment. She could hate me for a while. A little hate might help, she'll call me a twit or a moron, and who minds if a moron leaves?

Yes, now would be a good time. Her mother has already phoned so no interruption there. Nothing is about to start on TV. The mood has become sad. Go, go, catch the shifting mood of melancholy, use it, go with it.

Strike now.

But suddenly she starts to sing. The mood brightens in an instant. Singing and cooking. She is weaving her magic and turning a gray sky to blue. This is a happy moment again.

I can't spoil it.

She opens the fridge door, takes out a bottle and thrusts it into my chest: my cue to do the corkscrew thing while she reaches for glasses. Her long body stretches and I will miss it. And my heart feels tickled, but it's a dread tickle, a tickle of sudden fright.

I imagine a hand reaching down her back onto her bottom. I see her smile but the smile is for someone else. (Oh it will be, soon. You can be sure of it—flip forward a few pages and you'll see.)

She takes the open bottle from the counter and pours one glass. I say, "You used to drink spritzer. Back in the early nineties. It was the early nineties drink, remember?"

"That was when you wanted me but couldn't have me."

"I wanted you so much. So damn much. You bitch."

She laughs. "And you always drank Newkie Brown. And what's changed?"

"Now I drink it ironically."

After filling my glass she reads the label on the bottle. "This wine is light and crisp. The ideal accompaniment for poultry, fish or perfect as an aperitif with *friends*." She looks incredulous. "With *friends*," she repeats. This is a feed line—I know Victoria is waiting for the joke.

"Friends? What about family? Or business associates?"

"Only *friends*. If you tried it with your mum it wouldn't taste right. But what about lovers?"

"Lovers can be friends, too."

Will we be friends? We will. I must keep her in my life somehow. Keep her for another day? Stand in wait, perhaps. Something could go wrong with Stefan. I am retreating now, but one day I could come riding back and reclaim what is rightfully mine.

The moment to strike has gone. So, we will have a glass of wine, and be together one last time. Perhaps I will watch one of "her" programs just to be nice. *Casualty, Corrie?* Everything will be ok tonight. We will eat, drink and be merry. We might even make love. I will know it's for the last time. It will be so sweet, so cruel and sweet, to make love to this other man's girl. And as dawn comes and the central heating creaks into life, I will stroke her awake and say that I can't sleep. I will kiss her warm, damp forehead and push back the hair that sleep has stuck to her cheek. I will say that we need to "talk". . . about "things," about "us."

FIVE

In the two months following the plate-spinning farce, and the nearly-punching-Giles's-lights-out debacle, Victoria and I became good mates. I allowed Victoria to think that the girl who followed me around everywhere (Charlotte) was my kind-of girlfriend and this made seeing her without Giles fairly straightforward. At last I was doing what only art students do——having girls who are just friends. But I always knew my first instincts were right: we were made for each other. Bloody made *for each other. Just the funniest, wisest, kindest, strongest girl I'd ever met and . . . oh, what's the use? She was Giles's girlfriend and it looked like it would stay that way.*

There was one particularly sad moment——"sad" in the new, not the more-or-less archaic sense. She invited me over to watch a video of The King of Comedy, *which she'd never seen, and I pretended I hadn't, either. I brought the only dish I can cook with confidence: popcorn.*

Victoria commented on the film as it went along (a habit that irritates me in everyone else). I agreed with what she said. I kept agreeing with everything she said. I then found myself looking at Victoria instead of the screen, and laughing almost involuntarily at the same things she laughed at. As the credits rolled I realized what had happened. I'd become Victoria's Charlotte. *I had been following her around and was always available for whatever she wanted to do—plate-spinning, or seeing videos the whole world has seen twice.*

I now knew that if I ever told her how much I loved her she would sit there snapping chips, I would throw wine at her and call her a tactless little shit. She would go to get me some tissues from the toilet and I would disappear in an attention-seeking huff. So, rule one: I must never pour my heart out, I must not make Charlotte's mistake of letting my feelings show. In fact, just to make absolutely sure I don't end up as Victoria's Charlotte, I will be a little cold, a little standoffish, even dismissive at times.

That'll do the trick.

What bloody trick?

Have her think I'm not interested? That's hardly going to have her running into my arms. (In my experience women are not attracted to indifference, whatever the lad mags tell you.)

That will get me nowhere. What I should do is drop the occasional ambiguous hint and leave it to Victoria to run with or ignore as she sees fit.

Of course, there were times when I dropped hints so heavy I could hardly lift them. One time I came out with one so transparent that it was really more of a written declaration of love. We were going for a drink one night and I had promised myself very solemnly that the stalemate had to end.

I had prepared my line, which was this: "I am very fond of you, you know."

Her line was inevitably going to be: "I'm very fond of you," and there'd be a little silence as we both thought about what we've said. Then I would say, "I know it's a bit odd because we're such good friends but we'd probably get on really well as a couple."

And she agrees, and the rest is going to be smooth sailing. I must proceed with the plan no matter what. Too many other plans have fallen by the wayside because of some feeble excuse about the timing not being right, the mood not being right, and a thousand other procrastinatory inventions. This time, no excuses.

Trouble is, at five minutes to closing time (which was my self-imposed deadline), the conversation is about a Jay Jones, a mutual mate of ours. Victoria's talking about what happened the other night.

"Jay Jones offered to walk me home after going to dinner at Tim and Rachel's, and he stopped outside my flat and out of the blue said he was 'very fond of me.' And then he tried to snog me. I was quite shocked."

"Right. What's wrong with that?"

"Well, everything. For a start, he's a mate, for a second, he must know I don't fancy him."

"Let's be having you, ladies and gentlemen," says the barman as he starts gathering pots. My deadline looms.

I must strengthen my resolve. I must not allow Jay Jones to affect me—I promised myself NO EXCUSES. Victoria continues: "And it's not something you expect a mate like that to do. What was he playing at?"

"Make your way to the exit now, please."

I must act now. I say, "I'm very fond—"

"That's why you and I, we get on so well—you're one of the few blokes I really get on with as a friend."

"Right, glasses please. Haven't you got homes to go to?"

"We'd better go."

"Just a minute, Victoria."

"Come on, you two lovebirds."

"I'm very fond of you, you know," I say hurriedly as we put on our coats. "I mean, I am fond of you in the same way that Jay Jones . . . isn't. I mean in a purely . . . friendship kind of way."

"Exactly," says Victoria, and smiles, it seems to me, with relief.

I made up my mind about several things on the walk home: one, I wanted Victoria very much, and two, I would never let her talk about me in the way she talked about Jay Jones. I wouldn't make some obvious move that would disappoint and annoy. I would, unlike Charlotte and Jay Jones, retain my dignity. I would decline some of her social invitations, instead of always saying yes. I would not agree with her about everything, and maybe I'd have to pretend to disagree even when I agreed.

I would certainly not look at her instead of the TV. I would never give her the slightest reason to think I had fallen hopelessly in love with her.

The longer I knew Victoria it seemed the harder she was to read. For example, we go walking together on the Thames and stop off for a roast at one of those huge pubs in Putney. Out of the blue, she suggests going away together. Giles can't come and she's got this almost free offer for a weekend in Paris and some circus is going to be there. I am trying not to say yes to everything, but this is too good to miss. I suggest she comes to lunch next day to finalize arrangements. Lunch comes and goes and she doesn't show up. She phones at half-past two saying she "forgot" but would call me later in the week. How can you make a move on a girl who forgets to come to lunch? How can you stop being in love with a girl who forgets to come to lunch?

Oh, I did try. After a year of unrequited passion I decided not to call her. She didn't call me, either. I try to banish the following thought from my head:

She feels the same way! She is in the exact same dilemma! She's too scared to make a move, doesn't want to lose your friendship! Ha, ha, ha!

But that thought keeps coming back. The immigration officer in my head can't stop it from slipping through. The only possible defense is to have a careful look at the data. I go through the data over and over again till the message sinks in:

She doesn't call me nearly as much as I call her.

She keeps going out with other people. Men who are not me, other men, men with whom she chooses to have sex, men who are not called James Hole, and it's not some careless mistake.

She has actually said that it is nice that we are just friends and not lovers. Actually said it with words, English words, loud and clear ones.

She never, ever, ever, flirts. No really, I'll give you a very typical example:

VICTORIA: *(RE: THE BARGAIN HOTEL ROOM WE NEVER WENT TO)* It's great. Ensuite bathroom, TV, minibar, swimming pool. It's just got the one double bed—we can share, can't we?

JAMES: *That sounds like fun. (WITH A FLIRTY GRIN)*

Here are all the flirty things Victoria did not say in reply to "that sounds like fun":

Promises, promises. (Followed by flirty laugh.)

I hope so. (Followed by flirty laugh.)

Maybe. (Followed by flirty smile.)

You never know your luck. (Followed by flirty laugh.)

That's what double beds are for. (Followed by flirty smile.)

I'll pack my best undies. (Followed by flirty smile.)

Why do you think I booked a double? (Followed by flirty smile.)

I didn't know you cared. (Followed by flirty smile.)

You don't think we're going to Paris to sleep, do you? (Followed by flirty smile.)

Good, because I want to fuck you so badly. Come over here, Big Boy. (Followed by xxxxxx)

What she does say is this:

VICTORIA: (LOOKING AT LEAFLET WITHOUT A FLICKER OF A SMILE) It's only five minutes' walk from the Seine.
(FOLLOWED BY AWKWARD SILENCE.)

Feel that silence around you now. Can you feel it? Does it bring back memories for you, too? Embrace it, learn to live with it, make it your friend.

So having looked at the evidence the conclusion is pretty watertight. SHE IS NOT INTERESTED. So clearly the thing to do is STOP BEING IN LOVE WITH HER.

I try to be scientific about it.

Objective: neutralize burning passion.

Method: list everything bad about Victoria. Concentrate on the list till passion cools.

Equipment: pen, paper, a packet of Silkies, a heart unheated by burning passion.

You see the problem. So, life goes on like that for a year. Sometimes I think she's getting interested, but it always turns out to be an emotional mirage. Some mornings I wake up and think, I'm cured!—as if love is a spot that can disappear overnight. By midday I know I'm sick again, and I'm disappointed and ecstatic.

Victoria goes out with men, I meet them, I befriend them, I am apparently not regarded as a threat. Nice. It appears that I am not the kind of bloke who makes other men jealous. I am the harmless friend, no worries about good old James Hole from near Taunton, the beekeeper's son who really ought to be mixing with the science boys. Victoria's men fascinate me.

Why them and not me?

What do they have that I haven't? What do they have in common? What can I learn from them? What are the do's and don'ts of loving Victoria? Why does she go out with bastards and wankers? Is there a me-shaped hole somewhere in Victoria's heart?

I use my close friendship with Victoria to compile a complete mental dossier on her men. Will she realize that I am better than the lot of them put together? Or will I realize that I am not? Either way, I will end up knowing more about my future girlfriend's ex-boyfriends than it is healthy for a man to know.

VICTORIA'S MEN.
NUMBER ONE—GILES CARLTON

Giles Carlton, the would-be film producer, was the first. The first man I saw her with, I mean. He was about two inches better than me but about fourteen pounds worse. He had a fantastically graceful walk. It was as if he was being pulled by a string from his navel and his feet were on skates. His head didn't bob up and down like most people's—it seemed to glide. (I tried doing the Giles Walk myself but I looked like a stoned ostrich.)

Giles was a grammar-school kid who dropped out of Oxbridge entrance because *he wanted to produce a short film about Spike Milligan, which won him some sort of prize—Best Short Film About Spike Milligan, I think. He never bought cigarettes, but always had a cigarette, often perched on his ear. There was no shame in his cigarette-scrounging. He would scrounge all day long, often from the same person (me) over and over again. It was as if he was testing his popularity, his power, his ability to manipulate.*

So this is the kind of man Victoria loves. The high-flyer, the high achiever, the manipulator. A man who rides the wave of political correctness like a champion surfer. (He had that in common with Stefan—both of them can throw ideas into the air and they always land in a formation that justifies their own behavior.)

Giles even strokes girls' bottoms—all the time. All girls, all the time. The girls never complain, not even the ones who go on about feminism and date rape.

I ask Victoria about it when we're both drunk enough to be frank.

"He's always stroking girls' bottoms. Don't they mind?"

"That's just Giles," says Victoria dismissively. For a moment I feel as if I am the pervy one for having mentioned it. How could I think there was anything seedy about it? I must have a seedy mind myself.

"What do you mean, 'that's just Giles?' " I say.

"You'd have to be a woman to understand."

"Victoria, that is bollocks. 'That's just Giles?' Let's try it with some other names. That's just Adolf. That's just Attila. That's just Judas, he's always betraying people, it's just his way. That's just Saddam—ooh, there's no stopping him once he gets going. Just his way."

"It's not what you say or do, James, it's who you are. There are men who could take my arm on the dance floor and snog me before they even say hello. Another man doing the same thing might get a kick in the balls. It's style, chemistry, a feeling, Giles doesn't make women feel leched at, just liked and appreciated."

"Well, blow me. I want to make a few women feel 'liked and appreciated' tonight, as a matter of fact."

True enough. I, too, would like to stroke girls' bottoms (all girls, all the time) and I would like them to say, "That's just Jamie."

But Giles, in the scheme of things, is harmless enough and he certainly grew up a bit after the screening of our film he "executive produced." His credibility as film supremo and artist-about-campus nosedived dramatically. The film was atrocious, even by student film standards. It was so serious and earnest that it was just plain silly and the worst of all things happened—people began to giggle. Well, how could they not? It featured lines like, "Life is like an onion, beneath the layers, you just get more layers, and just when you think you've reached the center, there's nothing there."

Not only was the dialogue terrible, but the acting was giggle-worthy. I felt sorry for Victoria (whose acting was fine) because she was supported by these skinny English boys pretending to be U.S. Marines. The funniest thing about it was that just before the viewing Giles made a little speech. He "confessed" that the script had not been sent to him anonymously by someone who had fought in the Gulf (as he had told everyone), but that he had "penned" it himself. He had fibbed because "I wanted the actors to feel free to make constructive suggestions without embarrassment." But of course Giles made this "confession" because he believed the film was going to storm it, and had decided that now was the time to take the writing credit.

After the humiliation of the giggling and occasional heckling there was a Q & A session in which Giles tried to backtrack and say that a mysterious "friend" of his had been responsible for "most of the actual scripting". I don't know what the difference between "writing" and "actual scripting" is, but I saw at that moment that Giles had a fantastic future ahead of him—in advertising or politics.

Then, halfway through the barrage of questions, Giles blames certain problems with the film on "a lack of proper funding—that's why the British film industry is in a mess, and that is why we all need to campaign for a properly funded student film department." A few people cheer. Actually, Giles could probably make it in any field he chose.

After the speech he sidles up to me, perhaps thinking my close friendship with Victoria might stand in his favor. He looks defeated. He has been found out, and even the Giles Walk looks slightly ridiculous now.

"What did you think, James, my friend?"

This is the first time he has sought my critical judgement.

"I thought it was rather idiosyncratic."

"Oh, thanks."

I could have added that it was an observation, not a compliment, but instead I decide to be magnanimous in victory.

"I couldn't . . . ? Just the one? Gasping."

I oblige.

I am pleased to say that the Giles magic wore off Victoria fairly soon after that. She phoned me one night at about ten and asked if she could pop over. It was raining, her hair was all wet and her eyes a little sore. She told me that she and Giles had been out for pasta. He had had spaghetti vongole and the waiter had asked him if he wanted Parmesan cheese and he nodded.

Victoria intervened, in what she insists was a lighthearted manner, "One's not meant to have Parmesan on vongole. It doesn't go with clams, apparently."

Giles got annoyed.

"What are you talking about? It doesn't matter what you're supposed to have! God, you are such a slave to convention. I am not prepared to go out with someone who doesn't respect my different way of doing things. That is what my work is all about."

Victoria tried to tell him he was overreacting and that spaghetti was not "work" and he was wrong to take her approach to pasta as an indication of her general hostility to innovation. There followed a heated debate about how each of them seemed to want different things.

"What do you think I should do, James?" she asks as I pour my emergency bottle of Newcastle Brown into two coffee mugs.

"Well, do you love him?"

"No." Oh joy. "But you don't have to love someone to go out with them."

"No, of course not. But do you like him?"

"I like lots of things about him. I like his determination. I liked the way he got that crap film together——he's a motivator. Trouble is, I think his ability to motivate exceeds his ability to, well, do the thing he motivates people to do. That film was awful, wasn't it?"

"Pants with skid marks."

"He can't quite admit it. He's calling it a 'black comedy' now. Because people laughed. He says that the humor was intended all along."

"God, he is going to do well. I mean, he's irrepressible."

"He wants to write a play next."

"I'm not available."

"He does know a lot. I think he should be a critic or something. He knows so much about plays and films and art movements and history."

"But the vongole incident. Is that forgivable? I mean, not wishing to stir things up, but he seems to have taken it to heart."

You see what I'm doing. Posing as an entirely disinterested observer with my "not wishing to stir things up," but of course I want Victoria to ditch the man.

Any man.

I want to stir things up, all right.

"For once I knew something he didn't——that's what upset him."

"You knew that Parmesan doesn't go with vongole. Well, normally."

"Yes. And that irritated him."

"You can't stay with a bloke who thrives on your ignorance. I don't mean you're ignorant——but, you know, thrives off a knowledge imbalance, real or imagined." I sound like I have a clue.

In fact I know that a "knowledge imbalance" is precisely the sort of thing that turns Victoria on. It's sexy. I think she wants men to be taller than her, richer, older, stronger and more knowledgeable. Every time Victoria said anything positive about Giles I would agree wholeheartedly but find a way of slipping in a negative: the bottom-stroking, the terrible film, the fact that he was a bit of a laughing-stock, the cigarette-scrounging, his patronizing attitude to non-urban life-forms like myself, and of course this Great Vongole Crisis. Victoria agreed with me that this vongole incident would probably repeat itself many times and was indicative of worse to come. It was too much for their relationship to bear. Apologies would be fruitless, things had gone too far. Nothing would undo the terrible damage wreaked by this appalling act. Vongole had taken them down.

And so, with a little help from me, Victoria is becoming single again, while her head rests on my shoulder. Her head is becoming more mine with every sentence. I can feel her body warm against me. I try to memorize the feeling so I can relive it in days to come, but the feel of a woman is a hard thing to store. My lips are an inch from hers. An inch and a hundred miles.

"What sort of man would suit me, then?"

Is this a leading question? Yes, this must surely be a cue for me to describe myself. A man of medium build, probably with country origins, a scientific background but artistic temperament, a reformed delinquent, the likely heir to millions (of bees), not all that knowledgeable, and who may or may not amount to anything. Certainly not the natural "high-flyer" type. But someone who would love and respect you and not mind if you knew more about a subject than he did (unless the subject was fighting).

But I couldn't say all that. I couldn't even hint at it, not really. With her head resting on my shoulders? It would have been an act of gross flirtation.

So I say, "What sort of men do you fancy?"

"I don't have a type. I think I'd like to find someone much older than me for a change. Maybe someone who has a proper job, like in a bank or something. Someone who's lived a bit and knows who he is and what he wants and isn't going to feel threatened by me."

Victoria, why didn't you just say, "I'm looking for someone who's the opposite of you, James?"

So, what conclusions could I draw from Giles? That Victoria goes for well-spoken types like herself, high-achieving men with a rather lecherous manner. Giles is knowledgeable but this is in the end what lets him down—his fear of Victoria's knowledge. Giles is dumped because he is petty and doesn't like his woman to know more than he does about anything. But it should also be noted that Giles is dumped

when he is no longer the rising star of the film world but a bit of a laughing-stock.
Is this relevant? Is his status as "dominant male" important?

And what did Giles have that I didn't?

A nice accent.

Class.

Clothes from the obscure shop, etc. . . .

High status.

Poise, self-confidence.

The bestest walk.

Knowledge.

All this goes into my mental dossier. This information will be compared and contrasted with the men who'll follow. She may not think she has a type, but a pattern is bound to emerge—a pattern I will use in my struggle.

My long struggle for Victoria.

VICTORIA'S MEN.
NUMBER TWO—DANNY PHILIPS

After what seemed like an indecently short break of just three weeks, Victoria was boyfriended again. It happened before my very eyes. We were at a gig. The band consisted of four ex-history students called The Problemos. (Never heard of them? Where were you?) Victoria knew the drummer. She also had her car with her that week. (Yes, Victoria not only drove, but owned her own little BMW Mini.) She offered Danny, this drummer, a hand transporting his kit. I tagged along, ostensibly to help out, but of course really just to be with my beloved friend.

I had asked Victoria about Danny the day before.

"He's just a friend. He works at the bar in Soho during the day. He writes the lyrics. Plays drums."

"Romance possible?"

"Not my type."

Excellent.

"Why not?"

"His arms are too big and he wears plimsolls."

Wow.

Now, Victoria is not really superficial. Well, no more than most people. (I reckon that deep down we're all superficial. On the surface we're deep.) But the fact is that big arms and plimsolls don't do it for her. Maybe big arms alone are fine. Maybe plimsolls might be acceptable on a man with astonishingly thin arms. But a big-arms-and-plimsolls-combination is fatal. And who are we to argue?

Look at biology.

If any male hilder fish changed the tiny spot above its mouth from yellow to blue it would never be able to mate. Just one tiny and incredibly superficial change in its appearance, perhaps equivalent to a man donning a pair of plimsolls, and it has no chance. Norwegian laboratory tests show females swim miles to avoid dating a blue-spotted hilder, and no amount of sweet talk makes a difference. So what can humankind learn from the simple hilder fish? This: that small errors in fashion can mean you're going home alone.

I made a mental note never to wear plimsolls. And my advice to all men in the dating game: never, ever, underestimate the power of footwear. Don't try to understand it. Plimsolls may say something about you that only the woman you love comprehends.

But surely there are other things about Danny that make him a no-no? Huh, Victoria?

"Well, I don't like his band much. I don't respect what they do, really. It's all trying to be commercial without sounding like that's what they're trying to do. I think if they're going to be commercial they should stop posing like some underground band. I quite like Danny's company but he can be a jerk and he takes too many drugs. He needs to grow up."

This intelligence is invaluable. For I am a secret agent for Love, a double agent, in fact. I am posing as a mere friend, and all the time I am gathering information for the predator within. I must probe further.

"But he's quite a laugh, you said once. And didn't you tell me he's quite sexy on stage?"

"Not my type."

So let's recap. He is a plimsoll-wearing, big-armed, druggy, immature, unsexy jerk in a band Victoria doesn't respect. The secret agent can report back to Love HQ that the coast is clear. There will be no hanky panky tonight.

Three hours later I am in the car park, trying to locate Victoria's Mini and there it is—bouncing up and down like it was starring in an American teen comedy. The plimsoll-wearing, big-armed, untalented, immature tosser-in-a-crap-band has ignited a passion so strong that Victoria couldn't even wait for him to take off his plimsolls. There they are, jammed against the rear dash.

Conversation on phone the following afternoon:

"He was just dead-sexy on stage."

"I thought you didn't—"

"I changed my mind." Your mind?

"And he just put his arms around me on the dance floor afterward and started kissing my neck and it was great. I don't think it'll last but it's fun. Sorry about not giving you a lift but . . ."

"No, I saw. I could see his feet on the rear dash. I recognized the plimsolls."

"Oh, God."

So, do I change the edict to myself never to wear plimsolls? Do I develop outsize forearms? Do I behave like an immature druggy tosser and join a crap band? I think it was Barbra Streisand who asked, "How can I make you love me?"

Danny, Victoria and I went out as a threesome a few times. He talked about his band far too much and claimed he was the creative force behind it all. Basically a big head. Big-armed, big-headed and plimsoll-footed. On the other hand he was generous with his drugs, and he did have a slightly Irish-sounding lilt and these sweet, blue eyes that seemed to widen Victoria's own.

But the end came, as I hoped it would, just five weeks later. Danny was seen snogging some groupie. He told Victoria that he thought that he was having an open relationship with her. She said, and I completely agreed with her, that open relationships are fine in their own way, but you really do have to tell the other person it's open. And why, if it was so "open," did he have his little flings in secret, and look so embarrassed when he was eventually caught?

For my part, I could not understand why anyone would want to two-time Victoria. Not because I'm a saint—I like fooling around as much as any bloke—but I thought at the time that if I had Victoria, infidelity would be like owning Fort Knox and trying to get free chips from a confectionery machine.

So what did Danny boy have that I didn't?

A band.

Charming eyes.

A carefree, relaxed persona.

Drugs.

Big arms.

Plimsolls.

All this goes into the mental dossier. So, with Giles and Danny, can you see a pattern begin to emerge? Can you see a theme that might help in my quest to become Victoria's perfect man?

Me neither.

SIX

She sits on the wobbly kitchen chair, takes a deep breath to calm herself, but makes it look like she's just tired. She won't meet my eyes. Perhaps she knows this is the end. I had told her that I thought we needed to talk, about things, about "us." Now we'll have a conversation and at the end of it we will be single. She waits. There's a coaster on the table that she is trying to balance on its edge.

I take a last deep draw on my Silkie, drop it in the sink, and watch it die. I finger the soggy corpse and drop it in the bin.

"Victoria—"

"Right, ok. This doesn't have anything to do with the other night?"

"What?"

"You said something about Stefan on the way home from the pub. You implied I fancied him."

"I wasn't annoyed about that. I expected it to happen."

"But I don't fancy him."

"Maybe not now, but you will. Anyway, I'm not annoyed."

"But you *should* be annoyed if you think I fancy him."

"I arranged it."

I say this not because it's true, but because I want to see if it *sounds* true. If it rings true, then maybe it is.

What *was* I thinking, exactly, when I phoned Victoria from the pub and asked her to meet Stefan? Was it really a calculated set-up? Or was I trying to do something that I hoped would fail? Does trying-hoping-you'll-fail make any sense? Does anything I've said or done make any sense?

"What are you talking about, you 'arranged it'?"

"Don't worry. This will all work out well. You see, Stefan is the nicest person I know."

"So you *are* jealous about the other night."

"I'm not. I would have been a year ago, but not now. I've come to terms with it."

"Come to terms" is a handy phrase to throw into discussions with women. It sounds like you've really thought about your emotions and relationships and stuff.

"What do you mean, you 'arranged' it?" she persists.

"All right, I didn't arrange it. Whatever, whatever. I don't care either way."

The events follow the usual pattern of late: I say something annoying, in an annoying way, then Victoria gets annoyed. What is less predictable is that Victoria picks up a scented candle (vanilla, half burnt down, a little gift from me) and throws it and—*wallop*—it hits the wall behind me.

This is fairly unlike her.

Ok. Fair enough. I appear to be the baddy. Maybe I'm losing it a little. I don't seem to have perspective. Which is odd, because I have been giving things a lot of thought recently. I've been trying to look at things critically and objectively. Now, as you well know, I was in love—very in love—with Victoria for a painfully long time. But after two years of living together, I don't think about her as much as I did. Or long to hold her; and, to be brutally frank, I don't fancy her as much as I did. There. Those are the simple emotional facts.

You see, I'm trying to be as scientific as I can (putting my state-funded education to good use) and I reckon the love I have for Victoria has reduced by 10 percent year on year, in real terms. I was a bit obsessed, wouldn't you say? Now I'm not.

Now comes the deduction.

Victoria feels the same way. (My evidence is not scientific but I never said this was a textbook. If you found this in the science section, someone has seriously messed up.) Victoria, I deduce, is beginning to think this whole affair, which started with such promise, and gave us each the happiest year and eight months of our lives, has run out of steam, lost its sparkle.

I'm not talking about the trivial irritations. (But then again some trivial irritations might be worth a mention: whereas, before, the fact that I don't drive was ok and a little interesting, now is it still ok but a little irritating. The fact that I always leave something on my plate for Mr. Manners used to be a subject for merry banter. Now, like an overused catchphrase, it is beginning to grate.)

By and large Victoria and I can deal with the trivial. But there is something else lurking between us that I fear isn't trivial. If I could step back from the canvas for a moment I am sure I would see some large object that is totally out of place and needs painting over.

Victoria, being the game girl she is, will want to find out what it is, not paint it over, but deal with it head-on, make it better, reshape it, paint it a different color.

She'll want to discuss the issues, figure out why I'm unhappy, talk ourselves to the point where there's nothing more to say.

Why put her through that?

As the candle rolls over the tiles (which I laid on one stifling summer day), I feel guilty for being the cause of Victoria's wrath. That was really not my intention. I am simply trying to exit her life causing her as little pain as possible. This will all be for the best, she'll see.

"James, I really want to know what's wrong with you."

"What makes you think there's something wrong?"

"You know that poster of the rabbit with electrodes on its head they used in those anti-vivisection ads?"

"I think I've seen it."

"That rabbit looks happier than you do. He's a happy bunny compared to you the last few months. Especially in the mornings. You could be in an advert for euthanasia. A close-up of your face and the line, *Why let people carry on in such misery?*"

"You've noticed, then."

"Don't tell me you've been trying to hide it."

God, I really *had* been trying to hide the misery. For someone like me, misery is like nakedness. Showing sadness is like accidentally revealing my bottom to a crowd. (A dream I kept having at the time involved being naked in a fairground. I feel awkward, but it's just about tolerable, and I walk around. Then Victoria arrives with clothes and I'm mortified because she is the one person I feel most embarrassed in front of. I run away and she follows, saying, "But I've brought your clothes." She wants to help but I just keep running. It's one of those dreams that is so easy to interpret that you wonder why the subconscious bothers with symbolism.)

"Victoria, I try to keep my misery to myself. I push my face into the pillow in the morning."

"I know. Why?"

"So you can't see my sad face."

"Well, James, funnily enough, burying your face in the pillow for half an hour every morning isn't a very effective way of concealing misery. It does not make me think, Ah, what a nice time he must be having all scrunched up in the pillow. It makes me think, My partner is severely depressed, he won't talk to me, what am I going to do, call a doctor?"

"Well, it doesn't matter."

"It does."

"I just think that, on the whole, I am not doing you any good."

"James . . ."

"No, listen a minute. This is all very clear, very simple. You are going to leave me soon."

"What are you talking about?"

"I know that may seem strange but I know these things. Like you know things. Or used to."

"I used to *think* I did. I was wrong most of the time."

"But I'm not. It is totally crazy that we should be together. It's mad. It was great for a while. But now it doesn't feel healthy. For you, I mean."

"James, I love you, I don't understand what you mean. You don't mean what you just said. You don't. I am worried about you."

She gets up and puts her hands on my chest. She's looking in my eyes but there's nothing to see, I made sure of it.

"I've been worried about you for a while."

"I know. I do not want that. I do not want you to worry about me. I want you to look at me and think, He's great. However silly that may seem."

"I *do* think you're great."

She *has* to say that.

I continue. "I didn't desire you for eight years so you could watch me bury my head in your pillow. That's not what I want. In fact it's the last thing. I mean, there are men out there . . . who know how to use their talent to their advantage."

"What are you saying? Whose talent? What men?"

"Look at you, you're beautiful, no you *are,* you *are* beautiful, don't dismiss it, you *are* beautiful outside and in, and look in the mirror there—there are men who could bring a smile to that face. When do I do that? I don't. Not anymore. That's all I'm saying."

"James, the last two years have been the happiest in my life. Well, apart from the last month or two."

"Exactly my point. The last two years have been great. It's been fantastic. Helping you do up your flat—I actually *enjoyed* all that. Even scraping off the wallpaper. You make the most boring things fun. How do you do that?"

"I don't know."

"Because you are a naturally joyful person. You are pathologically happy. You are clinically chipper."

"But I'm worried about you—I'm not happy about that."

She has walked right into my trap. This is going better than I dared hope.

"Exactly. I make you unhappy. I manage to make a pathologically joyful person unhappy. How do I do that?"

"Oh no, that's not what I meant. I would be much less happy without you. Even when you're miserable. I love your miserable old bones."

"That's natural, that's fine, but a time will come. A time will come when you'll realize."

She sighs. "You are simply down at the moment. Low self-esteem or whatever. Look, trust me. I'm good at this. You're just feeling low."

I shake my head. She really doesn't get it. She doesn't understand that the low self-esteem is *hers,* not mine. She hasn't yet realized what a wonderful person she is, so she thinks all she deserves is me. You see women like this all the time. They go out with wankers, bastards and bores because they think that's all they deserve; because their low self-esteem tells them that. Men use this feminine foible to great effect (I have used it myself before now). Victoria deserves better. One day she'll know it.

We don't say anything for a moment. I'm standing there, feeling trembly on the outside, but my blood is running strong with logic. I have got this whole thing sussed.

Victoria has a frown. She can't keep up with the brilliance of my argument. I continue my roll.

"You did get on very well with Stefan."

"He's just a really nice, interesting guy."

Victoria never describes anyone as a *guy.* It's always *bloke* or *man.* What makes Stefan a *guy*? Is being a *guy* better? Are *guys* nicer than *blokes* or *men* or *boys*?

It was this constant laughter between them that clinched it for me. Laughter is how Victoria and I won each other—I suppose it's how anyone wins anyone. Me, I make Victoria laugh.

And so does Stefan.

Victoria and I made each other laugh the other night. First time for ages. We made humor together on the kitchen table. And we made love for the first time in two months and it was great. I was great, I really was. Passionate. Considerate. Patient. Loving. Dirty. I even stayed awake for a few minutes afterward—ha. And I made love to the *real* Victoria and not some fantasy

Victoria in some imaginary time. It was spontaneous, not dutiful. We weren't doing it because if we didn't we'd have to start asking ourselves scary questions like "Does not having sex mean this relationship is basically over?" Sometimes that question is just too scary so a bit of sex is required to chase it away. You see couples like this all the time. Well, you can't prove it, but you can guess. They don't look like a couple who spend time pleasuring each other. Otherwise she wouldn't be wearing the toweling tracksuit bottoms and he would have done something about the hair on the back of his neck. But they probably slog away at each other every other Tuesday just so they can tell themselves that their marriage is working.

There are other reasons for sex, of course. Without sex, romance doesn't work. The sunset, the wine, the panoramic view. None of it means a thing.

But the other night was *sexy* sex, sex for its own sake.

And after the sex there was love.

There was looking into each other's eyes and saying nothing. There were smiles about nothing in particular. (I can make Victoria laugh simply by smiling.) There was no trudging to the loo to wash anything away. No switching on the radio or opening of books to move things on. No conversation about what time we had to get up in the morning, or can you lend me a ten because I forgot to go to the ATM. Just time together, a stroke of her hair and a caress. This was good-bye. My body taking leave of hers. She leaned on her hand and said:

"You look sad."

"Yes, I am sad."

"Because?"

"Because all the best things come to an end."

"Silly."

"Youth, flowers, sex. Life. Happiness can only ever be short-lived. That's the only reason flowers are so beautiful. Because they're so transitory. An everlasting flower would be held in contempt."

"Why do you get like this after sex?"

"Do I?"

"Recently. Well, recently as in on the few occasions we do it these days. You come out with some rather melancholy statement about the human condition, while I'm trying to find somewhere to put the condom."

"Sex makes me think."

"You shouldn't be inventing lighthearted game shows. You should be writing gloomy detective series. Or *EastEnders*. Or one of those interminable radio plays."

We held hands for a while and looked up at the ceiling, pointing out various patches that needed painting over. She asked me when I'd get round to it. The answer's never.

"Maybe next week."

Victoria picks up the coaster and tries to balance it on its edge again. It falls over. If this was one of Stefan's films he'd have a close-up of that. It would be hailed as brilliant symbolism.

I'm thinking that the fact that she isn't simply laughing at the notion that she fancied Stefan is confirmation. Victoria either fancies people or finds the idea of fancying them absolutely laughable. (If you're female and your partner suspects you of fancying someone, laugh a lot. Laugh at the very idea. That's the most reassuring thing he could hear.) Victoria doesn't laugh. She has a serious face, like I could have a point.

"Anyway, look, I told you it's not about Stefan."

"What is it about then?"

"I don't know. Well, it's just that we aren't getting on very well. And . . . you probably need someone more, I don't know, different, *better.*"

When I was a kid I didn't think anyone was better than anyone else. It seemed to me that the bright kids in the class were probably either bad at games or got bullied or had a limp. The kid who was good at games was really poor or always in trouble. Swings and roundabouts, ups and downs, it all evened out in the end.

I also believed that everyone would have the same amount of luck in their lives. The kids who seemed to be miserable now would be happy when they were grown up. People with dead-end jobs would have great family lives. Lonely people would be comforted by success and riches. If everything was taken into account we are all equal—because what kind of God would have created us otherwise?

Then along came Darwin. And Stefan.

And as I saw more of life, it seemed to me that some kids were better, fitter than others. Some people were less lucky, less happy than others. If there was a Game Show of Everything, where every possible human attribute and condition was categorized and played for, there would be not be a big, cuddly, comforting draw. There would be winners and losers.

Some people are better than others.

There are men who are better than me. More desirable, sexier, more stimulating, more interesting, funnier, richer, kinder, healthier, luckier, better-smelling, happier.

It therefore seems perfectly reasonable, perfectly fair, and in the interests of both Victoria and Stefan, that I stand aside. Let a better man win.

Besides. I could not just walk out and leave Victoria on her own. No, I couldn't do that. That would be heartbreaking because of course she would be upset. She has invested time and love in me. She has set her heart on me. She wanted me to be the person she spends the rest of her life with. Of course she will mourn the loss of this hope—her dream that I would turn out good. All that striving, all that work for naught. Why put her through that, when the nicest man in the world is in town, and he's single? What a wonderful distraction for her grief. He will care for her, help her see that she doesn't need me. (I don't understand why everyone in the world isn't as levelheaded as me. I want this book to be a model for couples everywhere, a handbook for love.)

While I've been congratulating myself on my mastery of logic. Victoria has been very slowly shaking her head from side to side. There is a flicker of a smile on her face, but it's not joyful.

"So you are leaving me because you think I need someone better." She lets out a little laugh. "Well, you know you could be right. I could do with someone who doesn't lie about why he's leaving, that's for sure. Have you met someone else?"

"No."

Victoria is relieved but not for long.

"You're behaving like a man who has. It's all making sense now. You don't go to bed with me, you bury your head in the pillow to avoid my attention. You want out but you're too fucking scared to say so. So you come out with all this you're-not-good-enough-for-me crap. For a man who hates clichés, you've got enough for a whole episode of *Casualty.* How about this one—*I've met someone else.*"

"I haven't."

"I don't want to know anything about her! I don't even want to know if she exists or not! I don't want you to even deny it!"

She is on the kitchen towels now.

"So what are we going to do?"

I don't like to see her rub the hard tissue against her soft little nose. I go and bring some Kleenex from the sitting room, wondering if this gesture will come across as patronizing or insulting, like a boss politely shaking the hand of someone he's just sacked.

"Well? What are we going to do?" she repeats.

"What do *you* think?"

Wasn't she going to take the option of giving me the elbow? It was there on a plate.

"I'm asking *you*." She throws the coaster at me and it bounces off my shoulder. Seeing her cry gives me a deep hunger for her but I can't give in to it. I retrieve the coaster from the floor. An altogether too-controlled gesture, but I need to seem controlled. I need to do normal things. I can't crack up. I want to cry because she is leaving me, abandoning me. I want to sob like Sandra at Pizza Hut after seeing *Betty Blue*. The sensation I have is in my eyes and in my stomach. I suddenly realize that I have had the feeling before, a long, long, long time ago. It's the feeling that I suppose everyone has had—of turning round in a big shop to find that Daddy has gone. It's the feeling of being cruelly abandoned and suddenly the shop is a horrible place full of danger and the whole world seems like one giant trap and all you can do is cry and run, but when you're running you don't know if you're getting nearer to Daddy or further away, and it's all your fault for not paying attention and wandering off.

Victoria's tears are gentle, no hysteria. She cries beautifully, with tears rolling down a smooth face in repose, no contortion. I want to hold her and tell her everything will be all right, feel the drops on my tongue, say that we'll be together forever.

"Stefan mentioned that there might be a job for me if his film goes ahead," she states flatly.

"I know."

"I won't take it if you don't want me to."

"It's a good job, you must take it."

"But I'd be spending a lot of time with him. Wouldn't you mind?"

She's trying to be nice. But it's just making me think that I might indeed have cause to be jealous. But the *very idea* should be laughed out of mind.

"So what do you think we should do?"

Here goes.

"I think we should split up." But I can't leave it there, not just like that—it's too painful. It needs modifying. "Maybe just for a while. It's been two years, maybe we need to be apart so we can take stock. We might change our minds and decide that we *are* right for each other after all. This doesn't have to be the end of everything."

"Spare me the bullshit."

She bangs into the sitting room, slamming the door. I hear more bangs. She's piling up a few of my CDs, I guess. "I don't understand you, I just don't, and I don't think I ever have!"

Now we are no longer a couple. We are two single people, detached, unattached. I'm saying it to myself but I don't believe it.

On hearing of a death people always say "I feel stunned" but that's not really a feeling at all. They should say, "I feel nothing."

But then, here it comes, a quiet, floaty sensation, like being underwater, but something's coming, way off in the distance, something big and strong, like a great wave.

SEVEN

Me and Gerard are not having a good morning. Gerard is a flood of ideas and I am sitting in my own world, trying to understand how it feels without Victoria. It feels bad and strange and unfamiliar.

The night before I had told the love of my life I wanted to split up. The logic that had governed this decision has disappeared overnight. It was careless of me to misplace it. I must find it again.

I slept on the sofa. Or rather, the sofa is the thing I lay awake on, trying to get comfy with my set of reasons, as if they were giant cushions. When I began to think that I might have made a terrible mistake, a comforting circular argument helped me out. It went like this: only a coward leaves someone because they think they aren't good enough for them (a given). Therefore, I am a coward. A coward is not good enough for Victoria (another given). Therefore I am not good enough for Victoria. Brilliant, isn't it? At least my powers of reasoning are as finely tuned as ever. But I am having trouble finding some of the other givens. Someone has taken them.

I don't feel up to this game-show lark. I've got this permanent tremble running through my body. The shakes, I suppose. My whole coordination system feels suddenly unreliable. If only emotional pain didn't feel so physical I think I could stand it.

A mountain of Silkie butts is growing in the pan lid we use as an ashtray. I need an injection of nicotine, a mere cigarette doesn't do it for me. I want to drink pints of pure tar.

I lie back on the rancid old sofa and close my eyes for a moment. Lovers, think about this one. Does your lover love you? Suppose you had to start from scratch, could you win them again now, like you did the first time? If the answer is "no," then what are you supposed to do?

"Shark Survivor."

"Huh?"

I am supposed to respond, but my powers of crap-detecting have left me. I don't know which ideas are good and which deserve to be shot down in midair.

"Throw six people in with some sharks, whoever survives, wins."

Something tells me this is one of the maddest ideas in the world, but something else tells me that I'm not sure about anything anymore. It's crap, but maybe it could be made into something good. Maybe they are robot sharks that don't actually kill you. Or it's a computer game or a board game. Who knows? Who cares?

"Well? Is it a goer?"

"I don't know."

"You don't know? You have been saying that to every idea

I have come up with for the last two hours. You are the crap-detector. Not knowing is not an option."

Gerard says all this to a wall. His nose about four inches from it, which is actually slightly further away than normal. His hands are tightly clasped behind his back and I find I address these hands and use them as a face substitute. They move, they tense up, they relax, they frown, sometimes they seem to smile.

"*Whose Pants Are They, Anyway?* A panel of punters is given a pair of pants and they have to guess which celebrity they belong to."

I say nothing.

"When they have all guessed, the celebrity comes on, modeling the pants. It's got mystery, titillation and comedy. And pants."

Gerard seems to be working himself into a frenzy of creative destruction.

"*Who's the Stiff?* We exhume three corpses. Three widows guess which is their dear-departed husband."

Gerard moves away from the wall and stares out of the window for inspiration.

"*Climb Christopher Biggins!*"

"*What?*"

"We build a hundred-foot statue of Christopher Biggins. Two mountain climbers scale the monument—first one to his ears wins a dinner for two with Christopher Biggins. It's a banker."

"Oh, stop it."

"*Are Friends Electric?* Get two friends. Tie electrodes to their temples. Electrocute them."

"And?"

"There's no *and.* You just electrocute people. It's a winner."

"Leave it."

"*Pets Win Owners.* Abandoned puppies do tricks. The winners get caring owners. The losers get the needle." He mimes a syringe being emptied.

"No."

"You haven't given it a chance."

"I don't need to."

"*That's My Lung.*"

"Gerard . . ."

"Three lungs go past on a conveyor belt. Patients who've had their lungs removed press a buzzer when they think they spot their own. The winner gets an internal organ of their choice from a peasant standing by in the Sudan. If no one guesses the peasant gets to keep his organ."

"Perhaps if it wasn't lungs but . . . I don't know . . ."

"You're right, too vague. How about kidneys?"

"No!"

"Colons? Too messy. But it's got jeopardy, human interest and lots of gore. What more could a viewer want? Let's kick it around."

I feel sick.

"*Porn Idol.* For an adult channel. *Pop Idol* with split beavers. No, they're probably already doing it."

We're both going nuts. This has to stop.

Gerard says. "I'm not feeling right."

"*You* aren't feeling right. *I* am going nuts before your eyes and *you* aren't feeling right. We have six months to sell a game-show idea and *you* aren't feeling right."

Gerard turns to face me. "What is wrong with you?"

"I'm sorry, Gerard. I'm no use to you. I've lost it."

He looks down at the floor then back at me.

"Victoria and I are splitting up. She's going out with someone else."

"Jesus. Who?"

"Stefan Catchiside."

He heaves a sigh and sits down on one of the upturned crates. "How did you let that happen?"

I shrug. I don't know.

"Stefan is so sodding lucky. He walked into success as if it were a coat being held open for him. He's a Tim Rice in the making."

"No, Gerard—not now." But it's too late.

"Sir fucking Tim fucking Rice. And something else—Stefan is a *nice* man. I *like* the guy."

"What do you mean, *guy*? Why is he a *guy*? What are you?"

"I'm a *bloke*."

"What's a *guy* then?"

"What are you talking about?"

"You said *guy*. You never say *guy*."

"How do you know? Have you been monitoring my *guy* count?"

"I tell you what *guys* are. They are cleaner than blokes, more polite, and have good hair and are probably more sensitive and creative. A *guy* is a woman's idea of what a bloke should be."

"Bollocks. Loads of women fancy blokes."

"So you admit there's a distinction."

"Something strange is going on here, James, and it scares me."

"You're not scared of anything."

"Oh I am. People changing scares me. I like people to remain the same. But you are not the same bloke who—"

"Bloke!"

"Or *guy* . . . or humanoid entity you were a few days ago. You have not made tea. For the first time in two years. It's scary."

"So not making tea is scary, is it? Never join the bomb-disposal squad."

I take out my millionth Silkie of the morning.

"Anyway, he's good-looking, funny, bright. Why did you let him sniff around your woman?"

"Would you have kept them apart?"

"Of course I fucking would. I would have ditched Stefan completely if necessary."

"I did, kind of. I don't see Stefan much. But suddenly I feel that the game is up between me and Victoria."

"The game is never up. A good game keeps the suspense right up to the very end."

"This *is* the end."

"When did it all happen?"

"It hasn't. But it will."

"So none of this has happened, you just think it will?"

"I *know* it will."

"Do something, then! Stop them seeing each other."

"How do I do that?"

"Tell her not to see him. Or you'll bend her over your knee and spank her."

"Please."

"Come on, you're always on about evolution. Fight for her, play the caveman. Fight for what's yours."

"I don't own her, do I?"

"You were a fighter. The terror of Taunton School. Give him some."

Attractive though Gerard's suggestion is, I try to cling on to the nonviolent sensibilities that I have been nurturing since I started befriending Stefan at the age of fifteen.

"Jealousy is the least appealing of qualities. By showing my jealousy I would be revealing the worst thing about myself. That's not exactly going to augment Victoria's love for me."

"I can't believe it. I am supposed to be the mad one. You are supposed to be sensible. You are talking like a complete loser. I hate losers."

"You hate winners, too."

"Ok, I hate everyone. This is inviting someone to ruin your life. It's like leaving your front door open because you're going to get burgled sooner or later so might as well get it over with. This is like rejecting all our ideas because someone else is bound to turn them down sooner or later."

"But that's exactly what I do! With a few exceptions. I am really good at looking at things and deciding that they're crap. I have looked at myself and thought, I am a crap boyfriend. I have looked at Stefan and thought, He's not. If I were Victoria I would ditch me and go out with him. I can't stay with her with those thoughts in my head."

Gerard sits down, quite a rare occurrence.

There is a silence. Gerard seems deep in thought, not something I have seen before. He is an erupter, not a considerer, not a weigher-upper. But he seems to be weighing something up in his madhouse of a mind. He frowns slightly as if he is analysing an idea he's had, looking at it from all sides and making a rational assessment. Suddenly he springs to life and almost jumps up in the air.

"Do you want a cup of tea?"

That is by far the strangest thing Gerard has ever said. The game-show stuff might seem a bit off-beam to you, but Gerard offering to make tea is, believe you me, a pinch-yourself moment. What is happening to us? The delicate balance of madness that has brought us so much, er, success over the years (well, nearly brought us it—oh come on, we did get close) is in danger of coming down like a house of cards. We could simply drift into a mad world of game-show freakery from which there is no return.

We try to get back to work but Gerard dries up and I seem incapable of coming to a verdict.

"What should I do?"

"Kill him. Or her. Or yourself. Or try to sabotage their relationship. How about going out with someone else? Make her jealous. Threaten to commit suicide, prey on her guilt."

I should have known that Gerard's suggestions would be as sensible as his game-show ideas.

"Gerard, what are you talking about?"

"I'm trying to make constructive suggestions."

"Those ideas aren't constructive, they're crap."

"I come up with crap ideas, that's my job."

He has a point. We can't get any work done so I might as well listen to his crap ideas about my personal life.

"Go on, then. Fire away."

"Change yourself. Make yourself the person she wants you to be."

"It would take too long. I would have to pretend to be something I'm not."

"Make Stefan worse, then. Corrupt him, mentally cripple him."

"Crap."

"Change her. Make her into the sort of person who deserves you."

"I can't."

"Have a sex change, go gay, try to get her back. Beg. Campaign. See a shrink. Beg him not to see her. Bribe him. Poison his mind against her. Poison her mind against him. Poison your own mind against both of them. Become a celibate. Become an Islamic fanatic."

Gerard comes up with a few dozen more loony ideas before we decide to call it a wasted day. As I put on my coat he has one last shot.

"Just go to her flat and tell her the truth. You left her because you were jealous. You can't help it. But now you want to come back. You're very sorry."

That is, of course, a perfectly sensible suggestion. It's a goer, worth developing certainly. It has legs. But sensible is not how I feel at the moment.

On the way home I get an evening paper. A man in Dorset went berserk and killed his wife, two children and then rigged up a tractor so it would run over him and crush his brains. No explanation was given and there appeared to be no motive. It shocked the whole neighborhood, which was described as "quiet and peaceful, a very close-knit community." I have often wondered why anyone chooses to live in quiet, close-knit communities because so many ghastly murders happen in them. In fact they seldom happen anywhere else. I amuse myself with this thought when I notice the picture of the wedding photograph. The murderer and his bride, beaming with sickening smugness. They look familiar. His name was Timothy and hers was Barbara. "They had been together since university," said a close friend.

Timothy and Barbara. The couple I brought together because I thought they were made for each other. The drizzle suddenly turns into a shower. I use the newspaper as an umbrella and run to the bus stop, dodging puddles on the way.

EIGHT

VICTORIA'S MEN.
NUMBER THREE—MARK FRANKLE

I have Mark Frankle to thank for my first glimpse of Victoria nearly naked, and indeed it is pretty much down to good old Mark that I went to bed with Victoria in the second year. Our first bed scene. Victoria and I, in bed, our naked bodies touching for the very first time. It's something we can both laugh about now. Well, not now *exactly, but years later. What happened was this:*

Victoria's going out with Mark Frankle. He is a mature law student of about twenty-six, which seems ever so grown up. The bastard has a car, a flat to himself, a laptop computer, and a decent pair of gloves. I am impressed by the leather gloves because I think owning any is something I might never get round to doing. It seems an incredibly mature and sensible way of spending twenty quid—equivalent to twelve student-bar pints, or twenty-four cups of student cappuccino. I will never, even when grown up, have the courage to make that kind of long-term investment. And even if someone gave me a pair of gloves they would be lost within days. The responsibility of glove-ownership is beyond my capability and I can only respect

Mark's sophistication, albeit grudgingly. When I discover Mark also owns a fully operational umbrella, respect turns to awe.

Mark had been a buyer for a big supermarket and now wanted to get the qualifications for a pukka profession, hence his return to Studentville. The man wears "nice" clothes and is so mature-looking that you don't want to swear in front of him. He stands up when Victoria enters a room, and he buys a round of drinks without telling everyone how much it cost (obligatory in student circles to this day, I believe) and I suspect he washes his hands with soap after just a wee.

What's most unusual about Mark (or should we call him Mr. Frankle? Or Dad?) is that even though he's a student, he enjoys studying. He actually looks forward to lectures and never misses them. He suggests getting together with his fellow law students for "informal discussions" about recent cases. He is polite, clean, friendly and kind.

And do you know, despite all that, he isn't such a bad bloke. A tad straight, a tad off-home-early, a tad music-too-loud and a tad not-for-me-I-don't-drop-them-anymore. I like to think that in bed he is a tad not-tonight-darling-it's-a-weekday. I like to think that, but in fact I am quite wrong.

"It's the best sex I've ever had."

Well, knock me down with a feather.

"I think it's his experience. Or, well, I feel relaxed with him. And . . . oh, I don't know."

"What?"

"Nothing."

"You were going to say something else."

"No I wasn't."

"You were."

"I can't say. Really. It's just . . ."

"Go on."

There is something she's dying to tell me but it is too intimate, too crude, too damn sexy to reveal. My mission is to get at it. I must have the information. Endless guessing is the best way to wheedle it out.

"He knows how to find your G-spot or whatever it is?"

"No. It's . . . no, I can't."

"He's hung like a donkey."

"No. But you're . . ."

"I'm warm. He's got vibrating balls. Vibrating, detachable penis. He's got a clitoris-sensing device in his fingers. In his tongue? He stays awake for ages afterward."

"Look, all right, I'll tell you. He just feels great."

"Feels? What? His skin? Or his . . ."

"He feels really good . . . you know, inside."

"Right, so he's got a big cock, I already guessed that."

"It's not the size. Or maybe it is. But there's . . . no, I can't."

I contemplate bending her little fingers back until she talks.

"You cannot stop there, it is cruel and inhumane."

"I can't tell you everything, James."

"Victoria, listen to me. If you don't tell me it could give me some kind of complex. I might feel all inadequate. I might not be able to father children." (This is what American college kids used to say to their dates if they got an erection that went untreated.) Victoria smiles. Part of her was dying to tell me but on condition that she could claim, if only to herself, that it was arm-twisted out of her.

"I'll have another wine first."

A minute later I set a pint of Newcastle Brown and a white wine down on the table and wait for Victoria to straighten out the grin and find the right words.

"It's his cock. But . . . I don't know . . . what is it about his cock? It just feels fantastic. It looks and feels fantastic. I love his cock. I love touching it, sucking it, feeling it inside me, everything. That's all I can say. It's the most wonderful cock I've ever met."

I don't know for how long my eyebrows stayed raised in a quiet "how interesting" position, but I'm sure I beat my personal best. How to respond? A congratulatory kiss? By shouting. "Three cheers for Mark's cock!"?

I slowly nod my head, trying not to seem too impressed. Not many words, just raised eyebrows and a slow nod. What is there to say? The man has a great cock. Good for him. Good for her. May all three of them be very happy together.

As the weeks go by, Supercock frequently drops by my flat for a cup of tea on his way to a lecture. I can't engage in his conversations about the law. I'm too busy thinking about his cock.

"Do you realize that, in law, if you're a married man, even if your wife falls pregnant by another man, it is assumed you are responsible for the child? Hardly fair."

Is the shape of his fingers any clue? They are rather stubby. Is the way he crosses his legs an indication of what treasure lies between? Is his choice of trousers a sign of a buried gem of unimagined beauty? I must admit I glance down at his crotch often enough for me to wonder if he might get the wrong idea.

"Most English law is founded on principles of rights and responsibilities, until you get to children. Then all that goes out of the window. Your parents split up, didn't they, James? And you live with your dad, is that right?"

"What makes your cock so special?"

"Pardon?"

"Slap it on the table and let's have a look."

Of course I don't say this but it becomes a mild obsession. I accompany him to the Gents a couple of times but I never get a decent glance, and trying to coordinate my bladder-emptying with his might end in tears. I wanted to see his cock, wouldn't you?

Then one day a nice opportunity presents itself out of the blue. He pops round to my place for a coffee and while the kettle boils he unravels a wet towel which he wants to dry off. He had been swimming at the local pool.

"A bit of physical exercise recharges the mental batteries. Like a dynamo. Also breaks up the day. One can go back to the grindstone with a bit more lead in your pencil."

I wouldn't have thought your pencil needed any more lead, mate.

"Sitting at a desk all day makes me stiff."

Are you trying to annoy me?

"I'm determined to keep it up."

Stop it.

"You should have a swim yourself."

"Yeah, why not?"

"I can give you a lift to the pool."

"Definitely. What time are you thinking of?"

We decide one o'clock every other day would be best. Next day he comes to pick me up and off we go. The greatest penis in all the world would soon be within my sight.

Swim One

On the way he tells me his water-resistant watch became water-logged last time he swam, so he bought himself a flashy new diver's watch. Another item to go with his car, flat, laptop, gloves and umbrella. We arrive at the changing room, but he changes on the other side of a waist-high partition. I manage to sidle up to the barrier but only see an alarmingly smooth and hairless ass. It's a marvelous ass, an ass made in Ass Heaven by ass-making angels. A smoother, shapelier ass would be hard to find. He showers with his trunks on. Is he trying to hide something? Or is he politely sparing me feelings of inadequacy?

Swim Two

I make my way to a more communal changing area and he follows. However, just as he takes off his pants, a man plonks himself between us. Again he showers in his trunks.

Swim Three

This time Mark has brought some soap and shampoo and takes off his trunks in the shower. He has his perfect ass toward me permanently and so I can't get a look at his front. I sit down on the bench and resign myself to another day without a sighting when he comes over, stark-naked, and sits next to me. I can see it all.

"Look at that."

"Yes. I can see. It looks . . . fine."

"Oh, it looks all right. It looks great. But it's not working."

He holds his watch in almost the same line of vision as his cock, and both are clearly visible.

"It's been working fine but now it's stopped. I've given it a shake but the damn thing seized up. You're supposed to be able to dive with it!"

We only need a bit of sax music and a scantily clad girl to chase and we could enter Benny Hill's parallel universe.

And what of the cock in question? Is it an extraordinary vision of loveliness? Does it shine with radiant beauty? Well, no. It's just a cock. In fact I'd say it's a tad on the modest side and there's nothing about it that shouts "super" to me. It strikes me that my soul does not possess a Platonic ideal of "cock." What would the perfect cock look like? I have no idea. My musings on the male genital come to an abrupt halt when I realize that Mark has put down his wrist and I have been looking at his crotch for what must be a good few seconds. He grabs his towel defensively and moves quickly to the other side of the partition.

That's the last time I go swimming with Mark. "I think it's best to conserve energy really, James, what with finals coming up."

"Yeah, you're probably right."

"Maybe you should go with someone else." By which I think he means someone gay, like me.

To be truthful there is only one cock in the world I am directly interested in and, no, I'm not going to describe it. Suffice to say that the lunchtime swim with Mark banished any thoughts about perfect cocks and imperfect ones. I was at peace with my tool.

For exactly two months.

I am sitting on my bed, two months later, watching my old black and white portable TV, doing a disappearing trick with two liters of Newcastle Brown. It's 9:30 on a *cold winter's night and the thought of venturing to the union bar or indeed anywhere is not appealing. I opt for having my second, or possibly third, five-finger shuffle of the day.*

Just as I'm cleaning up the five million mini-me's from my belly with an old sock, the phone goes.

"Is that you, James?"

"Victoria?"

"I'm really scared."

I could hear it in her voice.

"A man came round earlier and asked if I wanted my hedge trimmed. I said no. He's still hanging around outside looking at the house. There's a window open downstairs."

"You're alone, I take it?" Dumb question.

"Everyone else has gone out till late! There's a window open! He could get in! Shall I call the police or what? Am I making a fuss over nothing?"

"No. What was he like?"

"Very creepy, very odd, I knew something was wrong. Why would he call about trimming a hedge at this hour and anyway he doesn't have a van or any equipment. Oh, God."

"Is he still there?"

"I don't want to look. All right, I'll look. Oh God. I'm so scared—please come over! He's looking up. He's going to kill me."

"Listen. He is not going to kill you. Can you close the window downstairs?"

"I can't go downstairs. I can't, I can't, I want to stay up here."

"Call the police. I will come as fast as I can. Do you know the neighbor's number?"

"No."

"Have you tried Mark? He's got a car and a mobile phone. Where is he?"

"Forget Mark."

"What?"

"Just come over. I'll get the police. Please, please hurry."

"I'm leaving now—don't answer the door and don't worry—he won't hurt you. Tell him someone's on their way if he gets in."

"He's coming up the drive! Don't go, stay on the line. No, go, I mean come here."

"See you in five minutes."

So I run out into the freezing air, hands trembling with excitement and cold, I unlock my bike and go like mad. My heart is racing with dread and fear. What would I do with this man? Fight him? What if he's armed with a knife or even a gun? Will I risk my life for Victoria? Will I die for Victoria so she can continue shagging Mark? Where is Mark? Will the police arrive just in time? Is it all a fuss over nothing? Is it just PMS? Will I be disappointed if the man has already gone? Do I want to be a knight coming to the aid of a damsel in distress? Am I glad this is happening? Will it make her love me?

Am I a shit for thinking these thoughts? She may be being raped or killed at this very moment. And I would have been glad it happened?

How can I stop thinking these thoughts?

Will she realize she loved me only when I'm gone? Will she weep over my grave? Will I weep over hers? Is she dead now? Is he fucking her dead body now?

I race through red lights and up a one-way street, across the park and over a pavement area. My breath is fading and my chest aches with the cold air suddenly rushing through it. There's a big hill leading to Victoria's road and I must reserve energy for it. As I approach, my legs and chest feel incredibly heavy and I'm not sure if I can make it. I overdid it, it was too sudden a rush, too sudden a change from re-laxing in a warm room to the physical and mental excitement of this, and the ice-cold air. Maybe the Newkie Brown has an effect, too. My legs will simply not obey me. The bike gets slower and slower till it teeters and zigzags along at walking pace. I get off and sling it down on the pavement (never to see it again). I make better progress on foot, all the time shouting at myself to move faster, faster, there's a life at stake. I keep my ears and eyes on the alert for police approaching, but there's nothing.

I approach the corner of Victoria's road and stop to catch my breath and harness my courage. There is no point in arriving totally breathless; I have to look like

I have the energy to put up a fight. I take some deep breaths and I turn the corner. I stand as erect as I can and try to look composed and not totally exhausted. I am now ready for a fight, and though I have no idea who I'll be up against I feel my body and mind are committed. That's really half the battle—you have to be committed. The fights I lost in the shopping center and street corners of my youth were mainly down to lack of resolve. A really committed weaker man can overcome amazing physical odds.

I am back in Taunton for a moment, ready for anything, not wanting trouble but not going to run away from it, either.

There is no one in sight. The window is open. There is a thud against my chest. It's a feeling that I have experienced before, but such a long, long time ago. When I was someone else, almost. A child, hiding under the covers because Dracula is in the wardrobe. This is not Taunton shopping center. This is dark, quiet, and empty. It's spooking me.

I call Victoria's name loudly. Nothing.

The light is on upstairs but none below. I call her name again as I approach the window. I find myself suddenly and strangely fearless again, utterly determined to do whatever is necessary. If I fail to stop the villain, it will not be through cowardice or lack of resolve. Pain or death are the only things that can go wrong and neither of them seem that bad at this moment.

Then another weird feeling takes hold. I suddenly get embarrassed. What if the chap is, I don't know, a vicar looking for his lost dog, or a neighbor who's dropped his key trying to find a way into the rear of the terrace? All this aggression has been mobilized and suddenly I would be faced with having to have an awkward chat. I would almost prefer the real danger of a psychotic killer than have to say, "Ah, sorry. Thought you were up to no good. Can't be too careful these days." Perhaps only a truly English person would prefer dicing with death to a slightly awkward situation.

I climb through the open window, and perch on the back of a sofa before jumping onto the floor. Again I call Victoria's name.

No answer.

Now another wave of fear does come a-crashing on my ribcage. (I am convinced that fear really does move in waves.) This fear is not for myself but of what I might find. Perhaps the madman has gone, fled out the back when he heard me call. Perhaps Victoria is dead now, her body waiting for me, and it is too late to say the things I wanted to. If she is alive I will tell her I love her and always have done from the moment I saw her.

As I begin to climb the steps I hear talking. Victoria and a man. Then she calls me.

"In the bedroom, Jamie."

I try to assess the tone. Fearful? Desperate? No, it's apprehensive, nervous, but in some way the nervousness is being concealed. I enter the bedroom with my stomach clenched, ready to take a punch. I then realize what an idiot I am for not having grabbed a weapon—a kitchen knife, a hammer, anything. Too late, I see Victoria sitting on her bed talking to a man in a blue tracksuit. He's about thirty years old and has thinning, reddish hair. He is wet with sweat and the room smells foul.

"This is Kevin."

"Is everything ok?" I say, but hardly recognize my voice.

"How do you do. You must be James. Victoria said you would be popping round."

I shake his hand. For Christ's sake, perhaps he is a man looking for a dog. I am almost disappointed that nothing dramatic has happened.

"So." I say. Useful word, that.

"Kevin just popped in," Victoria tells me. She makes her eyes very wide momentarily to communicate something to me but I don't know what. I sense things are under control.

I assess the situation thus: Kevin has some kind of mental problem and took a shine to Victoria. Perhaps he has been stalking her for a day or two. He came in through the window in order to talk to Victoria and Victoria engaged him in conversation because she thought that was the most likely way of delaying or preventing anything nasty from happening. Talk to the hostage-takers, in other words. Gain their trust, buy time.

And that is pretty much an accurate assessment. The police arrive about five minutes later, Kevin is taken away to the station while Victoria spends an hour answering questions and having a good cry. The police have come across Kevin before and he has a previous conviction for attempted rape. Victoria knew I was coming, and this fact enabled her to act calmly, and inform the intruder that her boyfriend was on his way. If I hadn't been, she probably would have panicked and screamed and who knows what would have happened. Victoria and the police both think I probably prevented a rape.

Am I a hero?

I certainly didn't feel like one. I just felt like a man doing his automatic duty. Who would not come to a woman in distress like that? In a way I felt privileged to have performed such a crucial role. Not everyone gets to be a real knight in shining armor and isn't it every man's dream? Am I even glad that it happened? Glad that Victoria was put in peril so I could rescue her? Even though it might give her nightmares for years? What does that make me?

Is there a word for it?

Then the phone rings at ten and I answer it for Victoria. It's Mark Supercock asking how Victoria is. He sounds very concerned. I give him the low-down and tell him she's fine. He says he'll come over in a minute. Victoria takes the phone and tells him not to bother and then hangs up.

Victoria and I wish we had some wine or brandy or a bottle or two of Newkie but the shops are shut so we have a cup of tea. She thanks me for the fifth time and for the fifth time I say it was nothing. It was simply an obligation. One doesn't decide to come to a woman in distress, it is an automatic response that any reasonable man would make.

"Then why didn't Mark come?"

"Did you call him?"

"I called him first—before you."

"And?"

"He said he was in a middle of one of his impromptu seminar things."

"But you explained the situation?" This isn't one-upmanship or rivalry or gloating or any of that. I am genuinely incredulous.

"He was three minutes away by car. He said that you could get there quicker by bike, which isn't true."

Obviously this is all music to my ears in one way, but in another I am quite horrified.

"I never want to see him again."

"That's a bit harsh. He's a good bloke. He probably didn't realize how serious it might have been. Give him a chance to explain." Feel the insincerity.

"Do you think he was reasonable?"

"Well, actually . . ."

"Fuck him."

And thus the verdict is announced and the jury is unanimous. Brilliant cock or not, he got his priorities wrong. Send him down.

Victoria decides then and there to break it off with him. Another one bites the dust.

Victoria and I are, as so often, sitting in a kitchen drinking tea and talking into the early hours. And as usual I begin to wonder how it will end. Whether the chemistry on this particular night would be different. If suddenly, instead of ignoring my occasional flirtations, she would play ball and one thing would lead to another. It seemed like the perfect moment in some ways. After all, I had nearly lost her—or so I thought. "If Victoria isn't dead, then I will tell her I love her." But that was a few hours ago and in an emotional turmoil. Now we have touched down at Reality Airport and things are exactly as they were.

Then suddenly: "I don't want to be alone."

"Ok . . . I'll hang about till morning. Is there somewhere I can crash?"

"Would you mind staying in my bed with me? I know it's silly but I'm scared."

"Ok, fine."

Calm down. Take a look at the facts, young man. The girl has just been scared out of her wits, she is alone, of course she wants someone to stay with her, and "in bed" does not mean what you think it does. And she said "would you mind." Those are not the words of a seductress. Would you mind are the words of someone in need of a protector, not a predator.

While Victoria is in the toilet I imagine the reports to her girlfriends. "He came to rescue me from a sexual assault, then he goes and takes advantage of me in bed when the whole reason he was there was to make me feel protected. Fucking dickhead. I'm never going to see him again." I thank the Lord that I have the wisdom to see this, and that I am not, say, three years younger when I probably would not have had the maturity and presence of mind to work it all through. I would have made some crude lunge at her the minute she got into bed (if not before) and then, when she pushed me away, I'd moan to myself that she's probably frigid. But now I am mature, seasoned and reasoned, balanced and considered. I am able to make the proper decisions with the wisdom that comes with age.

Yeah.

Not only, I tell myself, am I blessed with the presence of mind to understand the sexual politics of the situation and not misread the signals, I have the foresight to think a shower might be a good idea. I had worked up quite a sweat on my bike and I certainly did not want Victoria to get a whiff of what I was like most of the time. Three years earlier I might have given my pubes a dust of tale and my armpits a squirt of Right Guard but that's it. But new, improved James scrubs up well and even cleans his fingernails.

In the shower I have yet another gloriously mature and selfless idea. I will avoid the inevitable torment that a platonic night with Victoria is going to entail. (I would be lying there with an erection, unable to talk or think properly, and, let's face it, talking and thinking may be required till the early hours. She may even want a friendly cuddle. I cannot perform this talking and hugging effectively with an erection. It will be distracting and could make cuddling up potentially hazardous.)

So I must discharge myself of desire. So I embark on my third, or possibly fourth, lamb shank of the day. It was heavy going but suffice it to say that after a few minutes in the shower I feel completely relaxed and satisfied. To increase the *likelihood that this state of purity will last, I turn off the hot tap and give myself an invigorating ice-cold douche, for several minutes, aiming the nozzle at my bell end. I exit the shower feeling spiritually and physically cleansed. No carnal thought will spoil the sweet and tender night ahead of me. I have put my weapon beyond use.*

It's all very well for you to say you know what's coming. I mean, it's painfully clear NOW. But come on, would you have done any different if you were me? Ok, daft question, because people who are me always do what I do. But wouldn't you have done the same? Even if you were you?

YOU: *No, it was obvious that sex was at least a possibility.*

ME: *But don't you think I behaved with admirable selflessness and decorum?*

YOU: *I would say you were naive and over-cautious. So what if you had an erection? Nothing to be ashamed of.*

ME: *Not ashamed, embarrassed. And distracted. I would have made a desperate pass no matter how unwelcome it was.*

YOU: *She was probably gagging for it.*

ME: *You're a bloke, aren't you? I thought so.*

YOU: *I am beyond gender.*

I'm lying in bed and Victoria is removing makeup at the dresser. We're still talking about the incident. How weird, he should be locked up, mind you, he was clearly a mental case, and so on. We're both repeating ourselves the way people do when they've had a shock. Victoria begins undressing herself before my very eyes. She gets down to her bra and knickers, and what will she do next? She gets into the bed beside me (without so much as a T-shirt) and cuddles up. She thanks me yet again.

I am aroused mentally and visually, of course, but not genitally. Excellent. All is going according to plan because we're still talking and being all affectionate and I am not trying anything on. She must be impressed. So controlled, so gallant. A lot of blokes expect a shag just for paying for the taxi home. Me, I have practically saved her life and yet I ask nothing in return. I am the most brilliant man in the world.

And she rests her head on her hand and we talk some more and I am actually making sense instead of thinking "sex, sex, sex," and I can't tell you how smug I feel.

YOU: *I think you have managed to get that across.*
ME: *Ok.*

And then the conversation moves on to the people we mutually loathe. That's always a great bonding experience, I find, and it's times like this that one has to thank loathsome people because without them, what would couples talk about?

We lampoon that Welsh git of a director, we laugh at dear old Giles, we pour scorn on the entire film unit. We are united against a world of pretension and two-facedness. We are bonded by a sense of other people being a bit crap.

And then she puts her hand on my chest. "Right, interesting," I think. She strokes my chest, in a way that is . . . well, let's face it, there is only one way.

This can't be happening. She is not really expecting . . . sex?

Tonight?

Now?

With me?

I stiffen. A very bad choice of words but I will leave them there, shining with monstrous irony.

Victoria smiles, waiting for something. I know she wants us to kiss. But what then? Sex would have to follow the kiss. Then she kisses me. A brief kiss on the lips. (I wish I could remember how it felt but the kiss was on Planet Earth and I was on Planet Nerves.) She smiles. She knows that one thing is about to lead to another. I could not at this stage get out of it or proffer any excuse.

I don't often want to get out of sex. But is it me, or do a lot of women believe that the male is constantly up for it, and should be grateful for any opportunity, any time, with anyone at all? Call me presumptuous, but I have often felt required *to have sex. A girl, usually the kind who wears big, baggy trousers and chunky sweaters, invites me to dinner and cooks me a nice meal. I arrive and she's made the effort of a dress or skirt. After a meal, a joint, a coffee, a conversation about ex-boyfriends, a few nice words about her china frog collection, some slagging off of loathsome colleagues, I shuffle around and talk about getting the night bus. And then I feel, from the looks I get, that I have eaten under false pretenses. The three-course meal and the coffee from her new cafetière and little chocolate mints were not for nothing, oh no. And they weren't laid on because I am such fascinating company or even because I got her cistern working again. I'm supposed to stay the night.*

Sometimes drying the dishes is not enough.

Not only that, but I have to give (and I do mean give) her an orgasm which can often entail getting repetitive strain injury—and not just in my fingers. But I stay the night because I can't stand The Look. The disappointed look. That forlorn, cast-off, hurt face that I know would turn to anger and "stupid bastard" if I left now. Either that, or (and this goes out to someone called Kate Marsden) they claim to their friends that I am "gay" or "asexual" or "immature" or "hung up" because I didn't fuck them. Hardly fair.

So in order to avoid The Look, and to keep my reputation as a sex god alive (if only in my own mind), I do the business. Yes, I have been to bed with one or two girls just because they'd spent the day cooking and I felt obliged. So next time a man sleeps with you after you've filled him with lasagna, look at yourself in the mirror and ask, "Am I really that irresistible or did he just want to avoid The Look?"

Then again, sometimes I have been unsure about whether I want to have sex with someone. It's not always cut and dried. I spend the evening on the fence between fancying them and not fancying them with this kind of internal monologue going on:

". . . nice eyes but she never smiles—oh, she's smiling now but she has odd teeth—God, can I really sleep with someone who has never heard OK Computer? Am I a cultural snob? Oh, nice bum—but oh no that is the third time she hasn't understood that I'm being ironic—now she's apologizing again for something—she's rather sweet though really I wish I could get a better look at her

skin——she's probably a bit desperate——she might be quite a good one-nighter though but I still don't fancy those lips much maybe I could get to like them——oh I'm too tired and I can't be bothered——on the other hand it's all experience and one day I might regret not having taken every opportunity going so what the hell——but her hands are a bit chubby but——oh she's apologizing for something yet again——her legs are very nice, dear me they are lovely——can I really go to bed with her just because of her legs?——why not?——but then she might expect me to be her boyfriend and I can't do that just because of her legs——but she's also very sweet and she's quite charming really——all the more reason not to string her along——oh no she's talked about her parents for far too long and doesn't seem to have read a newspaper since last year and she's a bit of a hippy chick——we don't have much in common but maybe a quick snog and out the door——but those legs are great and I haven't felt a nice arse for ages and I'm getting a bit hard now so I might as well go for it——no fuck it I'll get my coat."

And then I get The Look.

So here I am, the woman I have waited to love for two years near-naked beside me, feeling her body next to mine, and there is no simple, mutually satisfactory way of not having sex. She will assume that being a Bloke I am always up for it. In a few moments I will be getting The Look. The forlorn, hurt, cast-aside, confused Look. And what conclusion will she draw? Gay? Hung up? Don't fancy her? Psychologically disturbed? Impotent? A painfully terrified virgin? Riddled with disease?

Oh God. Her hand is moving gently down. She is about to find it——if she can——it's probably shriveled to a quarter its normal size. Oh well, let her find it. What's the worst that can happen? And then I remember that this hand, this searching hand, has spent the last six months fondling the best cock in the whole world, the brightest, hardest, most fantastic supercock ever touched by woman. The hand is going from Wonder Cock to I-wonder-where-it-is-cock. She is about to feel a cock beaten into submission in the shower, then given a cruel, cold hose treatment. If it could run it would be halfway across the road by now. I must stop that hand. It's going down, it's going down, it's closing in, it's going to touch my——

"Victoria . . . the thing is . . ."

"What is it?"

"Well . . ."

"I know. We're friends, we shouldn't be doing this . . . I suppose."

"Well, it's . . ."

"You don't have to. I mean, if you don't want to that's fine. I'll . . ."

The Look. The Look.

"No I . . . well . . . our friendship is very important to me and this might . . ."

"I understand completely. I shouldn't have . . ."

"No, that's fine. I do fancy you."

"Then why . . ."

"Because I . . . I am a bit involved with someone and . . . you know."

"Oh my God. So sorry. I thought you might be. I mean, sometimes you seem to be and other times not."

"Yes. I know. I suppose. It's fine for us to be in bed and . . . and stuff. But it does preclude sex. And I really like you and fancy you and have done for ages."

The next thing I remember is waking up to the smell of burning toast. Moments later Victoria, fully dressed and businesslike, places a cup of tea and a plate next to me. Not so much as a good-morning kiss. She says she's in a hurry for her first lecture and will catch up with me in the week.

"How about Thursday?"

"Sure."

"Use this key and push it through the mailbox when you leave."

"Ok." She rushes out of the bedroom. "Bye, then!" I call after her but the front door closes with a crash.

I listen to her footsteps clopping along the pavement. I look at the room and breathe in the various scents of lavender and, I don't know, soapy things. There are some clothes I recognize strewn on the floor, some books we have discussed over the months on the shelf. Her bed feels so much softer and cleaner than my own. I would like to let my head sink deeply into the big white pillows, and sleep soundly until night.

NINE

Splitting up with someone isn't just an emotional thing, of course. It throws up all kinds of practical challenges. You put everything of yours into the hallway. It's depressing because you're nearly thirty and you still own a Bullworker. And your vinyl collection consists of *Bat Out of Hell* by Meatloaf and *Kind of Blue* by Miles Davis and that's it. CDs are more numerous but they are a constant reminder that your taste was a bit suspect. The CDs bought five years ago because they seemed to be the height of good taste are now embarrassing to behold. You look at your most recent purchases and wonder how long it will be before even they seem the epitome of naffness. The only time you're safe from taste-remorse is in the last year of your life, a thought you comfort yourself with as you place a bright-red waistcoat into a garbage bag. (Not because you're throwing it away, of course, but because you don't own a suitcase.)

Victoria is upstairs putting on her makeup. I make a fair bit of noise on purpose but I don't really know why. I don't want her to help and I don't even especially want to disturb or annoy her. I have a collection of fossils that are heavier than the rest of my possessions put together. Dad and I collected them. He thought fossil-hunting might get me interested in natural history and it half worked, I suppose. And here we are, the fossils and me, trundling around together until I have a son and I can say. "I found these when I was a boy just about your age," and he can pretend to be really pleased but wishes they were a new computer game. (Of course I have hoped, on and off for the last ten years, that my son might be Victoria's too, but hey ho.)

The taxi arrives and it all fits in. I retain the key for some vague reason I can't define.

There are no good-byes.

The taxi drives past a Dumpster, and I'm tempted to dump everything I own there. I ask him to stop for a moment. I pick up the Bullworker and sling it in. It seems like a cheekily cockney thing to do but the driver gives me a bit of a tut and says that dumping things into other people's Dumpsters is the same as putting your hand in their pockets and taking their money.

I wait by the front door for a moment wondering why Charlotte has not heard the taxi and come out to greet me. I pull the knocker on the mailbox and let it fall. This will be ok, I think. I can cope with this. I am lucky to have friends who care.

Charlotte's live-in partner opens the door. Brian is a chartered surveyor for Hackney Council. Used to be an architect until the recession hit and he had some kind of breakdown. Anyway, he's a good few years older than me and this will be his second marriage. I think. He helps with the bags and doesn't make any remarks about what a load of crap it is.

"I've already started looking at studio flats," I lie reassuringly as we climb the stairs to the spare bedroom. This is actually a kind of dump room. I am pretty crushed by the lack of space and crumminess.

"This is perfect. I won't be here for long, anyway."

"You've got your own sheets and stuff?"

"Oh yes," I have a duvet, but that's it. A trip to John Lewis beckons.

"Nice view from here."

"Yes."

"And the bathroom's downstairs, right?"

"Right."

"Good. Well . . ."

Brian is not a great conversationalist but it is not just his fault. I am really crap at making conversation when I am a guest in people's houses. I can't be myself. I feel it's rude to disagree with anyone who provides me with lodging, even if they say, "Here are the towels. By the way, Osama bin Laden is alive and he lives next door." I'd probably reply. "Really? I might bump into him later, then. And this is the switch for the immersion heater, is it?" I would find it hard to disagree with the opinions of Saddam Hussein if, while explaining his worldview, he was also hanging up my clean towels for the morning.

It's this thing I have about staying as an overnight guest. I think I first noticed it when I stayed at Victoria's parents' years ago. An intense unease, a feeling that I am a bad fit, and I know that my discomfort is noticed by my host, who thinks it's their fault, and I feel bad about that, and so the circle of mutually assured embarrassment is complete.

"Sorry about your news, by the way."

"Right, yes well, you know," is my brilliantly articulate response. I really don't want to have a chat with Brian about Victoria.

Brian leaves me to get settled and I flop down on the rickety single bed. I try to resist asking myself how I feel. It's a habit I have been attempting to kick for years because it always makes me feel worse. As soon as I ask myself if I'm happy then I'm not. If I ask myself if I'm *un*happy then I become even less happy because not only am I unhappy about whatever-it-is, I am now also unhappy about the fact that I am unhappy. If I could just stop being unhappy about my unhappiness then half the unhappiness would go away and I would be happier.

It should be bloody obvious.

Instead, I stare at the long-lasting lightbulb above my head and try to imagine what Dad would say to all this. I don't need to ask his advice because I know what he'd say: that Stefan is no better than me and I am crazy and Victoria loves me and he's sure she would not prefer to be with Stefan, and Stefan has no more going for him than I do.

But Stefan has a *lot* more going for him. He is making films and getting paid a fortune. I mean he is a serious filmmaker and I am simply a failed game-show deviser. Even if I became a *functioning* game-show deviser, Stefan is surely going to be more successful in Victoria's eyes. And I know Victoria: she likes success, she goes for it every time. Look at Giles: he was the big man on campus—but he was dumped at around the time he became the big laughingstock instead. Maybe the *vongole* crisis would have been dismissed as a mere peccadillo if Giles had still been Mr. Films. Mark Supercock had money, a sports car, gloves, his own umbrella. Danny Plimsolls was a performer, he was rock 'n' roll. Victoria will love being with a star like Stefan.

But that's not all Stefan is the kind of "guy" people talk about. People are impressed that I even *know* Stefan. Some of Victoria's friends think that the most interesting thing about me is that

I used to go to school with Stefan Catchiside. In fact, I wouldn't be surprised if you are thinking at this very moment: "I wish this book had more about the Stefan guy—he's *far* more interesting than that James bloke."

YOU: Now that you mention it, I *would* like to know more about the Stefan guy.

ME: What am I, his publicist? He should be *paying* me to write this book.

The bottom line is that if I were Victoria I would not go out with me, I would go out with Stefan.

My phone rings.

My heart squashes itself against my ribs, like it's trying to hide. Of course I want it to be Victoria—I want to hear her tears for me. Stefan's name appears on my phone.

"Hi, James. How are you?" he says in a concerned tone. He has obviously spoken to Victoria.

"I'm fine."

"Really?"

"Yes."

"I just phoned your home and Victoria told me. Do you want to go for a drink or something? I could get away for eight."

"No, really—I'm out tonight."

"James, I can't believe it. You waited eight years for her."

"Well, time to move on. Is she ok?"

"She's bewildered. Are you ok?"

"Yes."

"I know we're not very close these days, James. But I'm here if you need me."

"Thanks, but maybe you should comfort Victoria. She liked you."

This is said without the merest hint of pique, you understand.

"James, I have something kind of awkward to say."

"Oh, don't worry. I won't be upset. Victoria and I are history. I just want her to be happy, whatever she does and whoever she's with."

"I just rang to tell you that I'm offering Victoria a job on my film. Formally, I mean. I've got the budget now and everything. Just thought you . . . well, you know."

"That's great."

"You don't mind, do you?"

Are you saying I might mind because I'm jealous of you? If you were a big, fat, ugly bloke of sixty would you be saying, "You don't mind, do you?"

I quickly try to respond as if Stefan *is* a big, fat, ugly bloke of sixty. As if jealousy were a complete stranger to me.

"Er, mind?" I act confused. "Why, I mean, is it a dangerous shoot?"

"No, no . . ."

"Then why would I mind?"

"I don't really know."

He's blown it.

He really can't get out of the fact that he has, in effect, said, "Do you mind if I work with your ex because clearly you will probably think, with good reason, there is a chance we'll get off together."

"I just thought that—if I gave her a job that might be disloyal to you. I'm not sure why."

Well done, Stefan, yet again you have proved yourself kinder, more considerate and wiser than me. This is a nice thing to do—

to call me about the job, and to assure me that you aren't siding with Victoria in any dispute. This is typical of you, Stefan. You're good. Just what Victoria needs.

I would love to get my reader on my side against you, Stefan, but it's not going to be easy. Not unless I make stuff up, but what would be the point? I would like my reader to think of you as a villain but you aren't. (If you were a villain, why would I have made way for you?) My reader is probably rooting for you, Stefan, and I would be too.

"You've been in love with her for nine years."

"Nearly ten." Why bother correcting Charlotte about this trivial point of fact? It's the scientist in me; funny how it never leaves you. Maybe I am a boffin after all.

"Ten, then. Do you want to chop some onions?"

"Ok." She hands me a knife and indicates the chopping board. The steamy kitchen, the smell of food being prepared, this is coupledom. The scent of coziness I've left behind.

"How can you threw in the towel with her?"

The thought of a proper discussion eases my awkward-guest feeling. It will distract me.

"People throw in the towel all the time. Half the people who resign do it because they believe they'll get fired anyway. And do you know something? During the Black Death some people tried to catch the plague."

"Why?"

"They wanted to get it over with. They hastened the inevitable. Same thing happened in the trenches in the First World War. Boys wanted bullets in their bodies because they preferred the bullets to the *fear* of bullets. Sometimes that's why they went over the top."

"You are great at rationalizing. Basically, you've given up. Can you grease this, please?"

"There's nothing wrong with giving up. We live in a ridiculous culture that says giving up is weak or wrong. But what if your goals are unrealistic? You know who never give up? Stalkers. And most failures are people who never give up. Go to the pub tonight. Talk to anyone who is sitting alone and sad. They'll probably tell you about some dream they never gave up. People who give up and move on are the strong ones."

"You're talking to the woman who gave *you* up, James."

She is referring to the fact that she was in love with me. This is a subject we've eschewed for many years. It's history, forgotten, never mentioned.

"Exactly. You had the sense to realize things wouldn't work out between us. You've got a great man there."

You see what I did? Shifted the subject to Brian.

"You think so?"

"I like Brian."

"He's great."

We look out of the kitchen window. Brian is finishing a garden shed—not from a flat-pack. It's designed and built by him alone. He's another one who gave something up. The architecture. The great buildings that would change the skyline for generations to come. But somewhere along the line he realized that some dreams have to be given up or they turn into the kind of nightmares where you keep chasing something that remains inches from your grasp. The great award-winning tower designed by Brian Howditch will never happen. Brian is now a common-or-garden chartered surveyor.

Nice shed though, Brian.

It starts to rain but Brian is oblivious. He doesn't even look up at the sky or hold his hand out. He just carries on sawing like there was really a point to it all.

"Thanks for putting me up. I hope Brian doesn't mind."

"Brian's fine."

Why did I ask if Brian minded? I move on quickly.

"I envy you."

I don't envy Charlotte, I just want to say something encouraging. And I remember that's what Stefan said to her the other night in the pub. It's just flattery, really, but I want her to be pleased with her life. And I want to believe that she and Brian are happy, that this kind of coupledom isn't a sad routine, but a something worth striving for.

"Why envy *me*?"

"House, getting married, job. You'll probably have kids soon. My room's going to be the nursery, I take it."

"Yes. Yes, we have a nice life at the moment."

"You look good on it."

"Thanks."

The last bit is true. She is much slimmer than she was and the spots that disfigured her as a student have left with no trace. She now has a figure—with a waist that goes vaguely inward and pleasing hips. I think to myself that in the years I have known her she has gone from being unshaggable to shaggable. (There are a million more sophisticated ways of putting that, but none clearer.) She bends over to reach for a pan in a cupboard and I imagine pulling down her leggings and fucking her right now as she holds onto the counter. It means nothing of course. For men of my particular ilk that kind of thought is as common as plankton in the sea and about as significant. This carnal thought is only worthy of record because it is not one I would have entertained ten years ago. Ten years ago Charlotte could not have caused even the slightest movement in the pants department.

"Are you sure you aren't doing this because you prefer not having Victoria to having her?"

Here we go. Unsolicited psychotherapy. Why do they do it? You don't get bankers suddenly stopping the conversation to ask if you want a new flexible savings account. Surgeons don't have a quick poke around your gall bladder in the middle of a dinner party. But everyone in the therapy trade (and let's not forget the blessed amateurs) thinks they can dole out their tosh without so much as an introduction.

However, I'm a guest in Charlotte's house and so I comply, and you never know, she might just be on to something (which is when the psychobabblers are at their most useful and annoying).

"What? Why do I not want Victoria?" I ask, as if I really think she has the power to understand my squiggly, all-over-the-place doodle of a mind.

"That's what you're used to, isn't it? Not having Victoria. Eight years of it. You lived in the reverie of knowing that one day you'd have her."

"I didn't know anything, and it wasn't a reverie."

"You were the most hopeful man I've ever known."

"I was also sad, frustrated."

"That's the addiction."

A psychological theory looms.

"An addiction?" I know what she's going to say, more or less.

"All addictions have a kind of hopefulness about them, don't they?"

"Gambling, obviously," I suggest.

"Exactly: hope, followed either by disappointment or euphoria.

The smack addict has the craving, the chase for the fix, and the euphoria. The sex addict has the thrills of the chase, the despair of rejection, the hope that for once the sex will somehow fulfil expectations. A lot of addictions are about thrills and spills. Don't you miss the thrills and spills of *not* having Victoria, the tantalizing, thrilling roller-coaster ride?"

Whenever someone says something that challenges your world view, the best thing to do is change the subject. I don't quite change the subject but I at least try to turn it into a thing about Life In General rather than Me In Particular.

"Why is it better to travel hopefully than to arrive? No one ever told me the answer to that one."

"Because the arrival is *imagined* by the traveler. It is a fantasy that they can play in their mind and it is always perfect. But when the traveling stops the arrival becomes *real*. And that's the problem. Reality is never perfect. You don't like reality, chum."

I don't like reality, chum. Well thank you for that pearl of wisdom.

"Look, I don't mind a bit of slightly dull domesticity. As long as it's only *slightly* dull and no one asks me to barbecue anything. Or varnish anything. Oh, or visit anyone who owns a toddler. Or wear slippers from Woollies."

"Really?"

"Absolutely."

"No, I mean do you really not miss the chase a bit?"

"I am perfectly comfortable with comfortable."

Best leave it there, son. Don't over-egg it because you know what they're like, sound too sure about something and you're *in denial*. Then it strikes me she might have a point about the reality thing because right at this moment I feel like watching the most unreal, escapist film ever made.

Do they have a copy of *Sleepless in Seattle*, I wonder.

Charlotte turns and faces me. "I don't know if you've changed over the years or not."

I touch her shoulders, after first checking Brian is in his shed. This awkward limpet of a girl has always been there for me. The unshaggable to shaggable change is paltry. Charlotte has changed from a spotty barnacle into a person I care for and listen to, even if it's a psychological theory.

Pieces of wood fall onto the crazy paving. Brian arranges them into a lattice, then raises himself to his full height. He arches his body, and with both hands supports the small of his back.

TEN

Gerard and I have had a day off. Everything's fine, but under the circumstances we agreed that a bit of a rest from each other would do us both good. Time to recharge our creative batteries and other clichés. It was all his idea. He really seems to be rising to the occasion of my malaise. Perhaps the madman is maturing and mellowing at last. I approach his house feeling shaken and unsure if I can really put my mind to the task. I think about Victoria every minute—no, pretty much every other second. All the time, really. My mind is a constant dialogue with her, about her, listening to things she has said, things I hope she'll say and things I fear she will say.

I ring the doorbell, trying to focus. The vision that greets me is scary. Gerard is wearing normal clothes. I use the word *normal* in an extremely inclusive sense. A gray sweatshirt thing and pair of brown front-pocketed slacks. Gerard's hair has been washed, combed and I was going to say *brushed* but that's going a bit far. *Patted down*. He's barely recognizable. Three days ago if he walked into a bank the tellers would no doubt gently place their feet above the alarm buttons. Now, they would regard him as a harmless prankster. I probably look a little shocked.

"Morning," he says. Which is also very odd. Normally he opens the door and walks away barely looking to see who it is.

"Morning."

The place is not quite tidy but there are clear signs that it has been *tidied.* The sitting-room furniture has been moved around. There is a smell of domestic cleansers.

"How is the Victoria situation, James? I am concerned about you, but I didn't feel a phone call would be right. I didn't want to intrude."

I look at him with wonder. This is something a *normal* person would say. What is going on? Is he having some kind of crisis? I have had enough turmoil in my life. I don't need this.

"I put the kettle on."

"*You* put the *kettle* on?"

"And I put your notebook and pen all ready. Or will you use the laptop?"

This must be some kind of joke but I don't think Gerard is capable of even *pretending* to be this normal.

"What's happening, Gerard?"

"What do you mean?"

"Two days ago you made tea for the first time—or offered to, anyway. Now you're wearing normal clothes and hair and the house isn't quite as squalid as it was. And you asked about Victoria—and you put the *kettle* on."

"Yes."

"So? What's wrong?"

"Does there have to be something wrong?"

"No one changes this radically unless something's wrong."

He doesn't answer. Right before my very eyes he makes the tea. A normal action for so many people all over the country but I watch as if he were levitating. This is practically a miracle.

"Gerard. Have you had some kind of weird experience? What's happened? Tell me."

"Nothing."

"That just can't be true. People change for a reason."

He turns to face me. Even this small gesture is so unusual as to be slightly alarming.

"It was yesterday. I . . ."

"What?"

"Just got tired of my own mind."

"You got . . ."

"You know. Mind-fatigue. It's too chaotic in there. I'd like to straighten things out a bit."

"Right." This is a bit of a curveball. Not sure what to say. I'll try something very normal and British. "Yes, well, maybe we have been overdoing it. I think we've put ourselves under too much pressure."

"We're desperate, desperate, desperate. We're two prisoners planning an escape that'll never happen. It's not working, James."

"And this all started yesterday?"

"Yes. The way you sat there all depressed about Victoria and couldn't even crap-detect anymore. It dawned on me that we're both crap. I wanted to change."

"Gerard. Listen to me. Listen. I am the sensible one. And I think we still have a chance of getting somewhere."

"Are you the sensible one? Maybe you're nuttier than me."

He might have a point but I'm going to ride over it.

"We're going to give it six months, aren't we?"

"I'm tired."

Gerard beckons me over to a cupboard, which he flings open. There's nothing in it except a pair of Wellington boots and a couple of months' worth of my notes.

"I'm thirty-one and I have nothing. Nothing but a pair of Wellies and the world's biggest-ever collection of crap game-show ideas."

For some reason this makes me laugh. Gerard is serious but I find it funny. I find the pathetic emptiness of my friend's life amusing. I have always found Gerard funny—sometimes when he means to be, and sometimes when he's trying hard not to. Gerard is one of the funniest and saddest people I know. As soon as I laugh Gerard begins to laugh too. This is how it works. I feel I want to say something serious but I can't get the words out.

I first met Gerard when he came into Print Stop with a hundred sheets of A4 he wanted us to copy. He looked like a scarecrow at a job interview. There were bits of straw or hay or grass stuck to his big green sweater. His trousers were too long on one leg and on the other too short. (He later told me that he had shortened the wrong leg and never got round to correcting the mistake.) I think I can put it best like this: if you looked at Gerard's head, then panned slowly down like a TV camera to his shoes, you would find that his *shoes matched* and you would be *surprised*. "Matching shoes!" you would exclaim.

Yet this man had the confidence of someone who was about to marry a beautiful, rich, pregnant woman who was also his boss. All the great hurdles of life—love, money, career and procreation—were being dealt with in one go. All this confidence from one who looked like he couldn't afford a free newspaper.

"I will be back in half an hour to collect the copies."

"Ok."

"Your best paper."

"Conqueror?"

"The best."

"Ok."

He then takes a bottle of champagne out of a holdall.

"Please have a glass of this. At the end of the day or whenever."

"Really?"

"To celebrate. I'm hitting the big time. Where can I go for a nice drink round here? Somewhere nice."

"The Horse and Groom?"

"Ok. I'll be back in half an hour."

Gerard did not come back to the shop in half an hour. Or for the rest of that week or the next. I placed his top copy in a cupboard for the regulation six weeks before we would have to throw it out. It's strictly against protocol, but I couldn't help glancing at it. There were all kinds of weird TV-show ideas, some so ludicrous I nearly cried laughing. Others felt new and exciting but impossible. I thought to myself that this man is half genius. His was a kind of powdered brilliance—it would come to nothing without adding water. Perhaps I could be the water.

Two months later Gerard returned with a different set of clothes but looking equally bizarre in a pinstripe jacket and tracksuit bottoms. Again, he seemed to be brimming with confidence.

"A copy of this little lot, if you would."

"Oh, I think we still have the last little lot." I had kept his top copies all this time.

"Yes. Sorry about that. I will pay, but I don't want to see those papers ever again."

"Really? But—"

"It would send me into one of my depressions. No, burn it all, it's rubbish."

I thanked the stranger for the champagne he'd left the last time and we started talking. In a few minutes I knew that I really wanted to be with this weirdo, to get inside his mind. I knew he was mad as pants, but we'd make a great team.

Gerard and I stop laughing eventually. I try to wipe the smile off my face. Come on, this is serious.

"Gerard, what's gotten into you?"

"I want to be a little normal. Take a walk on the mild side."

"Have you met a woman? This is woman's work, isn't it? Some slut has nobbled my creator."

"It's not a woman. I want to be a bit more normal. I don't know how to do it. I haven't really got a clue. But I would like to give it a go. Maybe you could help."

"You are never going to be normal. It wouldn't suit you."

"Then at least I could try to be sane."

"That's crazy."

"It's not. I think I am finally going stark-staring sane."

"That's the maddest thing I've ever heard. How are we going to make our million? Where are the ideas going to come from?"

Gerard sits down on the sofa where I normally sit and gets the pad—my pad—out and assumes the position—*my* position.

"I'd like *you* to think of some ideas. I'd like you to come up with crazy thoughts and weird notions. I'd like to sit around deciding if they're crap or not."

Jesus.

"Gerard, you are a great ideas man. You are a generator, no, a volcano of ideas. You don't have the doubts I have. You just explode with inspiration. It is brilliant to behold. Don't turn into me, you wouldn't like it. It's too depressing. You know the film about the kid who sees dead people? Well—I see problems. Problems invisible to others."

"Even problems that aren't there?"

I know what he means—maybe more of his ideas *aren't* crap than I thought.

"That isn't fair."

"How do I know?"

We sit in silence for a while. Maybe we should give the whole thing up. It's something I've thought about every day, although I chase the thought away with dreams of success, riches, recognition, praise, acceptance. But the dreams aren't working now and the thought of giving up squats in my mind like a little Buddha. What was I saying only this morning? It's the strong who give up, who have the strength to move on.

It seems utterly hopeless right now.

We're just two schoolboys in some fantasy about building a space rocket and flying to Mars. *You don't like reality, chum.* Maybe this has been my way of avoiding it.

I look at Gerard.

His whole countenance has somehow changed. Is he on medication? Or has he stopped? Can someone really go stark-staring sane? Is Gerard getting *on* his trolley and his rocker? Is his loose screw tightening and are the fairies he was away with bringing him back?

"Let's forget it," I say. And I mean it. I think. "I was saying only this morning about giving up not being a shame, but a realistic option. You have one life, why gamble it away when the odds are against you?"

"So we agree."

I pause. All I need is for Gerard to leap in the air with a great idea and I would be back in the game. But it's not going to happen.

"We agree."

In the silence that follows I wonder what Gerard is thinking. Does he feel as crushed as I do? We're not just throwing away the future we planned here, but also our pasts. So much time we've spent together on this fabulous adventure, all that past will now be remembered with regret, sadness, even embarrassment. It could have been remembered with warmth—"the two years of struggle that got us where we are today." But now the memories will simply remind us of what fools we were. Our past has suddenly changed and that's as hard to accept as our dream blowing away with the wind.

"What'll you do, Gerard?"

"I don't know yet. I think I'll try getting a job again."

"I suppose I'll have to do the same. I mean it's good enough for ninety percent of the population so it should be good enough for us. You know our trouble?"

"We thought we were better than them." Then he says, "I'll miss you both."

He means Victoria and me.

"Nah! We'll still be friends."

Victoria and Gerard had a special little relationship that didn't make me jealous. Victoria mothered him. She once came over to pick me up at Gerard's and came in for a cup of tea, which I had to make, naturally. You know what she did—and this isn't Victoria at all—she offered to come round at the weekend and "sort the place out" for him. To Victoria, Gerard was a "poor love." Now, I would never want a woman to call me a "poor love" but I concede that it has its advantages. Victoria spent a day tidying up—and discovered that Gerard had no sheets on his bed. And never had done. Last Christmas she bought the poor love a full set of bed linens. And she even put them on the poor love's stinking rotten bed for him. As far as I am aware (and I don't want to be more aware than I am) Gerard has never cleaned or changed them since. Still, it's only been nine months.

Victoria had a theory. "Speaking as the progeny of two psychiatrists . . ."

"Here we go."

"I think Gerard is manic depressive."

"But he never gets depressed. He's the happiest, most optimistic person I know. He's a manic manic."

"Have you *seen* that house?"

"He's filthy and crazy. But he is the archetypal pig in shit. As in *happy as* . . ."

"Believe me. He's hanging on by a wire."

The poor love.

We're at the door now and I'm wondering how to leave things. Gerard and I have a kind of friendship, certainly. But it's not so strong as to last without the work thing. Or without Victoria. Like a lot of blokes, friendship alone is not enough. A shared hobby, a sport, a job, even a shared location such as a pub is necessary to keep it going.

Here goes a friend. No point in making a big play about keeping in touch. Gerard has a great nose for insincerity.

" 'Bye then. Good luck."

"Right. You too, James. I hope you work things out with Victoria. Or someone else or whatever. 'Bye."

I walk down the steps. I don't hear the door slam behind me. He can't be waiting to wave, that would be too normal, even for the new normal Gerard.

"James."

"Yes?"

"How is she taking it all?"

"Well, I should imagine she's . . . I mean she's fine."

So, how *is* Victoria taking it all? Exactly how concerned am I for this woman I claim to love? Exactly how much thought have I given to the possibility—however remote—that she might be heartbroken? I am sorry to report that the answer is: not much. My conviction that she was about to large it with Mr. Perfect bludgeoned any notion that she might be shedding tears for me.

"You're the mad one."

I smile, and if this were an American film I suppose we'd hug now. As far as I know, me and Victoria are Gerard's only friends in the world. I am letting him out of my life because we have run out of the glue that held us together. There was him, me and a glue called Shows. I wonder if all relationships need glue. Did Victoria and I need glue? What was it? We had shared interests in food, television, theatre, music, America, flowering plants, nature programmes, soft porn and soft drugs. But the glue was none of those things. I sometimes think it was just the way we looked at each other, and made each other laugh with our faces.

Gerard takes a few steps down.

"I don't know much about love . . ." What on *earth?* "But I think you should get her back."

"All you have are some Wellies and a thousand bad ideas for game shows, and you're giving advice. Do you mean it?" Silly question, because Gerard would not say anything he doesn't mean.

"She's lovely."

I wonder how he will fare in the big, mad, crazy, sensible world.

ELEVEN

VICTORIA'S MEN.
NUMBER FOUR—JOHN TEACHER

John Teacher was Victoria's first man after university.

The year after you leave college is when "the rest of your life" is supposed to begin.

On your marks, get set, now what?

I get a flat-share in Haringey. While trying to get a career in films I pay my rent by taking a series of temporary jobs. One of these is at Print Stop, which is a temporary job in the same way that the Eiffel Tower is a temporary construction.

Victoria goes to live at her parents' house in Kentish Town. Can you blame her? Lovely house, central London, rent-free, full fridge and drinks cabinet.

I believe that now that we are away from college one of two things will happen: I will suddenly become mature enough to stop this silly infatuation, or, do something about it. But maturity doesn't come with age or even experience. Maturity only comes with maturity. It only comes to those mature enough to know what it is, and so there's no point in the rest of us even trying for it.

But this situation with Victoria cannot go on forever. I want the book on Victoria to have an ending—happy or sad, but please let it end.

YOU: *Why didn't you see someone, get help?*

ME: *Because I knew what a shrink would say. He or she would say: "Many people have infatuations for unattainable people. It's the fact that they are unattainable which makes them attractive, and it protects them from intimacy, which is frightening. Perhaps you are afraid that if you started a relationship she will find you out—discover your imperfections. Relationships are scary, so unattainable people are the safest." And I would say, "Do you really expect me to pay you forty quid for that?"*

YOU: *Did you ever consider just not seeing her?*

ME: *Considered. But Victoria was my joy-bringer. Without our monthly get-togethers my life would have been such a barren place. Mark, Simon and Estelle at Print Stop have never once engendered a genuine laugh from me, and I am getting sick of the sound of my false one. Victoria makes me laugh, makes me feel understood like no one I have ever met. That's why the thought of going out with her scared me, I think—losing that friendship. I was a pretty lonely kid, I suppose.*

YOU: *Come on, you were a big boy—what, twenty-two? I assume you did see other women.*

ME: *Quite a few. Three months seemed to be the average fixture.*

YOU: *You've hardly mentioned them.*

ME: *Because this book isn't about them. It's about me and Victoria. The others don't really figure.*

YOU: *None of them influenced the situation with Victoria?*

ME: *I think the fact that I've hardly mentioned them speaks volumes. No offense to them, I mean some of them were, I don't know, great human beings—and now I sound like someone who can bestow greatness—all I mean is that they didn't have a long-lasting effect on me—but that's not to criticize them.*

YOU: *There must have been someone you liked.*

ME: *Every girl I went out with seemed to be shouting in my ear, "I am not Victoria. I am dull. Look, see how dull I am. The more you look at me the more you want Victoria." In the dark, all my girlfriends were Victoria, if you know what I mean.*

YOU: *No.*

ME: *Oh come on, don't make me spell it out.*

YOU: *Ok, I know what you mean.*

ME: *But you know, I felt guilty about it. It wasn't fair on them. Loving someone is quite a lot of baggage to carry. I wished I could have dumped it somewhere.*

YOU: *It's dangerous to leave your emotional baggage unattended.*

ME: *Hey, leave the funnies to me, please.*

We always go to the the Jorene Celeste, a congenial, traditional pub next to Kentish Town Tube. This has become our London Place. We always sit in the same booth if we can and, if we're feeling flush, stay for dinner. If we're not feeling flush (which is most of the time) we get drunk enough not to care and stay for dinner anyway. I like it that the barman begins to remember us and of course assumes we are a couple.

I always arrive early, being the gentleman that I am, and always buy a spritzer, Victoria's nineties drink of choice. When she arrives I hand her the drink, say-ing—Here is your nineties drink of choice. She always smiles at this bon mot. I don't know about you, but some jokes or bon mots, even really naff ones, get better with age, or rather with repetition. This is knowledge Bruce Forsyth (best game-show host of all time) was born with. And it is something I have learned. But only some jokes can do this and it's not at all about being funny. Anyway, this spritzer one is a regular.

We always hug massively tightly and talk each other into the ground. Generally I think we both put a bit of a gloss on our lives, not because we are competitive but because we want the evening to be as enjoyable as possible. Why spoil our moments with bad news? At least I assume that she feels that way too.

But I was wrong. I learn later, much later, that this is a tough time for Victoria. She is trying to become an actor, but not only is she not passing auditions, she isn't even getting the auditions. She barely mentions the subject when I see her—it embarrasses her. She thinks there's something naff or ridiculous about declaring to the world you want to act. Her dad keeps teasing her about it. Why don't you try and get a proper job? And other clichés. (Aren't parents wonderful? You really would have thought a psychiatrist would know better.)

This particular evening Victoria has had one of her annual image-changes. Her long blonde hair is now short and dark brown, almost black. She has also gone back to wearing lipstick and maybe there's a touch of foundation or rouge or something.

"This is my try-to-get-a-job look."

"You could get a part as a glamorous checkout girl."

And so begins a little game that we have played so often. It starts with me throwing out an observation which is a cross between an insult and a compliment. "Glamorous" is a compliment, "checkout girl," I figure, is not. Together, they make an attention-grabbing little phrase that should mean she is in the palm of my hand for the next few minutes trying to work out what the hell it means. It's completely meaningless, of course, and only serves as a starting point for the game. At least in my head it's harmless.

I realize now, looking back, that for Victoria at this time in her life her physical appearance is more than simple vanity—it connects with her career, her whole future. How was I to know?

"Checkout girl? Why checkout girl?"

"I said glamorous checkout girl."

"Yes. But checkout girls aren't very glamorous. Don't you like the new look?"

Now, I suppose, she is laying down a "slightly hurt" card, which compels me to lay down a compliment—after all, this is a game and no one is meant to get hurt.

"I think it's fine. Really great. You look great."

Compliment duly supplied. But the game goes on.

I say: "Yes, very nice. Very Kentish Town." Another meaningless remark. I have no idea what very Kentish Town means. But I know she will.

"Kentish Town!" Another mock-hurt expression.

"What have I said?"

"What's very Kentish Town? How dare you! That's really nasty. You think I look like a cliché." This is mock-offense, of course. But even at the time I had my doubts. Have I gone too far? Is she really offended? Have I hurt her? If so, I must reassure her straightaway. Hurting for fun is the sport of the insecure. And a game that hurts isn't a game.

"I have no idea. I have come to Kentish Town lots of times and the women seem to look nice. And you're from Kentish Town. But the main thing is that I think you look great. I like the hair and the makeup. Forget the Kentish Town thing, I just said it to tease you. You look lovely."

And I really do think she looks lovely and I wish I could tell it to her straight. I wish I could say she's the most beautiful girl I have ever met—even when I'm angry with her.

I wish I could tell her I want to kiss her now and touch her all over and fuck her and not fear that she will run away and tell her friends that I'm pervy about her.

But no, all my compliments, all my love, must be served with playful banter; my sexual feelings must be communicated through social games that lead to nowhere but a goodnight kiss, a hug, and the Tube home.

"I am sure many, many women would love to be described as very Kentish Town."

She screws up her eyes at me. She knows I have been toying with her a little. "You've got Taunton Shopping Center written all over you."

"That's the nicest thing you've ever said."

We smile at each other, which is something we do a lot but Victoria is always first to look away, sometimes for far too long. She would twirl her hair—when she had long hair. But now she puffs out the hairs that fall just below her right ear. Her fingers haven't gotten used to the short hair yet.

Does she know I am still looking at her? Is that why she has turned her head away? Because I am too intense, invading her space? Am I one of those awful lecherous men that women talk about? The estate agent last week, the man on the bus who keeps leering, the boss who keeps looking at their breasts, the tutor who stands too close, the landlord who inspects the room at unsocial hours and says how lonely he feels and how lovely her blouse looks? Am I the friend she has known for years, who keeps giving her looks that make her uneasy, embarrassed, so she must look away and make sure she isn't giving him the remotest of ambiguous signals?

YOU: *No, she has turned away because you told her she looks like a checkout girl.*

ME: *I said* glamorous *checkout girl.*

YOU: *Oh, sure.*

ME: *And you are operating with the benefit of hindsight. Normally she wouldn't have been so sensitive. She never told me how badly things were going for her acting-wise.*

YOU: *You were playing games. All games have risks.*

ME: *You know, it would be very easy for me to leave out the bits where I behave like a prat.*

YOU: *It would be quite a short book.*

ME: *Look, I thought she was indifferent to me when in fact half the time she was actually hurt. But I did try to retrieve the situation. I was not trying to hurt her. Just play.*

YOU: *Relax. You get her in the end, don't you?*

ME: *Not telling.*

These evenings with Victoria are the highlight of my month. Even hearing about Victoria's men has never made me jealous—it's just something I expect, and it is endlessly fascinating. John Teacher's arrival in Victoria's heart is particularly germane. I'd already heard a little about him from phone calls. His name is Teacher and he is a teacher. Not funny, and kind of tedious I suppose, but dozens, maybe hundreds of teachers are Teachers. Or should it be hundreds of Teachers are teachers?

". . . and he is incredibly kind to me."

"What else?"

"What else?"

"What else do you like about him?"

"Let's see . . ."

"You knew him at school?"

"Yes. We were really good friends. He was probably my closest male friend. But there was nothing in it. Well, nothing from my side. He was always in love with me, so he says now. Well, actually I always knew he was."

This is a particularly fascinating scenario from my point of view, you know, a close friendship turning into romance. I wonder how far I can push it before the comparison becomes too glaring.

"But how do two mates suddenly start going out together? Isn't that a bit odd? And how did you know he was smitten?"

"I think I always knew he wanted to take things further but was too scared to."

Christ, this is getting too close for comfort. Then thankfully Victoria breaks the tension. "He was obviously intimidated by my awesome beauty." She immediately pulls one of her grotesque old-hag faces.

"How do you know he fancied you?"

"Oh come on, they all do." And she pulls another face.

"Exactly, and I'm no exception."

Now any decent girl would take this baton of flirtation and run with it. Come on, you would if you were interested, wouldn't you?

But not this girl.

That is what I find so maddening about Victoria—hints, implications, innuendos, flirtations, none of these seem to get through. (It's as if we never went to bed together—however inconclusively.)

Now would be the perfect time for me to say, "You know, speaking of friendships that turn into romances, I have always . . . and this may come as a bit of shock . . . but I have always quite fancied you. In fact I have been smitten for years."

Why should I care that she's going out with someone? Teacher can look after *himself. Victoria can make her own decision. All I would be doing is telling her how I felt.*

If I had come out of the Love Closet I might have had six happy years with Victoria. Instead I had this need to go the other way—the exact opposite direction. I wanted, yet again, to bury any trace of love. Yet again, Victoria made this incredibly easy.

She buys a round and sits down. There is a momentary lull as we both think about choosing our next topic. She beats me to it.

"I can always tell if someone fancies someone else."

"Really. Oh yes, your psychological background."

"Yup, the psychological background. Having psychiatrist parents is bound to rub off."

I am pleased she hasn't also inherited her parents' snobbery and social sadism.

"I've pretty much assessed everyone in this pub already."

"Those two over there. Are they a couple or what?"

"They're just friends. She isn't interested, he would give her one but isn't that bothered. I mean she'll do as someone to chalk up, you know, get his shag-count to a respectable figure, but that's about it."

"How about those two?"

"Interesting. He is definitely interested in her."

"How do you know?"

"He's leaning in. Leaning in like that. And he's talking a lot and really trying to keep her interested—he keeps trying to make her laugh with his accents and stuff—I can tell that from here. But sadly she is not interested because she's in love with someone else. Probably a friend of his."

"I would really like to check up on this. I mean if we're going to be scientific."

"I can go and ask."

"No, don't."

"When one of then goes to the loo I could ask the other one."

"If you ask I am leaving. You can't ask them."

At that moment the man walks toward the Gents. Victoria is on her feet before

I can stop her and approaches the girl. The girl looks very curious at first. Victoria is obviously spinning something. The conversation becomes lighter and the girl laughs, and shakes her head. Victoria comes back to our table, triumphant.

"I have to say I was rather brilliant."

"What did you say?"

"I said I was writing an article about what makes people fancy each other. She said he wasn't her boyfriend and I asked if there was any chance he ever would be and she said no. I am right. I always am."

"Amazing."

If I had only realized it at the time, Victoria clearly had this idea that mind-reading was her birthright. Her psychiatrist parents had given her some kind of belief that a working knowledge of psychology grants one the ability to see into the human heart. But Victoria, you never saw what was in mine. You thought you had the power to see into it, and found it empty.

To me, Victoria was a mystery, an enigma I tried to understand but couldn't. But for Victoria, I was a certainty.

She had me all worked out.

An open and shut case.

"Tell me all about John Teacher the teacher."

And Victoria told me all about him.

So, let's assess John Teacher as a match for Victoria. John is an English teacher and his name is Teacher and I have now decided that that is silly and he has to lose a mark for that. If my name was Teacher teaching is the last thing I'd do—call me superficial, but I would find some other vocation. (My name is Hole. For that reason I would never become a dentist, a road-digger or a proctologist.) Teacher teaches at a very highly regarded secondary school. He is six months older than Victoria and he is already losing some hair. He has been in love with her for . . . ever. He was her best friend at school. But somehow he found a way of being promoted from friend to lover.

Perhaps I should phone him.

"So what happened, Teacher? For five years she didn't want you, then she comes back from college and she's changed her mind. Why? What did you do? Jump on her one night? Send her love letters? Did you tell her you'd got a diploma in cooking, massage, aromatherapy, listening and back-stroking? Did you change or did she? Or did you both change? Why don't you either change your name, or your job?"

From an evolutionary perspective John Teacher is excellent—an eight or nine. A good few points must be awarded for staying power—he has been around a long time, stable, consistent, reliable. He has a steady job that he is unlikely ever to lose. Income poor but everlasting and he might end up as a headmaster one day. A lot of points must be for kindness. That is the main thing Victoria enthused about. Quite a turning point; kindness did not seem to be high on the list before. Ambition, intelligence, looks, and sex appeal ranked higher up the agenda.

Could Victoria be in a nest-making mood? John Teacher seems to be a nest-making kind of mate. But no, Victoria is definitely too young and adventurous to be thinking along those lines yet. John Teacher will be dumped for being a bit too dull, or dumped for wanting to settle down long before Victoria is ready to.

Conclusion: John Teacher has arrived too soon.

He should have waited another ten years, when Victoria might have traded excitement and charisma for stable, good-dad material. Victoria will not be carrying his genes to the next generation.

Good.

TWELVE

The day after the day after the day after. It is two days after I split up with my live-in lover, cohabitee, partner, main squeeze, girlfriend, lover, bird. Actually, I prefer *sweetheart*.

Have all the usual rules of the jilted been observed? (Oh yes, I am the jilted one, you'll see.)

Mr. Hole, do sit down. Let's go through the checklist to make sure all is present and correct. Stopwatch. Clipboard. Pen.

"Nothing Compares 2 U" has been played.

Check.

Victoria's phone has rung and no one has been at the other end.

Check.

The dating sections of various journals have been surveyed.

Check.

Victoria has made a triumphant comeback in masturbatory fantasies.

Check.

"Nothing Compares 2 U" has been played again.

Check.

And again.

Check.

A cheap telephone chatline has been dialed, hoping for some seedy, emotionally distracting excitement that never arrives. The next day you receive a call from your mobile company advising you of a sudden surge in your phone bill and you realize that spending two hours on the phone at a pound a minute really will cost 120 pounds.

Check. ·

A new item of clothing has been bought.

Check.

This item of clothing is out of character and is intended to show Victoria that you have some new side to your personality she has not discovered, and she will think, "Ah, nice new unusual jacket. I had no idea there was such a colorful side to his personality, and therefore I would like to resume the relationship with him."

Check.

An inordinate number of cigarettes have been smoked. The thought of giving up smoking has been pondered as a way of impressing. "Me, *smoke*? No! I gave up, haven't you heard? It was easy."

Check.

A session in a tanning shop has been contemplated, booked, then cancelled on the grounds of it being a dead giveaway.

Check.

Ditto hairdresser's you wouldn't normally be seen dead in.

Check.

Gay Simon has been phoned repeatedly on spurious grounds,

hiding the real reason—which is he must know everything that is going on in Victoria's life because he lives next door to her. You want to say, "So, has it been quiet round there lately? Huh-huh. You haven't noticed groaning sounds from the bedroom then, at all?"

Check.

The last conversation with Victoria has been analyzed and reanalyzed and sent to a lab for tests, to determine whether or not the stuff between the lines means she loves you or doesn't give a damn.

Check.

"I Will Always Love You" has not been played but only because you don't own a copy.

Check.

A photograph of Victoria has been used as masturbatory fuel.

Check.

Fantasies about The Other Boy being killed in a special-effects accident had enjoyed, then enjoyed again in slow motion.

Check.

An old flame has been phoned, out of the blue, nothing important, just to see how she is, and she immediately says, "What's wrong, have you been dumped?"

Check.

For the first time, the suggestion of visiting Dad at the weekend does not come from *him*.

Check.

Anything positive or interesting that's happened since Thursday has been noted down so that when you speak to Victoria you will have something interesting or positive to say about your life.

Check.

But it's still pretty dull so you have made stuff up.

Check.

Your next phone conversation with Victoria is worked out in exact detail word for word and has been rehearsed over and over again.

Check.

This imaginary conversation ends with Victoria thinking to herself: That two-minute conversation has really changed the way I think about him. How wrong I was! I will phone back immediately and beg to resume the relationship.

Check.

Mr. Hole, you have passed the test, please take your Being Jilted proficiency badge. Wear it with shame.

I'm on Kentish Town Road after having downed three pints of Newcastle Dutch Courage. I'm walking reasonably soberly, a quarter of a mile from our flat—sorry, that should be *Victoria's* flat. It always was *Victoria's* flat—bought with money from her psychiatrist parents. I didn't even contribute to the mortgage. She sometimes called me her "kept man." I smiled. You don't want to show vulnerability by seeming to mind. Besides, it was *silly* to mind. Victoria used to give me money to buy shoes when the ones I had were so worn the soles were half off, and flapping all over the place. If you're with someone much richer than you, they will eventually keep you, and there's nothing you can do about it.

I turn onto our road—or the road that used to be ours and is now hers. Some people get butterflies in their stomach; I get poo in my pants. Well, not literally, but it feels like it. How much nicer it must be to have lovely little butterflies fluttering gaily than a pint of diarrhea getting ready to squirt.

But there is no turning back now. If Victoria's in, fine, we'll have a chat and she will notice that I am now a shorts-kind-of-guy and I am wearing surprisingly clean clothes. I also have some interesting anecdotes, some of which are funny, and I carry a book that I would not normally read, *The State We're In*. Oh yes, I'm quite intellectual.

I will of course put a positive spin on the Gerard/James split. I won't tell her that I miss him and that he occupies whatever little space in my head that she doesn't. It almost feels like I've walked out on our only child. I will tell Victoria that Gerard and I have decided to spend some time apart in order to explore our individual creative . . . oh, I'll think of something. I'll tell her that since working on my own, I've had some interest from the BBC in a couple of ideas, can't tell you, I'm afraid, all very hush-hush, early days, but could be Big. She will think I have bought the new clothes because I've actually been paid for something, but in fact I have just two hundred pounds in the bank. Again.

I will not smoke.

No, that's impossible. But I have changed brands since the split. I am now a Camel smoker, and for some reason I think that is better than being a Silkie smoker. It shows I am broadening my horizons, branching out, growing as a person.

If she's out, I will let myself into her flat.

Well, it's still *"our"* flat, really—I know a moment ago I said it was Victoria's, but let's not be too pedantic here. I mean, she hasn't asked for the key back and there are still one or two things I have forgotten to take with me.

YOU: Such as?

ME: Such as . . . there are some bottles of stuff in the bathroom.

YOU: Such as?

ME: Dandruff shampoo which costs four ninety-nine a throw, so I think that's justified. Plus some Vaseline moisturizer for my forehead that suffers from dryness and occasional flaking. Plus I'm sure there are some other things such as . . .

YOU: Oh come on, this is pathetic.

ME: The duvet cover and matching sheets! Of course! They were a moving-in present from Dad.

YOU: To *both* of you, surely?

ME: Oh come on, he's *my* dad!

YOU: That is just about justified. And you did mention not having sheets when you moved in with Brian and Charlotte.

ME: Well remembered.

With my pretexts arranged, I ring the doorbell.

"Hi. I just popped round to pick up a few things. And to see how you are, of course. Congratulations on the job. Really? Do I not normally wear shorts? You need the legs for them, ha. Yes, Camels now."

There is no answer so I press the rickety old bell again.

"Hi. Just popped round to er . . . They're shorts, yes. And these are Camels. You were a long time coming to the door—I hope I wasn't disturbing you or—oh, are you with someone? No? Well you took a long time. Is it Stefan? You can tell me. Please, just tell me! Tell me! It's Stefan! Eaeaeaeargh!"

Still no answer. Which is a relief because I might really have embarrassed myself like that. I take out my key and put it in the lock. I go through my rationalizations for this act of trespass once more:

We did share this house till only last week.

She did not ask for the key back.

She still has my duvet cover. Plus a bottle of Vosene and moisturizer.

Yes, rationalizations all present and correct.

I proceed.

Well, blow me, it's still the same! Same coats on the hook, same lampshade that's wonky there in the hall, same pair of trainers, same my . . . God, the exact same oranges are in the fruit bowl and they still look just about edible-when-drunk.

Has nothing changed?

Where are the undies cast off by Stefan on the stairs leading to the bedroom? Where are the empty bottles of pink champagne they drank? Where are the expensive gifts and flowers? Where are the boxes with tissue paper which contained silk bras and teddies and knickers that he gave her?

Jesus, even that old copy of the *Guardian Guide* is still on the mantelpiece and it's two weeks out of date. Somehow I had expected things to have changed. I move into the kitchen looking for clues.

Has love been committed here?

If so, with whom?

I wonder if those private detectives who spend their lives following adulterers have ever been tempted to draw a chalk outline around the humping bodies.

On the kitchen table is an envelope of photographs fresh from Snappy Snaps. These must be the ones that we took on our last visit—our last-ever visit?—to Taunton to see Dad. I take them out knowing that it won't make me happy. There are some things we do knowing full well that they will not increase our happiness, or do us any good—even for a moment—yet we still do them. What's the evolutionary reason for that? Is misery life-preserving?

The first picture is one I took of my beautiful girl in Dad's garden. She is holding a hose and watering the plants, something she loved to do, and she yearned for a garden of her own.

She has a smile like peace itself.

I remember thinking that the smile must be just for the flowers because she didn't know anyone was watching her. But more likely it was for no one, just an involuntary reflex caused by a happy thought.

I often watched Victoria.

I would watch her cook, garden, tidy, soap herself in the bath, walk down the street, drive, and I would never tire. She moved in a gentle, happy way. There was a benign quality about the way she touched her world and . . . oh, this is romantic drivel really, isn't it? Am I expecting you to believe Victoria is any different from any other girl? Did she really "touch her world" more kindly than anyone else? What about when she lost her temper and kicked things? She certainly thumped the steering wheel often enough. God, she was difficult.

But, but, but, when she was in a good mood (which was most of the time) I could watch her for as long as it took her to say, "What are you looking at—is my hair a mess?"

"I'm just watching you."

"Why?"

"I like to."

"Why?"

"You can't ask *why.* It would spoil it. Some things should be left unsaid, undescribed."

"Go on, I need a compliment."

"*Awe,* that's what it is. And awe should always be silent."

"You can be very charming, very occasionally. Or are you just avoiding the washing-up?"

"Not avoiding or being charming. Look, if you went to Victoria Falls would you say, gosh, isn't it beautiful?"

"No. I hope not, anyway. It would be superfluous."

"Some people would."

"Especially Yanks. They'd have to say things like, 'My, Esther, isn't nature wonderful?' "

"God, I know. In fact Americans were the first to use the word *awesome* as an exclamation."

"Awesome!"

"Awe should never be exclaimed," I proclaim with the pomposity of one who has polished off two bottles of Newkie. And then suddenly Victoria collapses in a heap on the kitchen floor.

"What are you doing?"

She laughs like a schoolgirl.

"Oh no," I say, "that is your worst ever."

Victoria falls, you see. (Perhaps such moments should be left out of books, but I don't know.)

Before looking at the next picture I pour myself a glass of Glenfiddich. My justification is that Victoria is generous with her booze, a giving person, I'm in a bit of a state, and she doesn't drink Scotch whiskey anyway (I think that's why her dad gave it to her—to "educate" her in the way of whisky snob values.)

And it makes a nice chaser for my three earlier pints of Newkie.

The next picture is of Dad's cat, Foster, who replaced the previous cat called Foster whose ninth life ended a year ago. I wonder if getting a new Foster is a compliment or an insult to Foster One.

(It's a shame people can't be replaced as easily—the idea of a "new Victoria" is somehow worse than no Victoria at all.)

The next picture is almost immediately blurred by a soppy tear in my eye—it makes Victoria and me look like we're in a garden underwater. She has her head on my shoulder, her hand on my thigh, we're both smiling and I am holding a glass up to the camera like I'm saying cheers. God, we made a great couple.

We look good together.

What on earth has gone wrong? It was too good to last, I suppose. Too good to be deserved. Too good for me not to want to run from it.

Idiot.

Look at her, she loves you, she needs you, she even *likes* you. But you're right, you don't deserve it.

There are more pictures of smiling faces, warm, summer days. That's me lifting Sammy, the neighbor's dog, over the fence after he had jumped over to our side, the mad old mutt. This is Victoria sunning herself in her swimsuit. That's cousin Geoffrey. This is Dad. That's Dad again. That's Dad *again.* This is everyone except me. That's everyone except Dad. And this is what I have been looking for—it's Victoria fast asleep on the grass.

It's come out nicely, this one.

There's a concentration on her face as if she is trying to sleep very, very well. She seems to be saying, "I am really trying hard to sleep as well as I can, and I think I'm doing pretty well." It's my favorite. I slip it into my shirt pocket.

I finish my Fiddich and pour myself another large one for it seems unlikely that I will see Victoria tonight. I might as well get myself into a stupor. I look around the kitchen. For . . . something. I'll know what it is when I see it.

There's a cookbook open on the counter. It's for this dish that involves fish and potatoes and stuff that Victoria whipped up for practically every dinner party we used to give. We were quite good hosts and Victoria always said that I was the most "demonstrably affectionate" boyfriend she'd ever had. It's not often I blow my own trumpet—well, not in this book anyway—but I used to get ten out of ten for that. Hugging, pecking on the cheek, all that. Sure, it's a bit too lovey-dovey for some people and to tell you the truth I never did it much with any other girl. But Victoria brought out so much good in me. (Dad, you always said Victoria put the sun in me, and I denied it, but you were right.) Why some people like public displays of affection puzzles me but I'm not going to look ten-out-of-ten in the mouth.

I look around, somehow surprised to see so much unchanged, and an old anecdote of Dad's springs to mind. (Skip this if you like, it's not crucial.) A ten-year-old boy is furious with his parents because he can't watch TV or something. He is so angry he sneaks out of the house, never, ever to return. He makes his way to the local park. After what seems absolutely ages and ages and ages he eventually decides to make his way home for he has punished his parents enough. He arrives through the kitchen door and the parents don't seem to have even noticed that he'd gone. Slightly hurt, the kid looks around and says, "Ah, you've still got the parrot, I see."

That's the kind of story Dad tells—chin-strokers. (Oh well, I did say you could skip it.)

Anyway, like that kid, I feel as if everything should have changed. Ah, she's still got the Paris poster, I see.

A rather attractive poster of a French fringe production of *Hamlet*—in English. It is the worst thing I have ever seen and Victoria and I sat at the back for two hours trying desperately not to laugh. During the death scene a dead body sneezed and one of the others scratched itself. Neither of us had enjoyed ourselves in the theatre as much in our lives. We wanted a momento and so we asked for a copy of the poster. The girl at the box office took it as a compliment and seemed delighted.

It was our first-ever holiday as a couple. I assured Victoria that we did not need to book a hotel.

"But Paris must be bursting with people."

"Ah, not on the weekends. They all go off to the country," I said knowledgeably.

"Wouldn't it be best to just book somewhere?"

"Trust me, I've been before. Paris is one of the biggest, most cosmopolitan cities in the world. There *will* be a hotel with vacant rooms. We'll just walk around and find one."

The first hotel we stopped at was full, and the second, third, fourth. "Don't worry, we'll be fine. We're probably too near the Gard du Nord."

The fifth hotel was full, and the sixth, seventh, eighth, ninth, tenth, eleventh, twelfth, thirteenth, fourteenth, fifteenth, six-teenth, seventeenth, eighteen, nineteenth, twentieth. After fifty hotels (and look, I really, really do mean fifty—I know it sounds unlikely) we went back to the station. Now, any girlfriend I have ever had in my life would by now be exacting revenge—you id-iot, I *told* you to book, you wouldn't listen, my feet are killing me, you've ruined our break . . . you know the sort of thing. But not Victoria. No recriminations. She even said, "You weren't to know this would be the busiest weekend of the year." Apparently there was some festival on. There was nothing doormat-like about her. She'd simply found some way of enjoying a potentially frustrat-ing experience. And I thought for the hundredth time: this girl is good. I am a lucky bastard.

Then we spied a tourist information office and after half an hour queuing up we found a rather nice hotel in the Latin Quarter.

We fucked, showered, and went out on the town.

"James, I know why you didn't want to book a hotel in advance," she says over a typically greasy lump of Parisian offal (*why do the French still think they can cook?*).

"Why's that?"

"Because you wanted to *catch* me one. You wanted to hunt me down a nice fat trophy of a hotel, while I admired your hunting skills."

"You think it was some primeval need to hunt, rather than simply a need to find shelter?"

"Yes. Else you would have booked. But you wanted to catch a fish rather than go to the supermarket. It was romantic."

"And stupid."

"I admire your total persistence. You would never have given up if I hadn't asked you to. And then when I asked you to, you did, even though I know you felt so defeated, like a warrior lost in battle. It was thoroughly heroic."

And she was only half joking. She enjoyed my dogged attempts to find shelter.

Yes, that's what those early days were really like. I thought even then that one day she'd find me out. She would wake up one morning, scales would fall from her eyes and she'd realize that the things she'd found funny yesterday were really just irritating, bullheaded and selfish. The James Hole Show would become tired, predictable, due for the chop.

Maybe Gerard was right—I'm the mad one. Maybe I should start behaving like a normal person. What would a normal person do right now? Leave Victoria a long letter telling her why they had left and that it had all been a ghastly mistake. I scramble about for a pen and paper which I eventually find in the cutlery drawer—ah, so Chaos still resigns supreme.

I sit at the kitchen table and pour myself another drink. (Drink isn't the answer, of course, but I do find it helps with the questions. I can ask myself questions that are too frightening for the sober mind.) I will write down all the possible motives for my actions. This will form the basis of a letter.

I write the digit "1" on the sheet of typing paper. It feels very businesslike. I then put a little dot by it. Time to face the truth about myself. I will write a list of where I'm at. These will be the possibilities, the leads, the emotional prime suspects.

This is finally The Truth.

No self-deception or illusion. No more procrastination. I make the dot a little clearer and refresh my glass. I am beginning to work things out in my mind. After a few moments' thought I turn the dot into a bracket. This seems more appropriate. There.

All neat and tidy and ready to begin.

Something is emerging and I feel I have reached a crossroads, or perhaps a turning point, a moment of clarity. I decide to make the bracket into a circle. Looks neater. There. Is the pen working properly? Scribble a bit. Yes, fine. And then it happens. I start writing.

Here are the possible reasons I left Victoria:

(1) I am just a jealous guy—bloke.

(2) I am not a jealous bloke, it's just that Stefan is a particularly perfect guy and so it is quite reasonable for me to be jealous of him.

(3) I am simply jumping before the push.
    (Am I that spineless?)

(4) I am frightened of commitment and other clichés.

(Boring. Commitment isn't frightening, being single is. And fear of it is the reason a lot of people get married and stay married. Fear of singledom is so universal that inventing a word for it—such as "monophobia"?—is unnecessary.)

(5) Charlotte's theory: I prefer being in love with Victoria to loving her. I prefer her as the great unwrapped present in my life.

(Appealing concept and I would say twenty percent true.)

(6) I genuinely think I am not right for her and that Stefan really is even if they don't realize it yet.

(Very appealing to cast myself as martyr. I like this one.)

(7) I am a miserable bastard.

I don't want Victoria to see me in this self-hating, depressed state. Running away is all I can think of doing.

(8) You don't know what you've got till it's gone. Absence makes the heart grow fonder. The measure of love is loss. And other clichés. I have given up Victoria in order to measure my love. I reckon my love for Victoria is about a mile and a half there and back the slow way, which is a lot.

(9) The ninth reason is the one I don't know about—perhaps can't ever know about. It is a number I will reserve for the unknowable.

I put the pen down and admire my work. Amazingly lucid for one who is ever so slightly pissed as a fart. Three pages of squiggle but it's perfectly readable. I stand tall as I stretch my legs and flex my tired fingers.

The plants seemed to have grown a bit since I was last here. Victoria's garden is the size of a bath mat. I smell a pot plant; I have no idea what it's called though I do remember Victoria telling me a hundred times.

I breathe in the scent.

I never look at a plant without imagining that I'm a bee. Well, I grew up with the darlings. The busy little creatures kept us in house and home. I try to give a bee's appraisal of the scent, the color, the stamen. Then I look at it as a man, and I wonder what evolutionary purpose is served by my appreciation of this flower's beauty. Or indeed by the fact that I am now drunk as a skunk and am about to talk to a plant.

"You are a very beautiful flower." I probably slur a bit, and give it a drunken kiss on the petal. "May you attract many pollinating insects and may your seed spread far and wide."

Then, if memory serves, I begin to sing "Daisy, Daisy" (predictably enough) as I leave the kitchen and make my way up the stairs. I am in something of a dream, I guess, because the sound of the key in the front door makes me start and brings me crashing into the here and now. But it is a here and now covered in mist and with cotton wool in its ears.

I feel like a thief caught red-handed.

If I was in the kitchen I'd be fine, I could just tell Victoria I had let myself in, was waiting to see her and see how she is, but somehow being on the stairs is different. It is literally and figuratively a step too far. I instantly think of going down but she would see me at the bottom—it would look furtive.

I impulsively proceed upward.

I make it up to the landing, go into the bathroom and gather the Vaseline and the Vosene, which are surprisingly easy to find. The Vosene is disappointingly empty, however, which makes my mission seem even more pathetic. I turn back to trot down the stairs when I hear Victoria speak.

"You can leave it there." A coat or a bag or something, I suppose.

And then comes the reply. In glorious baritone.

"Ok. Hey, this is really nice. I like the mirror."

Could this really be his first visit? What had taken him so long?

"Coffee then?"

"Actually, have you got any herbal tea or anything?"

Now would have been the time to saunter down with nonchalance but I am frozen to the spot, knowing that the window of opportunity is closing fast. I must go now or . . . or what? I will be a sneak, a spy, a stalker.

Then there is silence. What can they be doing? No movement, no conversation. It can mean only one thing, surely.

I have the Vosene and Vaseline, he has Victoria.

THIRTEEN

Two months go by and Victoria isn't returning my calls—or rather she is, but in that way people have of calling when they expect you to be out. Messages are duly left—"we keep missing each other."

I'm missing her.

Maybe we're drifting apart in the way people do a year or two after leaving college. Or maybe this John Teacher, the teacher, is preoccupying her. I like to think of course that she isn't seeing me because I am a threat to their relationship.

Oh, I do enjoy thinking that.

Meanwhile, my life is trudging along like an old tramp in the snow. Every day I send ideas and my CV to film companies, TV companies, radio companies, theatre companies, newspapers, magazines, advertising agents, PR companies, local papers, makers of in-house training films, producers of comedy voicemail messages, comics, teen mags, porn mags, comedians looking for jokes, sketch shows, producers of bubblegum cards, greeting cards, novelty gifts and Christmas crackers. I receive some nice replies. My prayers are being answered, but with the words "no, thank you." The scatter-gun technique isn't working.

It's a strange thing when you have a very strong desire in your working life and a strong desire in your love life. Try this questionnaire:

A flatmate tells you that someone called but didn't leave a message. Do you:

A.   Hope it's someone offering you a job/deal/contract.

B.   Hope it's that special someone wanting to see you.

I would pick A. I would pick A because if my career took off, I would not need to wait for B to happen. I would be full of the courage that success gives to a man, and phone the girl myself.

Then, once upon a time, I get a message. "Hey James, it's been fucking ages. How are you? Things with me are fine. I have something to tell you. Just a bit of news. Quite exciting news, so give me a call if you want to find out what it is. I bet you're dying to know."

Oh God, let it not be marriage. It can't be, she's far too young and ambitious and doesn't want to "settle down." And I know she dislikes the idea of marriage. And she loathes that word settled *as much as I do. Parents use it all the time. "It would be so nice to see you settled." Do you know what "settled" means? Excuse me while I look in my* Chambers New Edition . . .

Here we are: "to cause to subside, to dispose of, put out of action, stun, kill, sink to the bottom, come to rest." That's what parents want us to do. Why don't they call a spade and spade and say "it would be nice to see you subside and put out of action?" Because, let's face it, that's what happens to a lot of people who marry.

So it can't be marriage.

Then why is my heart banging around like a percussionist in a strop? Don't let her slip away forever! I wasn't given enough time! Four years is nothing! OK, if she's not getting married, I promise you, oh Lord, in whom I don't believe, that I will cab it round there tonight and do the ring thing myself.

"You'll never guess. You'll never guess."

"You got a job. A starring role?"

"Oh, I'm not interested in acting anymore. It's total crap."

"But I thought you really wanted it."

"But it's not realistic. I haven't got the face for it. I went to see three agents—all of whom said I looked too 'characterful.' "

"What does that mean?"

"Ugly."

"No!"

"Sort of glamorous checkout girl."

"What?" I had genuinely forgotten saying such a thing, even with this prompt.

"Never mind. It means I can't get love-interest roles because I'm too quirky or funny or something."

"You're too interesting."

"They want bland and pretty. I've just wasted a year of my life on that profession and now I'm practically unemployable."

"You're twenty-three!"

"That's old nowadays. Anyway, you guessed wrong."

"I give up."

"Guess."

"You won a million quid?"

"Better. It's the best thing that's ever happened to me."

"Not . . . marriage?" Please God, I'll be your best friend.

"No." God, I love you!

"I'm pregnant." God, you bastard!

There's a beat or two's silence from me. But the silence can't be left too long, not in this situation, it must be filled with gush.

"You're joking!" I try to sound pleasantly surprised rather than dismayed, but this hardly amounts to a gush.

"Isn't it incredible—but it's not official. No one knows except Mum and Dad and John, of course."

I can't understand it. Victoria has never mentioned kids or family before. Her thoughts have always been about her career—and she's just twenty-three, for

God's sake. I want to ask what the hell she's playing at but of course I can't. There is only one response when someone absolutely delightedly tells you they are pregnant, and that is absolute delight.

"I am absolutely delighted!" And other clichés. Dare I try a bit of probing? "So—was it a . . . surprise?" A terrible, regrettable accident, in other words.

"A surprise? More like a shock." Good. "We hadn't been trying or anything. And you know, I was unsure at first. It's quite earth-shattering. But we talked it through, John was really keen, he wants to be a dad—did you know he's an orphan?"

"No."

"Anyway, it feels as if fate has helped me decide what I really want in life. And Mum and Dad are over the moon. They adore John and seem to think this is a great move—they hated the acting stuff."

She can hear that someone else is trying to get through.

"Oh, better go. See you soon, ok? Come over for lunch on Sunday."

"Ok. 'Bye."

Ugh. Lunch with the parents.

Victoria's oh-so-clever psychiatrist parents are delighted and it makes me sick. It would be a different story if I'd been the culprit (because that's what I'd be, the culprit).

I'd met the Maginots two or three times over the years when Victoria invited me for Easter lunch, summer barbecue and a Christmas neighborly get-together in aid of elderly aunts and mince pies. I am always nervous around the Maginots. Dad Maginot (with the ludicrously spelled first name of Kollyn) keeps trying to catch me out and expose my country-bumpkin ways. The first time I met him we were just sitting down to Easter lunch and he notices that I'm looking strangely at the starter.

"Parma ham and melon."

"Oh. I've not had that before."

"Which haven't you had? Parma ham or melon?"

Before I can reply Victoria rescues her bit of rough.

"It's just an Italian fad."

"A tradition going back centuries, Victoria. Don't come the inverted snob just because Jim comes from the country."

"James comes from Taunton."

"Near Taunton." Shit, I have corrected her and she's on my side. There then follows an atmosphere you could have whipped into a "terrine" or a "roulade" or some other poncy thing I hadn't tried.

I remember to wait for everyone to be seated before I begin. (Thank you, Dad, for telling me that that's the way to behave in polite society though you never bothered yourself.) Now I couldn't swear to this, but Dad Maginot seems to notice that I am waiting, and decides he'll start even though Mrs. Maginot is still fiddling about by the Aga, which is an oven with no "off" switch. So now I am wondering whether I should start or not.

I start.

Then, would you believe it, this learned psychiatrist, thirty years my senior, infinitely richer, with a truckload more status, puts down his fork and pretends he was just having a sly nibble, so when the lady of the house comes to the table I am caught red-handed being the turnip-eater she had always taken me for.

Now this incident might seem a mere trifle, and hardly worthy of a book that otherwise deals exclusively with weighty matters of historic resonance, but it affected the whole weekend. I felt myself constantly trying to "do the right thing" but my confidence was so shot that I kept hedging my bets and doing sort-of half the right thing and half the wrong thing. It's as if embarrassment were a bug that I'd caught, an infection that had spread until I was ill with it. As for trying to get closer to Victoria, it just made me want to get away from her and her family and smell the green, green grass of home. (Since then I have never felt comfortable as a guest in other people's houses. I've got a kind of host-phobia. People I feel perfectly at ease with, normally, turn into terrifying demons once they become my hosts. Never ask me to yours for the weekend.)

So all hail, victory to the Maginots. Their beautiful daughter is not going to bear children who smell of cider and cow dung. Their superior genes will not be *mongrelized to form a grotesque hybrid that carries a briefcase and wears Wellies. She is going to marry a professional and a townie.*

Victoria is gone. It's as if there's a monitor flashing the words "Game Over" with hideous insistence. The battle of genes has been fought and won. And it confirms my worldview. You can't buck evolution, things take their natural course, I don't know why I thought things could have gone otherwise.

John Teacher (twenty-four, steady income, kind but unexciting, steadfast, middle-class urbanite of good family) has fertilized the female in a sudden and unexpected maneuver while other males were napping. The rules of the group dictate that the rest of the suitors must give up the fight, pay their respects to his dominance and trudge to the wedding carrying badly wrapped designer lemon-squeezers from Habitat.

He who hesitated is lost. He who kept asking "to love, or not to love?" was not noble enough to suffer the slings and arrows of rejection.

Idiot.

Personally I have no sympathy for that Past Me, that dithering fool. I hate Past Me. You are quite right to as well. Let's chant it in unison: Idiot, idiot, idiot! We hate you!

I immediately phone Dad in order to present Victoria's pregnancy as good news. Well, someone once said that "you are what you pretend to be"—and I want to pretend to be someone who's not in love with a pregnant girl. I think pretending to be that person might be a step towards being that person. Like, if you pretend not to be shy, maybe you'll stop being shy.

Dad answers. I am going to pretend to be someone who is not in love with a pregnant girl to help me stop being in love with one.

"Victoria is pregnant! Isn't that great?"

Pause. Dad, you aren't supposed to pause. You are supposed to express immediate and unqualified delight. Surely you can't see through my pretense.

"Oh dear, I'm sorry James."

So the pretense hasn't got off to a flying start but it's early days, it just needs a little reinforcing.

"What do you mean, you're sorry? It's great. She's going to have a little baby. She is overjoyed—I can't wait to see the little thing."

"You don't really think that, do you, Jim? This is Dad you're talking to."

Why does Dad always see through my attempts at bravado? Why can't he at least pretend not to? Clearly I am putting on a smiley face, in the hope it will send happy messages to the sad heart, and ask it to cheer up.

Can't he see that?

"You've lost her for good now." Thanks Dad. Just in case that thought hadn't occurred to me.

"Well at least now you'll be able to move on. You really have to forget about her now, Jim. Perhaps you shouldn't see her so often. You won't be able to fall in love with anyone if you keep seeing her and—"

"Oh for God's sake! I'm not in love with her anymore! All that's over!"

Poor parents. No one thanks them for telling the truth. Why do they keep doing it?

I hurriedly say goodbye and switch on the TV. Good, it's Auntie's Bloomers. (Terry Wogan will always be remembered for making the tackiest show—Blankety Blank—entertaining, which proves that tacky format + cynical host = hit.) There is one particularly funny clip in which a newsreader loses his script and the autocue fails. He has nothing to say and the embarrassment, his pain in other words, is a joy.

I make a mental note to describe this as funnily as I can to Victoria—and then I realize that that is what I have been doing for years: collecting anything remotely funny or interesting, no matter how banal, even banal stuff from crap TV, and saving it for Victoria like a bird bringing worms to the nest. That has to end now, because Dad is right.

I will never see Victoria again.

I will drop her a little note briefly explaining the reason, wishing her well, and *that's it. This is to be an absolute, clean break like people do when they split up. We will be like estranged ex-lovers. Shame I got the "ex" part and not the "lover" part.*

Never mind, mate, just keep watching the funny man on the telly, light up a Silkie, drink some Newkie Brown and before you know it you'll be out cold.

At last, at long last, the book on Victoria could come to an end. No more agonizing, no more beating myself up. Maybe it'll be a relief. Yes, I feel a certain relief now that biology (real biology, sperm 'n' egg stuff) has made the decisions for us all. The subject I so derided at university has spoken.

And so this is the end of the book on Victoria. There will be no sequel, no epilogue, and at last, no more chapters.

Wobbly screen, a harp glissando, and caption.

Two bottles of Newkie Brown later:

I pick up the phone.

"Hi—it's me. Are you around tomorrow?"

"When?"

"Anytime. I'd like to see you."

FOURTEEN

I go back into the bathroom and lock the door. I am safe for a moment and can mentally regroup. But my brain feels like Gerard's on a bad day—a frenzied game of Kerplunk. What would a normal person do now? Walk down the stairs, cough politely to gain attention, avert their eyes if there was any hanky panky going on, and briefly explain the situation. "I was just popping by to get my skin and scalp treatment. Didn't hear you come in, made use of the toilet facilities while I was here. No, won't stay for coffee thanks, you're obviously busy."

On second thoughts, that is not normal.

It might be Gerard's mad idea of normal. Those would be the actions of a man with no real sense of embarrassment. I like to think that my sense of embarrassment is finely tuned—after all, embarrassment is one of the things Britain is still good at and speaking personally, I never leave home without it.

It can only be a question of minutes before I'm discovered and although the more time goes by, the more painful the situation becomes, I cannot move. I sit on the toilet seat as if superglued. I hear laughter.

Oh, I knew they would laugh together, but so soon? And so fulsomely? (Good Sense of Humor abbreviated to GSOH is the most common description in personal ads. More than intelligence or attractiveness, it's the most desired commodity in a mate, and the gift we most proudly proclaim. Would a visiting David Attenborough from another planet conclude that humour in humans is something purely ornate, a non-functioning attractant like peacock feathers? Or is shared humor a sign that a relationship might endure, so that offspring will be sustained by two parents throughout their infancy, and so increase their chances? In other words, is it a bonding instrument that lasts even when you're tired of the same old body? But what happens when you're tired of the same old jokes?)

Stefan has a GSOH. In fact, he has a VGSOH. Everyone at school thought Stefan would become an actor, partly because of his looks, but mainly because he could hold an audience—even an audience with Sugar Puffs for brains. He gave a reading at assembly which became legendary. It was a speech originally made by Hoffnung the cartoonist—Stefan made it his own. The speech began whimsically enough, but chuckle built upon chuckle, and laugh slowly built upon laugh and, like a great whirlpool stirred from small eddies, everyone became caught in a vortex of hilarity. It was as if the whole hall had been filled with laughing gas. I saw teachers giggle who I hadn't thought capable of a smile. Fletcher, an embittered part-time teacher and supply sadist, had a grin like a cracked tombstone. Giffy, a master of maths and applied misery, clapped his hands and chortled. Miss Sarah Hemp, an inflicter of French and double tedium, was enraptured and wished she was ten years younger and not a teacher. The hardest

Neanderthals in the fifth year were guffawing and, perhaps for the first time in their lives, not at someone's pain or abject humiliation. Sixth-formers laughed without condescension. For a moment, one dreary boys' school, in a dreary town, in a dreary county, was united and alive.

When assembly finished, the corridors filled with the buzz of novelty and excitement. As I pressed through the crush I felt elated and obsolete. Me and my fights, my macho mates, all the posturing would have to go. I was about a million years out of date, a boy that evolution forgot. I needed to get closer to that kid.

The laughter from below increases in volume and intensity. This isn't just laughter, though; it's drunken revelry. Or is the fact that I'm drunk making it sound that way? They're laughing so much it seems like there are loads of Victorias and Stefans down in the kitchen. And then it dawns on me. They have found my draft letter. The list I wasn't even going to send till I'd given it more thought, more time. The letter that says I'm jealous, the letter that says Stefan is a perfect guy. They think it's hilarious. I'm sitting on a khazi, drunk as a lord, with brittle shards of laughter piercing my hard, dark skull. It feels like a thousand voices and a thousand fingers pointing, and I know that's melodramatic, but drink does that to me. How could Victoria be so cruel and how could Stefan? I have been wrong about both of them all this time. They are evil, evil people. They are devils. How can they be enjoying my misery? What would it take to kill them both now? *Then* they'd be sorry. No, I wouldn't want to give them the satisfaction.

Huh? Satisfaction at being killed? What am I talking about? And I am *talking*. I am rambling out loud, sitting in my ex-bathroom, on my ex-bog, planning the murder of my ex-friend and ex-girlfriend, and my head spins whenever I close my eyes. I am sick, I need help, I should turn myself in to the nearest hospital or mental asylum.

Footsteps come up the stairs.

Impulse takes over and I hide behind the shower curtain. Another impulse takes over which tells me that is a stupid thing to do and it would be far better to shimmy down the drainpipe. Yes, shimmy down, and take the path by the side of the house into the front garden. Then I'll run home, get my passport, get as much money as I can from an ATM, steal some more, and buy a ticket to Canada. Start a new life. They'll think I committed suicide. But one day I'll devise a famous game show and I'll come back and visit them in a metallic blue BMW convertible. Yup, I can see it now. I can see the look on their faces.

I turn to the open window. It beckons me as surely as if it had said, "Pssssst, shimmy down the drainpipe, you know you want to, Big Boy." Shimmying down a drainpipe is a very simple thing to do.

If you are in a film.

Whether that be a Hollywood film or an Ealing comedy, it's a quick slide and you're down, shouting, "You can't catch me, copper," and running off with a bag marked "swag." But in real life, it is scary. But real life + booze + shorts = bloody painful. Because the drainpipe is rusty and horrible and hurts your skin. You can't "slide" because the drainpipe is surprisingly unslippery and the rust eats through your flesh. Look, I don't want to sound like a wuss, but it's more tricky than it looks, is all I'm saying, especially with shorts and when you're drunk.

However, I always say that a lot can be achieved in life with a little desperation. The first few seconds, as I realize that I really am outside and that the drainpipe might give way at any moment, are scary. Scary because I can see myself falling on the railing below, breaking my neck, being fed by an elderly nurse with bad breath for the rest of my life, and being visited by Victoria and Stefan at Christmas and birthdays because they feel so guilty. I can't banish the thought.

I can't move my legs. I daren't move my hands, too risky. I can't get back in the bathroom. I can't go down. I can't let go. I daren't call for help. I am stuck. Please, let this nightmare end. Please, Victoria, I didn't mean any of what I thought earlier. Please ignore those thoughts, I take them all back. You are not evil or a devil. I love you, I really do.

I love you, love you, **p-l-e-a-s-e help me!**

My arms can't take the strain any longer, and so I have to move to get myself into a more stable position with my feet resting on a sticky-out thing. I find another sticky-out thing on which to rest the other foot and it feels firm. I think a doctor would describe me as serious but stable.

I breathe deeply.

I try to slow my brain down, take things one step at a time, buoy myself up with a mantra: "James, you have been in worse scrapes than this," which I say out loud a few times. I steadfastly refuse to look down, or even *think* down. I simply move one of my feet downwards to where I think another sticky-out thing will be. Yup, that feels like one. Progress. This is going to work. I do the same with the other leg. Good. Pause. Some more morale-boosting mantra? "You have been in worse scrapes than this. You have been in worse scrapes than this."

"Hello?" This is Stefan's voice.

"It's ok. I can manage. Please, I'm going to be ok."

I still daren't look down. I mean there's no point in facing your worst fears, I don't care what the psychologists say. Besides, I can see it all without looking: Victoria and Stefan have stepped out to the tiny patio in order to take some air, and enjoy the romance of the moonlight. They look into each other's eyes, they draw closer, he holds her hands, they kiss, they hear a whispered "fuck" and they look up.

There is an arse in the sky and it's heading right for them.

If this were a film they would no doubt do a double-take, but then if this were a film I would be running away with the bag marked "swag."

"James, it's you."

His voice feels as if it is coming inches from my ears. Funny how the mind plays tricks. I must proceed downward. I move my right leg down and it finds a really big sticky-out thing. This one is very large, indeed—in fact it feels more like a kind of platform and is very firm. So large and firm that I feel secure enough to put both feet on it. There. I begin to search for another sticky-out thing and realize that the one I am on is even bigger than I thought. It's vast.

"What are you doing?"

"Don't help me—the pipe'll give way!"

Then I see Stefan. He's right next to me. He even touches me with his hand.

"How the hell did you get up here?" I say, still feeling for a foothold.

"Up where?" says Victoria. I turn to my left to see Victoria on my eye level.

"You, as *well*? Get down before you both get hurt!"

"*James* . . ." This she says in her "you're being silly" voice. I look round. I look down. I am on the ground. The really, really big sticky-out thing is, in fact, Planet Earth.

Right. Safe at last.

Physically, I am totally safe, but emotionally I am swinging from a drainpipe twenty feet in the air and there are hyenas snapping at my bollocks.

Dignity, dignity, that's what I need now, because I must have been hemorrhaging the stuff while they were watching me hugging the drainpipe with my foot sliding around trying to find a foothold on the ground.

"It's ok, Victoria. I'm not a burglar. It's me." Yes, reassuringly, it is the man you have, until recently, been living with who has been hiding in your bathroom.

"James." Victoria simply looks confused. Not angry or even upset.

"Yes. I um . . ."

"James, look, this is . . . . . ."

"Don't mind me. I was, umm, just popping by to get my skin and scalp treatment. Didn't hear you come in, made use of the toilet facilities while I was here. Popped down the drainpipe because, well, you're obviously busy. So. I'll be on my way. I'll see myself out."

I produce a bottle of Vosene from my jacket pocket in order to corroborate my story.

"Is it ok if I take the Vosene?"

I'm not normally a chatterbox but since Victoria and Stefan have been struck dumb, this seems as good a time as any for a sudden attack of verbal diarrhea.

"I know what you must be shinking, I mean thinking . . . that I'm . . . that I'm in some jealous frenzy but . . . but I think the two of you are great together. Fantastic. My plan has worked brilliantly. I set you up, you know."

I reach for my trusty drainpipe to steady my swaying frame.

"Victoria, if . . . if we were on the African plains a million years ago then we'd be fighting [hic] over you. We'd be fighting for the [hic] girl. But you, Stefan, taught me that fighting is un[hic]civilized. You preferred poetry. You made me think that I, the tough kid no one liked but everyone was a tiny bit scared of, the kid with no mum, could asp[hic] asp[hic]ire to greater sings. Greater things."

The alcohol is coursing through my brain but even so there's a voice telling me that I'm going to regret this, big time. Here I am, telling the truth—or a kind of truth. No one should ever be this honest.

I sway, and the world sways with me. Victoria and her new lover whisper something to each other.

Do they want me to make an even bigger fool of myself? Well, all right then, I will. Watch me.

"The thing is, Stefan, I am not like you. Underneath. I did [hic] I did try for a while. Pretending to be the nice, s-sensitive type. The swaggering arty ponce. But I found myself out. I am not Victoria's type. You see? Actually Stefan, why don't we have a fight? All this talking things over nonsense—is it worth it? A good h-[hic]honest fight is what we should have. That's what walruses do, and walruses are happy. Have you ever seen a walrus in therapy? Have you ever heard a walrus say, *I'm having trouble dealing with my aggression*? No! One clean [hic] fight and the winner gets the girl. And the girl is happy. Isn't that right, Victoria? Have you ever heard a lady walrus say, *He fought off all his rivals but I'm not sure he's right for me*? No! He won the fight so he's right for you, lady, [hic] no [hic] no [hic] argument. We think we've got it all sussed, us humans, I mean . . . what was I saying? [hic] Lost track. Let's have a fight! Fight, fight, fight!"

"Victoria, is everything ok?"

I turn round to find three people I've never met before standing two feet to my right, huddled in the doorway to the kitchen.

"Should we call the police?"

I turn back to see Stefan and Victoria still looking at me with pursed lips. Victoria with a mixture of sadness and shame, Stefan with (wouldn't you know it) benignity, warmth, pity. (If you saw your oldest friend in a gutter with a needle in his arm, and he wouldn't let you help him—what look would you have? Now look in the mirror. That's Stefan's expression.)

Victoria begins normalizing the situation.

"This is James. James, this John, Harriet and Malcolm, they're all working on Stefan's film. We've just finished a shoot up the road."

And I add, "And so you decided to pop round for a quickie? A drinky? A quickie [hic] drinky?"

Having a brilliant memory is a real handicap if you are also brilliant at getting drunk. You behave like a twit and remember every detail. It's a pity we can't forget at will. You could take a pill and forget all about your last marriage, the office party and those ridiculous leather trousers. There, all gone. And the next thing you do is buy a pair of ridiculous leather trousers to wear to the next office party.

Our memory of some things is sustained by the effort to forget them. I would love to forget most of what I said next on that night, and the more I desire it, the more the words dance round me in the middle of the night like evil clowns.

"Perhaps you two should have some time on your own," suggests Stefan. "I think it might be best if the rest of us went back inside."

You see, Stefan's a great guy, isn't he? He's not even a wanker or a bit of a tosser or a prat. (My adversary is, sadly and very awkwardly and tragically for me, beyond reproach. It is, from the point of view of this book, an absolute disaster. Because the guy everyone is meant to hate is really nice. And the bloke you're meant to like (me) is, well . . . you'll say I'm fishing.)

I'm seasick and I wish the ground would stop oscillating.

"Come on everyone, inside." Stefan ushers people into the house like a cop asking people to move away from an accident. *Move along, there's nothing to see here.* But the crowd wants to see the broken glass, the blood, the hand dangling from the car.

"I've got yesterday's rushes on VHS. Let's watch them."

"That is a very sensible suggestion, Stefan," I say. "Stefan is a very mature guy. He makes sensible suggestions because he is mature. In fact, you are all very mature, I am sure. *Sure* you're mature. *Suuure* you're *matuuuure.* You all have careers and money and long-term committed [hic] relationships."

The ghouls watch this tragic scene despite themselves, and despite Stefan's vigorous gestures.

"James . . ."

"I am mature too, though, Victoria. I am very mature now. I wasn't last week, but I am now. Very mature. Sure I'm mature. I am more matuuure than any of you, for suuure. I challenge anyone here to be more mature than me. Come on, let's see who's got the most maturity. I am the maturist! I am the maturist!"

"James."

Now imagine a football chant rhythm.

"I am matu-ure! I am matu-ure! M - A - T - U - R - E *mature!*"

"Let's all go inside." Stefan says this so firmly that his team of media sophisticates obey, and in a moment the door closes behind them. Victoria and I are stuck in a ditch of silence and it's clearly my job to get us out. We say nothing for a while. Victoria looks beautiful and this of course makes me feel worse.

"I'm sorry."

Victoria shrugs her response.

"I've embarrassed you in front of your new chums."

"Oh, don't mention it."

"I'll go."

"Not yet."

"I mean I'll go completely. Finally. Forever. The James and Victoria story can end."

"James. I'd really like to know what happened to you."

"What happened?"

"Over the last six months. Before that, we were fine, weren't we?"

"We were the best. Really, I mean . . . yes we were."

"So?"

"So . . ."

"I knew you would leave, James."

"Of course you did, you know everything." She mistakes this for sarcasm. "I'm not being sarcastic. You know so much. You are so wise."

"You could deserve me, Jamie, if you let yourself, but I don't think you ever will. That's really why it took us eight years to get together, isn't it?"

"You were scared too."

"Not anymore. I want you to be strong. But I don't think you are, fundamentally. I need someone strong."

"Exactly. I am the weakest link."

"Oh please."

"Sorry."

"I can't wait around for you to think you deserve me. Because I don't think it'll happen. You understand, don't you? You've hurt me a lot and I can't let myself get hurt again. Hurting hurts. And you don't seem to learn. You keep making the same mistakes."

A collective, ugly scream of merriment comes from the kitchen.

"Are you going out with Stefan?"

She doesn't have to answer with a word. She glances to the ground apologetically, and follows this by raising her head, as if she regretted her earlier apology. She's saying that, yes, she is going out with Stefan and is sorry that I am upset by that, but no, she is not going to apologize for going out with someone new, she has every right to. I return the gesture with a very slight nod, which says I'm hurt but I understand, I'm an idiot, but I love you, and why don't those people fuck off and we can just be alone together, and where did it go wrong, and sorry for embarrassing you, and I'm drunk and dirty and do you still love me, blimey, you've got streaks in your hair.

"Right," I say, in order to emphasize some of the points above.

"What am I supposed to do? That's what you wanted, isn't it? And he is perfect for me."

"I knew he would be. I read the future."

"You *made* the future."

"I love you."

"I know that. Sometimes I wasn't sure. You're afraid of—"

"Yes I am."

"I didn't finish my—"

"You didn't need to."

One of the brave young filmmakers opens the garden door and says "sorry" and closes it again, as if she had opened the bathroom door to find someone straining on the loo. I suppose an intimate conversation isn't that different.

I want time with Victoria, time to explain, but I need acres of it. I try to gather it all up into a nutshell but it doesn't work.

Then suddenly she says, "I want to hug you and ask you to stay."

I melt, this is marvelous, this is beyond my wildest dreams. Can I really be awake? In one short sentence the whole nasty episode is over. Stefan has been found wanting. Victoria has made her choice. I feel like a king. My life, our life, is back together again. Suddenly—just like that. Yippee. I am just about ready to take Victoria's hand and dance with her in the street, all night long.

"You're so much better than Stefan in every way. I don't understand how you could think I would want him and not you."

Just a minute. High on the drug of victory though I am, there is something unreal about this, which is detectable even through my drunken haze. Her tone, her vocabulary, is not Victoria.

"You're the one for me, James, you always were."

This is a little like being in a nice dream—but one that could turn nasty at any minute. A crazy thought goes through my head that the real Victoria has been replaced by a robotic double.

"Are you going to forgive me just like that?

"I want you to make love to me like you did the last time. It was fantastic. Then I'll cook you breakfast in the morning and we can pretend none of this very hurtful business happened."

I hug her and kiss her neck. I feel such relief I'm practically crying—oh, all right, I am in fact crying, or at least teary-eyed. Then the robot sensation happens again—this does not feel like Victoria. This isn't my girl; I can't fathom what's different about her but I would swear some alien force has invaded her body. I stop kissing her. I squeeze her arms tightly to reassure myself she is flesh and blood and not full of wires.

"Something's wrong."

Her head is going to fall off to reveal the wires now.

"You really think I'm going to let you stay here tonight?"

Oh, I get it. Suddenly it makes sense. So it was a dream after all, sort of. Something not real, anyway.

"You think I want you in my bed ever again? After all you've put me through? You would quite happily come here, go to bed with me and pretend nothing happened? I bet you've hardly even given a thought to how I feel. You walk out with barely an explanation—do you know how selfish that is? You've probably only been thinking of yourself in that self-obsessed, self-pitying, self-everything way of yours."

Oh, dear—she's quite right. That's Victoria all over, she is right quite a lot. Being right is one of her most annoying habits, now I think about it.

"Well no, you can't stay here tonight and, yes, I might well sleep with Stefan. I've been living with the anvil of us splitting up for so long it's a relief to have it finally fall on top of me. I don't want to winch it back up."

She goes to open the kitchen door.

"Victoria—did you read my note?"

"I couldn't decipher a word. Are you on drugs?"

"No. It kind of explains things. Victoria—let me talk to you now."

"Get a cab."

"Do give my apologies to your chums. Say I'm sorry I had to dash off but I've got another two houses to burgle tonight."

She acknowledges that this is a joke, but doesn't smile. The kitchen door opens—it's Stefan. He fiddles with the latch to get it to stay open. How does he get his wavy hair to look like that? Rich, dark and wavy. How does he get the light to fall on his face so that he looks like he's in a movie?

He's lovely. (Say what you like, but I'm not going to fall into the trap of protesting too much.)

Oh, God, he's going to do something nice. Please don't.

"Brought you both a coffee."

What a nice person he is and what a selfish ass I am.

"How's the game-show business?"

"Ok."

"I hate game shows," says Victoria. I take comfort from the fact that at least she's not pitying me. Please don't pity me, Victoria, no matter how pitiful I become.

"You never said you hated game shows."

"Didn't want to discourage you."

"Well, do you know something? I hate game shows too."

"Good. You're wasted on them."

"I agree," says Stefan. "Not that there's anything wrong with game shows, of course. But you could be doing something better, I'm sure."

They've both said something nice. I suppose it's my turn to do something nice now. The nicest thing I can do is leave.

"I'm shooting off. Cheerio. Have a nice evening. Sorry for um . . . well, everything."

And James Hole exits the scene.

I walk round the side of the house, into the front garden and away. I can feel the breath of a collective sigh of relief on my neck.

I unfold my lapels and huddle into my jacket though it's not cold. I think of that advert they show in the "hundred best archive" shows. *Poor, cold Fred.* I think he's a man who is too mean to buy central heating or something. He's the guy outside in the cold all alone. What a martyr I am. What an outsider. What a romantic. What a loser.

What a drunk.

* * *

By the time I get to Charlotte's my head has cleared, as if the fresh air had gone in through my nostrils and out through my ears taking with it the drunken fog and the acrid stench of self-pity. I turn the key slowly so as not to rouse my hosts. I feel guilty about staying out so late. As a house guest I feel I have too fla-grantly followed my own pattern when really I ought to have fitted in with theirs. Rise when they rise, eat when they eat, eat *what* they eat, talk about the same things, *believe* the same things. How long will it be before I am indistinguishable from them? God, I am weak. (Thank God my host isn't Mike Tyson.)

The kitchen light is on. I feel obliged to turn it off in case they think I had been careless with their resources. I flick the switch without fully entering the room.

"James."

I start at this disembodied voice and turn round sharply. Brian is slouched at the kitchen table with a bottle of Jim Beam and a glass for company. The picture is of myself an hour ago in Victo-ria's flat. The ghost of the face that had dominated his evening is still about him. He tries to shake it off, but the wind has changed and he's stuck with it. It's a face of murder and dark deeds, and the settlement of scores. Fiery passions have drawn his skin into deep crevices, making the rest of his face taut and ready to crack.

He's had a skinful of strategies and heroic acts. The war in his head has been bloody and long. But he was bound to find glory; like a boy attacking World War II infantry with spaceships and transforming robots, winning was never in doubt.

"Bourbon?"

I try to fathom which answer he wants. Would he really like me to share a whiskey with him? Or is he thinking that I have spoiled his night of violent reverie? I feel the house guest's compunction to do whatever my hosts *really* want me to do, whatever the literal meaning of the encoded message.

"Just a very small nightcap."

Brian takes the top off his bottle with defiant clumsiness. He enjoys not only *being* drunk, but *looking* drunk, as if he's rebelling against all us sober mugs, and our petty concerns with coordination.

"Been out?"

"Yes. Over to Victoria's."

"Oh yes. How is she? Taking it ok?"

"Well, not bad."

I'm not sure how much Charlotte had told him but I guess he has reduced the situation to it being a simple matter of boyfriend-has-left-girlfriend.

He grabs a tumbler from the drainer, turns it upright and grips it as if it were a small animal trying to break free.

"So you leave Victoria and the next thing you know you're living here. With me and Charlotte."

His voice has the same flaunted inaccuracy as his movements. *Yeah, I'm a man and I'm drunk. Don't like it? Tough.*

Something tells me we aren't going to be chatting about immersion heaters and towels.

"Yes. It's very kind of you both."

"You never actually went to bed together, did you? At college."

"Not really."

"I'm talking about Charlotte."

Trouble.

"Oh. Well, same answer. Ha."

Well, well, well. Looks like this could be a long night.

"Have a seat. I'm not really used to this kind of thing. You know, talking things over."

Ah. So the big drunk act is not the bravado I thought it was. It's more of a license, a ticket that lets him into the world of heart-to-heart talks. He has demonstrated to me that he is sufficiently drunk to talk about "stuff" without looking like a girl. And it can be assumed (can't it?) that anything he says will be officially forgotten by morning or blamed on the bottle. That's the deal.

"You and Charlotte, Charlotte and you." He pauses. "Well?" There is a chill sobriety in his eyes now and I want the drunk back. I tell myself to wake up, there's work to do. Job number one: find out what the hell is going on here, on the double.

"Right," I say as if I know what he's talking about, but I have no more idea than you do. You can guess, but you're not sure, are you?

"She was in love with you. Charlotte. The love of her life. The total and complete love of her life. You broke her heart."

Oh deary me. Not the most meaningful words in our great language, but sometimes no other words will do.

The look on Brian's face says he has a plan. He has worked out how this conversation is going to go. He has put my lines in too. I'd quite like to ask to see the script—then we could read out our parts, go to bed, and deal with this properly in the morning.

Ah well, I must dither through this somehow.

"Well," embarrassed cough, "I can't imagine I'm the love of her life."

I wish no one had invented the word *disingenuous.* It would be so much easier to pull off.

"You want her now. You want each other. Perhaps you always have, I don't know. And I have given it some thought."

To say I feel uncomfortable doesn't really do justice to it. For me, being a bad houseguest is, as I think I have intimated, pretty much a Room 101 thing. Winston in *1984* had rats. A lot of people would have snakes. I think my Room 101 would simply contain a couple looking disapprovingly at me, and then down at a large stain on their carpet.

I look as contrite as I can.

"I've decided not to stand in your way. Because you two need to be together."

I can't disagree. Not because I agree, but because I *can't* disagree. I'm his guest. He could say anything now and I would have to politely concede. It is his house. He knows where the towels are, I don't. I am on his territory. There are rules going back millions of years about this. My evolutionary heritage is telling me loud and clear I should not be on this patch of ground. If by absolute necessity I must trespass, then an intricate set of rituals must be observed: rituals of absolute subservience.

"I will leave you both to it. I will stand aside," declares Brian with the resolve of a martyr.

Houseguest-anxiety has a stranglehold on my vocabulary.

"Well, obviously that is very generous but—"

Brian interrupts me but I have to interrupt him first to say that the line above is really quite alarming. I can't believe I said it. It would be so easy to delete and no one need ever know, but this isn't that kind of book (something I am beginning to regret). I mean, *generous?*

"So you're not denying it?"

"I don't think that it's quite right, what you're saying," I venture timidly.

"Come on, at least have the courtesy to level with me. I can accept disappointment. I wanted to be an architect. Well, I *was* an architect. Do you know why I stopped?"

"You were made redundant."

"No. I gave up because I couldn't reach the top. I couldn't be the best. I couldn't even be one of the best. Do you know why?"

"You weren't good enough. Shit. No. Umm . . ."

"Right first time. Don't be afraid to say it. I was not good enough. Say it! I was too proud, yes too proud, to design public lavvies and sub—post offices and fucking dry cleaners. I was too much of a man to do that. So I gave up. Zam. Good riddance."

I wonder how long this script is. It sounds like it could be a three-acter.

"Yup. Turned my back on a dream." He'd make a reasonable low-rent Willie Loman.

"So, I am now a chartered surveyor. And an average one at that. And see that there?"

He flicks a switch on the wall and a garden light illuminates the shed that he'd been working on. It looks embarrassed to be in the spotlight.

"That's what I build now. Buildings, sheds, same difference."

I nod. I nod vigorously. All the more vigorously for not agreeing. That shed is a long way from the Pompidou Center.

"Same difference. Now where was I?"

"Um, the garden shed."

"Before that."

"Architecture."

"Before that."

"Not sure. It's late." Maybe he'll just forget where he was and mumble himself into a tangled stupor. I make to rise.

"*Disappointment.* Disappointment. I'm always ready for it, it's round every corner."

"That must be quite oppressive. *Every* corner?"

"I'm not surprised by it."

"What if you turn the corner and everything's fine? Then you'd be surprised. Ha."

"But there's always another corner. And I'm on a one-way street."

What is it about drunks and metaphors? I once had a drunken conversation about no man being an island. It included the words *sea, peninsula, beach, ship, cargo, port, waves* and *pebbles,* all of which signified different aspects of social interaction.

"A man is only what he achieves. No more and no less. Not what he has. Not what he owns. Burn my shed down. I no longer have the shed, yes?"

"Yes."

"But I still have the achievement."

Please let me go.

"Is love an achievement?"

Untie me from this lasso of melancholia. But he is waiting for a contribution to the debate. How to find words that sound like I'm trying to engage with this, but not interesting enough to prolong the discourse.

"I am asking you. Is love an achievement? Do you regard Victoria as an achievement? You no longer have her. But do you still have the achievement of her? Do you want to achieve someone else now? Charlotte, for example?"

"What?"

"Don't just say *what*? Don't say *what*. *What what*. Answer properly."

I meet his intense, mad eyes then look down at the ripples on the badly laid linoleum.

"Well, I like Charlotte a lot. I'm very fond of her and have been for years but I've never been in love with her. I prefer to think of love as just something that happens when you're busy making other plans—to paraphrase Lennon. I'm a biologist at heart. A determinist." I find myself getting into this a little. Talking to a drunk (especially when you're still drunk yourself) gives one license to talk earnest cobblers. "I'm a boring old Darwinist. I've always been one—long before he came back into fashion. But you're wrong about Charlotte and me. We were best friends, I suppose, but I'll tell you something that maybe I'm only just beginning to realize. I really love Victoria. I mean I've been *in* love with her for years. But I think I love her now. Which is different."

And then I notice heavy rhythmic breathing. I turn to Brian and his head is slumped down onto his chest. It is deeper than the sleep of the dead. It's the sleep of the drunk. I watch him for a moment. All is quiet.

Sitting on the knackered old bed I untie my laces. It's cold now. A half-moon shines through the Velux window. I take off my shoes and then a sock. I throw it at the wall. I feel free. Free from Brian, who I left slumped on the chair, his head in alcohol clouds. Off with the other one. I feel free of something else too, which I can't identify. Something has lifted but I'm not sure what. I'm lighter.

I'm naked now, but the cold doesn't bother me. I get a notebook out of my jacket, search around for a pen. I write in large letters the words: I HATE GAME SHOWS.

I want to pin it on the wall but there are no pins, and no bits of old tape or Blu-Tack, so I place the piece of paper on the floor right in the middle of the room. I walk round, dodging the clutter of electric heaters, blankets and rugs. Looking at it from different angles might clarify something. I get my phone from my trousers that I'd flung on the floor.

"Gerard, I've got an idea—and it's not crap. Call me."

FIFTEEN

It's always pretty terrifying to try hundred percent for anything. That's why nobody ever works for exams. "I didn't do any work at all" is only partly a posture. It's probably not true that they did no work, but it's also likely that they didn't dare give it hundred percent. Where does that leave you if you fail? Trouble is, you could apply that thought to everything you do and end your days with your family gathered round you, saying "Ok, my life was a failure—but I did no work at all. I was a crap dad, a crap husband and I had a crap career but obviously if I'd really tried I would have been brilliant."

Such excuses are not available to some people, of course. Captain Scott, for example, never wrote in his diaries: "Well, the Norwegians really tried. They swotted. We did no work at all. We didn't even especially want to get to the Pole first. But we could have if we tried." Nor would it have been possible for Hillary to claim that he reached the summit of Everest by busking it, or swotting up the night before. Scott and Hillary were prepared to risk everything, in view of the world, and fail.

I suppose Victoria became my own private Everest, but I was no Hillary or Scott. While I didn't declare my love for her and beg her to love me, I wasn't really trying. That meant there was always the possibility that if I did really try I might succeed.

It's a great feeling, you should try it.

Instead of climbing that mountain and probably killing yourself in the attempt, you look at it every morning and say to yourself, "If I really tried, I could reach the summit." That is an absolutely fine way to live your life. You can imagine what it would be like to climb up there, you can look forward to the possibility that you might do it tomorrow. Not only that, but your life has a constant purpose and you never have to endure that feeling that you've lived your dream, so now what? Nor do you have to face the possibility that actually climbing that mountain isn't quite as much of a buzz as you imagined. So you sit around, doing some much easier things like brewing your own beer or learning to line dance, keeping that mountain as a wonderful source of inspiration and joy. I can't recommend this philosophy highly enough and it might have been a marvelous way to carry on if Victoria had not become pregnant. Because that's the mountain falling down.

We arranged to meet in our usual place and I waited with my usual bottle of Newkie and spritzer, her nineties drink of choice. I was, I kept telling myself, attempting something that was virtually impossible——to woo a woman when she's just declared that she's starting a family with another man. Of all the inopportune opportunities. I suppose a wedding might be worse, or perhaps the delivery room. I could arrive as the baby comes out, singing "It Should Have Been Me" at the top of my voice. I should call it off, for this is madness. I pick up my phone and find Victoria's number.

A voice is telling me that this flies in the face of the natural order of things. It even makes a monkey out of evolution——the last thing I should be doing is wooing a woman carrying another man's genes. Ok, let's look at it this way——I'm not really wooing (am I?). I'm just fessing up. But still, it doesn't feel morally sound, it isn't socially sound. This is desperation. I should leave Victoria to her man, her baby, her happiness.

My other voice (I have many——and this one pipes up after a few gulps of

Newkie Brown) tells me that the girl can always say no. Victoria probably will say no. But at least she'll know how I felt. And sod it, I have agonized and I have listened to the "don't do it" voice long enough. That voice can get lost for ever, says the voice with the Newkie in its hand. Ok, so it's wrong, and it may be futile but I love her, and love is . . . well, you know, it makes you do daft things.

If she turns me down, I will walk off into the sunset never to bother her again. If this was a Western then the voice at the end might say in a croaky drawl, "And James was never seen in that town again. No one knows what became of James. Some say he died of a broken heart. Others say he still works at Print Stop on Kentish Town Road. He was a man whose heart had become a battleground between fear and love, and the fear won. Victoria and her husband, the teacher called Teacher, had nine children all of whom were teased mercilessly."

Victoria appears, windswept and bent sideways by a bag of shopping. The tradition of the tight hug is honored. Our booth is occupied by a gay couple apparently in the midst of a row. No matter. This is not going to be a romantic evening.

"Congratulations again."

"Thanks. But look, it's really early days. Top secret. You haven't told anyone, have you?"

"I did tell Dad but no one else."

"And how did he react?"

An odd question. How did he react? As if there could be any other reaction but delight and congratulation.

"I'll tell you when we sit down."

We sit down straightaway, so that wasn't much of a delaying tactic.

"You want to know how he reacted?"

"Yes."

"You might be surprised."

"Well, don't tell me if it's bad."

"You're happy, Victoria. Nothing he said will affect that." Spit it out, son. "Victoria. Dad was upset because he thought—well, hoped—that one day we would get together—you and me."

"He thought that?"

"Yes."

Her nose seems to shine suddenly, and redden, while the rest of her face remains unchanged. And, to my surprise, her eyes fill up. I really didn't expect this. I don't know what I expected, but my handful of words seems to have gone in, and hit something soft. The biologist in me is inclined to trust these involuntary—biological—responses, the ones that happen against our bidding.

"Dad always thought we would make a great couple. He looked forward to our wedding, the nutcase."

And Dad did. He wanted me to "settle." To settle with Victoria and I resented him for wanting it because I was afraid it would never happen.

Why had I chosen this moment to come clean to Victoria? I can see why now, but I didn't know then. I chose this moment because I had nothing to lose.

"I told him how I felt about you from the beginning."

She scrambles about in her handbag for a tissue. I search my pockets but it's just a reflex, I never carry them. A load of stuff comes out of the handbag and onto the table. Makeup, chewing gum, bits of paper, a purse, various tickets and finally she retrieves a desperate scrunch of pink tissue. She blows her nose loudly and it's rather lovely.

I wait for her to regain composure. How should I interpret these tears? They are tears of what, exactly? I suppress any urge to take solace from them. The red of her nose has now spread, her whole face is flushed and bright.

She blows her nose again. "Sorry. I don't know why I . . ."

"It's ok. It's probably all those new hormones you've got in your system."

"You told your dad how you felt about me?"

"He knows I've loved you since I first saw you in the coffee bar four years ago."

Victoria breathes in deeply then exhales through a small opening she makes with her lips. Where is she? In the past or the present?

"I don't really understand."

"I know this isn't the best time to say it."

She heaves a sigh to calm the tears. "I agree the timing isn't brilliant. I am pregnant and going to spend the rest of my life with someone else. And you pick this moment. You are a nutcase. You and your dad."

"I'm not trying to woo you." Oh really? "That would be crass." As if that would stop me. "I just . . . I suppose I just wanted you to know how I felt all that time. That's it. No other motive."

She smiles as if she wants me to continue and maybe fall into some trap of my own making. So I oblige, as she touches my hands sweetly.

"I suppose love that's never revealed is like a kind of . . . well, a crime that goes unpunished. I haven't expressed that very well at all. Very badly, in fact. But people want . . . oh God . . . I'm trying not to say 'closure.' But I think there's a natural urge to want to get the truth out. That's all I want to do. It's quite selfish, I know that. But you're strong. You've found a life. I figure you can handle it."

"Timing, timing, timing. Mind you, it could be worse. It could have been——"

"The wedding."

"Or——"

"The delivery room. I did that routine in my head while I was waiting."

"The honeymoon bed?"

"Ah. I missed that one. Maybe I didn't want to think about that."

I admire women for being able to laugh and cry at the same time. I've never seen a man pull it off.

"Is this true, what you're telling me?"

"What, that I loved you?"

"Yes."

"Why would I make it up?"

"I mean, maybe you think you did. But I was there, remember?"

"I'm sure. You can't be wrong about love."

"Oh, you can."

"So you think I'm mistaken?"

"You were not in love with me. I would have known."

"I was. I have the scars."

"You were not."

"Was!"

"Were not!"

"Was, was, was."

"Weren't, weren't, weren't."

"Well, at least we can discuss it like mature adults at last."

The barman asks if we're staying for supper—last orders soon.

"Yes, please," says Victoria.

We continue at lower volume. I decide to raise the debate with a philosophical approach, even though all my philosophical knowledge comes from a Made Simple book.

"You can't be mistaken about a feeling. If you think you're in love then you are. It's like, I think, therefore I am."

"Stuff and nonsense. People are wrong about love all the time. I used to think I was in love with Morrissey. Oh, God, and that one from Tears for Fears, what was his name?"

"Why can't you believe I loved you?"

"The skinny one."

"Victoria, listen to me."

"I'm sorry but I'm overwhelmed by this."

"You're amused by it. I don't mind." And I really don't mind.

"I'm incredulous."

"Why?"

"Your Honor, I am prepared to believe, with the all the evidence put before the court, that the plaintiff tried to fall in love with me as a distraction from Charlotte but he wasn't—"

"Charlotte? You aren't serious. This is contempt, m'lud!"

"You were practically married for a while."

"This is very, very alarming. You thought I wanted Charlotte?"

"I can always tell. It's my psychological background. Both my parents are shrinks, remember? Besides, you did say you were going out with her."

"I did but only once. I didn't expect . . ."

"You spent all your time with her."

"She was someone to be with."

"And you gave me to believe you really liked her."

"Oh, God."

If memory serves, somewhere in Philosophy Made Simple is a quote from Kierkegaard: "Life must be lived forwards but it can only be understood backwards." The past is falling into place like containers being hauled off a ship.

"Look, I began to realize that you weren't in love with her after a while. But I didn't think you had any feelings for me."

"Why? I thought it was pretty obvious."

"Pretty obvious? The way you criticize, take the piss, put me down."

"I have been nothing but nice to you."

"Oh, like the last time we met? 'Kentish Town Woman, Checkout Girl'."

"You don't take those things seriously."

"I was incredibly hurt."

"Oh God. In that case I have completely misread all of your reactions for four years."

My body caves in around my stomach. Could I really have been misreading practically every conversation I had ever had with her?

"I'm winding you up. Of course I wasn't incredibly hurt. Just a bit miffed— since the whole acting world was telling me the same thing at every audition. And it just confirmed my belief that you never found me attractive—even when we went to bed that once."

"I'll explain that another time."

"I thought the girlfriend excuse was a bit phony. I felt so rejected. And so stupid."

"I cocked up."

"So to speak."

So that's why she left the next morning with barely a word.

So I tell her the whole story. All of it. Mr. Supercock, going to the swimming *baths, putting my weapon beyond use in the shower. Victoria's reaction oscillates between hilarity and incredulity.*

"You did that? In my shower?"

"Needs must. But it's history."

"It's hysterical."

"I would like to know what you would have thought if I had told you. You know, just come out with it."

"That you'd just had a five-knuckle-shuffle in my shower?"

"That I really fancied you. I mean before all that. Would you have ended our friendship like you did with Jay Jones?"

"Jay Jones?"

"He walked you home and then tried to kiss you or something and you ditched him as a mate."

"Are you thick or something? Jay was just trying to get me into bed because he's a trier. He did it with everyone. He's a drunken lech. And never much of a mate."

"I'm a drunken lech sometimes."

"And another thing. When you stayed at my parents those times . . ."

"Yes?"

"You always wanted to get away. Couldn't leave early enough on a Sunday morning."

So that's what it looked like. Rejection.

"I always felt very uncomfortable staying at your house with your parents. I think it's given me a complex."

"What?"

"Every time I stay with anyone these days I get really anxious and can't sleep or be myself. I'm so afraid of offending or being in the way. I have a kind of thing about staying at other people's houses. Maybe I had it before meeting your dad, I don't know. Anyway, it's practically a phobia."

"What are you on about?"

"Your dad. He wanted me to feel anxious. Like I wasn't good enough for you."

"It's true, he's a terrible snob."

"Him and his Parma ham. By the time I left I felt I wasn't fit to trim their hedges, let alone woo their daughter."

Victoria shakes her head sadly and squeezes my hand a little tighter. "You're lovely."

"And you're pregnant."

Which means that I must surely be programmed not to want to have sex with her. To do so, in strictly biological terms, would be to waste my genetic material, or worse, possibly end up nurturing an offspring of whom I am not the biological father. If only I were a fruit fly, life would be so much simpler.

There's a long silence. Victoria is looking intensely at the pockmarked table, pressing her fingers into miniature craters. I suppose the past is being realigned. The neat phalanx of events has become untidy and must be put into a sensible new order. I don't want to interrupt the process.

I smile at a very old joke that pops into my mind suddenly.

"Victoria, here's a really old joke. You've probably heard it. A man is in a hospital bed. The doctor asks him what he wants first, the good news or the bad news. He says he'll have the bad news. The doctor says he's afraid that he has had to amputate both his legs. And the good news? 'The bloke in the next bed wants to buy your slippers.'"

The good news is that I had at last told Victoria how I felt. And it made me feel good. Really very good. Very, very, very good.

And the bad news?

She's pregnant.

SIXTEEN

Going to bed with a new idea is a little like having a one-night stand. You never know how you'll feel about it in the morning. Embarrassed, perhaps. Did I *really* like that person/idea? What was I *thinking*? I must have been drunk. Alternatively, this could be the start of something. This new person/idea could be The One.

Yet again I allow myself to test my feelings. How excited am I about this new idea? *I Hate Game Shows.* I say it aloud a few times as I look around the attic at the clothes strewn on the floor.

My nerve-endings send messages back to my brain informing me that I am a bit confused. Half the hormones rushing through my veins are going, "Yippee—this is the big game-show idea he's been waiting for," and the other half are going, "He's lost Victoria for good, there's really no point in going on." My brain is no more than a switching mechanism. If it thinks about Victoria, I am down, and the effort to even get out of bed seems too great, too dangerous. If it switches attention to the New Idea I feel like springing up and hugging something.

So Stefan and Victoria are together.

They had sex last night probably; maybe they've done it before. I don't understand why I'm not screaming quietly to myself. I feel calm, the worst has happened and I'm not dead. It's that old feeling that I had once before with Victoria—a feeling of having lost, of having nothing, therefore having nothing to lose, therefore I can go into action without fear because nothing can go more wrong than it's already gone. Like Victoria said last night, the anvil has fallen; it hurts but at least it can't fall again.

Only she was talking about her.

I think about them together. I wonder whether they did it last night after the guests had gone. It makes me horny and it makes me sick. I can see them now, reaching for each other. The thought of his hands on her body arouses me and my arousal disgusts me. They kiss, but they know they shouldn't, it's too soon, too soon after James. But they want each other so much. "No, we mustn't," she says, but she hopes he'll put his hand further up her skirt. He does, he can't help it. Up it goes. Further and further until it arrives. It's too late to stop now, the feelings are too strong. Their clothes fall off each other onto the bedroom floor. No, the kitchen floor. No, the hall. She is impatient for him—this is sinful so it must be done quickly, with the breathlessness of shame and excitement. He withdraws, remembering that he is betraying a friend, but she pulls him back like he hoped she would. It is painful, but I must go on imagining. It's a punishment. I am a masochistic voyeur. Her back is arched on the floor, she's gripping the hair on his head as it nestles between her legs, she's trying to make herself wait, but it's almost unbearably pleasurable. The spasms of guilt augment rather than diminish these glorious sensations. There are tears in her eyes. She lets out a whimper when he enters her, she can't believe how good he feels and how betraying me makes it feel better, which she knows is all wrong, but it's good. She doesn't want to come, she wants this to last, but she's overwhelmed by his presence inside her and lets out a surprised screech—as if she had not thought such intensity possible. He has her nipple between his lips. She gasps, he moans, and all three of us come together.

They lie in each other's arms feeling their sweat mingle and their chests rise and fall in unison. My house guest anxiety returns with the thought that I might have committed the ultimate faux pas: made semen stains on my host's bed.

I make myself a cup of tea and toast at ten past seven, hoping that if I can get out of the house early enough I can avoid Charlotte and Brian—especially Brian. Best make myself scarce. They won't even know I'm here today. But at quarter past seven I hear Charlotte's footsteps on the stairs and she arrives in her dressing gown, her arms folded tightly as if she's cold, though the house is perfectly warm.

"Cuppa tea?" I say.

"Thanks."

I'm tongue-tied by host/guest anxiety. It's intensifying, this discomfort at being in a home that isn't mine. I'm fine when the hostess isn't actually present, like just before Charlotte appeared, but as soon as I am having to make small talk and watch my manners, I suffer mental paralysis.

"Did you sleep well?" she inquires. This is a question people who are used to sleeping in the same house never ask, but those who aren't feel compelled to.

"Yes. I did. Thanks." You'd think I'd be able to chat with ease to this very old friend but the host/guest divide gets me every time. "Quite a late night, though. Came in at about one."

There is an awkward silence. By that I mean that neither of us speaks and I feel awkward about that. But that's the problem with mornings in someone else's house; the day is too young and too inexperienced to talk about, nothing has happened yet. We keep nearly bumping into each other as we go from toaster to fridge to kettle and back. I try to give a little chuckle each time, but it sounds less and less genuine. I resist the temptation to go to the toilet just to give myself a respite from the pressure not to offend. But I tell myself I must try to grow out of this—I am a big boy now. I am *welcome* here. They *invited* me here.

As we settle down at the breakfast table something alarming happens. Charlotte says something that is not a meaningless morning pleasantry.

"James. Um, Brian's unhappy. He didn't come back last night."

"Didn't come back?"

"He does that when he's unhappy. He sometimes goes to sleep in the attic room but you're in there so . . . maybe he went out somewhere."

"He was here when I got in. I left him asleep here."

I have upset the host and the hostess has found out. I am being a terrible guest.

"You don't know Brian well, do you, James?"

"I suppose I don't. I know he's not especially happy career-wise."

"I think he's gradually come to terms with being a surveyor."

Like being a surveyor is on a par with going blind or losing a limb.

"He seems ok to me, but as you say, we don't know each other well."

"He thinks you've got some magic spell over me."

"Really?"

"He knows about us. Our past. University and all that."

"But that's all so long ago. There's nothing at all like that between us now." That's not *quite* true, is it now? Unshaggable to shaggable. My words, I recall.

"And . . . why did you both let me stay here if——"

"He didn't want to admit that that's how he felt."

"I see." And I do. Well, it doesn't take a genius to see that there are certain parallels. Whacking great tramlines of parallelism that I suppose I'm meant to learn something from. Like, he feels about me the way I do about Stefan. He thinks Charlotte wants to be with me, and has even suggested standing aside, like I've done. And I'm meant to think, how foolish Brian is for doing that. Hang on, *I'm* doing the same thing, *I* must be foolish, too! Oh me, oh my! The error of my ways! I must explain everything to Victoria, ask her to marry me and we can live happily ever after.

God, if life were that simple they'd be no point in writing books. But it isn't, because the slight difference is that Charlotte is now sitting in front of me and saying: "I was so in love with you, James. And I still am."

Oh dear.

"But you and Brian seem so happy." Sometimes you just have to roll out the clichés, say the things you ought to say, never mind about how true or original they are. Just roll them out. Watch me.

"You two are great together. Made for each other. You have so much in common. He loves you. And I'm sure you love him."

But the clichés bounce off her ears like bad radio ads.

"You know how pathetic it is to be in unrequited love for twelve bloody years. Brian's right. Nothing's changed between us, James. I thought love was something that faded with the years like radiation. But it hasn't. I tried to distract myself so many times. But you can't trick yourself out of love. Love is too clever. It's like a parasite inside me. Sometimes it hides, lies dormant for a while, but it's always there. I can't kill it. I can't kill it!"

She cries and bashes the table with her fist. A spoon flies into the air and lands noisily in an empty porcelain fruit bowl.

I wonder at the chances of that happening. Then I recall that the last time Charlotte talked about loving me I thought about snapping crisps. How little we've all changed. She sighs heavily and pushes her uneaten toast away.

Sometimes I can watch another human in pain and feel nothing at all. No empathy, no real sympathy. I just go through the motions of seeming to care because it's the "right" thing to do. Maybe it's houseguest syndrome again—just wanting to do anything or say anything as long as it's blandly inoffensive.

"I'm sure this is something that has just flared up because I'm staying here at the moment."

More soothing, meaningless words. Meanwhile I'm thinking about how this situation confirms my own choices and predictions. Brian was *right* to be jealous. Charlotte *would* rather be with me. It all verifies what I feared about Victoria and Stefan.

Automaton-like, I touch Charlotte's arm—something I would not have done ten years ago. This touching helps me to feel a little. It makes her feel less like a hostess and more like a person. She looks so frail, this home-owning-woman-with-job-and-live-in-boyfriend. She's a child suddenly.

We say nothing for a while.

She sighs tearfully and I think how strange it is to be loved like this. What did I do? How did I do it? What does she love? I mean *precisely*? Is there one thing about me that, if it were removed, would leave her free from loving me? Or is her love really like a growth inside? I think that's nearer the truth. Charlotte would go on loving me even if I died today and my body was turned to ashes.

Her love would survive me.

And I begin to feel. Feel, I don't know *honored* isn't the right word, and nor is *flattered. Humbled* is as close as I can get without using a thesaurus.

"I wanted you to come and see my life here with Brian. To see that I managed to make a home without you. And I also wanted to help you because I always felt guilty."

"Why guilty?"

"Because I knew Victoria loved you all those years ago. I did what I could to stop you and her happening in tiny ways you wouldn't have noticed. Looks, gestures, little words to her friends that I knew would get back. I made Victoria think there was something unspoken between us."

I stroke her shoulders again. I am glad for the opportunity to forgive her. On the third stroke I hear a noise from the hall. I look up to find Brian standing in the doorway. To recoil from Charlotte would be an admission of guilt. But I have no time to think and recoil involuntarily, so the guilt is admitted. I put my hands by my side. Charlotte, with her head cradled in her hands, is oblivious.

She continues: "Even now when I'm with Brian I so often wish I was with you."

"Charlotte . . ." I say, as I look my host in the eye. "Charlotte, that's nonsense." I nod my head at Brian to emphasize the point.

"Now you are beginning to annoy me," says Brian. Charlotte looks up and well, *gasps*, I suppose. People do gasp. Not often, but they do.

And I probably gasp as well. I am a guest in the house, and I have been caught apparently touching up the hostess.

"Where have you been, Brian?"

"Asleep in the cellar. You can hear every word through the floorboards. No plasterboard or insulation, you see." Thanks, Mr. Surveyor. "But I knew it all already. How about fighting for her?"

"Brian? Don't be a wazzock. You're angry with me, anyway, not James. James isn't to blame, I am."

Brian addresses me. "You were a bit of a fighter when you were young, weren't you? Bit of a tough guy. How about putting your skills to the test?"

"Brian, are you drunk? You reek of whiskey."

"Come on, macho man, let's see how tasty you really are."

My host puts up his fists like some latter-day fop. He looks absolutely ridiculous. Then, just to make sure he looks totally absurd, he takes off his specs and folds them up, placing them on the sideboard before resuming position. Charlotte stands up.

"Brian, don't be a prat. You're a *surveyor.*"

I edge away from my aggressor and start rapidly thinking of ways to calm things down.

"How about we all have a cup of tea before I leave?"

This is a peace offering. It allows Brian a dignified way out. All he has to say is "milk no sugar" and the whole thing is forgotten. But he remains standing there, seething.

So, peace offer declined, the situation has just got one step closer to ugly. Guest-anxiety is replaced in my veins by a darker, richer, hotter fluid—that of aggression and self-preservation.

Without my bidding, my body is preparing and my brain is making automatic calculations. I do some "reconnaissance." Pathetic, but this is the word we used to use in Taunton for sizing up our opponents. Brian is a good fourteen pounds heavier, an inch or two taller, and I am guessing reasonably fit because of all that sawing of planks. But, most importantly, he is angry. So, quite a match.

On my side I have experience. One of the things about a fight (and if this doesn't sound too grand, exactly the same applies to war) is that there's no point in getting into one unless you are certain of winning. And the only way you can be certain of winning is to have overwhelming force. I know this, but Brian doesn't. Brian thinks he can win the fight by hurting me. But if I hit Brian in self-defense it won't be to hurt him, it will be to immobilize him completely. Hurting is for kids.

Brian is blocking my exit. A dangerous place to be because it increases the chances of a fight actually taking place. In my experience 90 percent of verbal aggression is bravado, not leading to actual violence. But blocking an exit ups the ante considerably, leaving no way out for your opponent. I am now feeling hemmed in: want to leave, but can't. The heart's starting to pump the adrenalin around, it's building up, looking for release. (Guest anxiety? What's that?) My whole body is getting ready for something. It's that old feeling again. Brian is making flight difficult, a fight more probable.

I am scared, not of what Brian will do to me, but of what I might do to Brian. I try to open the door to the garden to get away but the key isn't in the lock.

"Where's the key?" No one answers.

"Brian, you're being very silly."

This really doesn't help—I have seen this sort of behavior a million times. A girl (usually a middle-class type) will try to prevent her brother or boyfriend from fighting. By what method? Humiliation. Basically by calling him silly, a child, immature, and so on. "Don't be such a kid, grow up will you?" are not the sort of words to soothe that aggression away. Phrases such as "he's not worth it" are much more effective if you can bear the cliché.

"Brian, put your fists down. You look like a nutcase and you're behaving like a baby."

Many's the time I have thought if only the girls had kept quiet the fight might never have happened. The word *baby* is not the best choice. What does she expect him to say? "Oh, I'm a baby. Sorry everyone. You're quite right, I'll go upstairs and play with my rattle." All Charlotte has done is make Brian feel more aggressive. She has made having a fight a matter of pride, otherwise Brian will be admitting that he *is* a baby.

I am not a technical expert, but I do have a bit of experience and I know that if someone is primed for a fight, then the very last thing you want to do is touch their body in any way, no matter how friendly your intent. Do not, for example, try to pat them—or even gently stroke them—on the back or on the side of their arm. Their body is hypersensitive—a pat can be interpreted as a jolt, even a gentle stroke could set them off.

I know that trying to brush past Brian would be foolish.

I conceal my right hand so that I can make it into a tight fist without provocation. The fist must be very tight to avoid damaging the knuckles. I think a fight is unlikely, these are just simple precautions. I hope that very strong nonaggressive signals from me will be understood, and the dominant male (upon whose territory and female I have trespassed) will prevail without recourse to violence.

Then, just as I am beginning to sense a calming of nerves, Charlotte goes to touch Brian, her hand makes contact with his arm, he jolts, I brace myself, and . . . here it comes . . . he takes two steps towards me, brings his fist back, and before he knows what's happening I have landed a powerful punch and he's now bent over trying to stop the flow of blood. And this is when I should go in for the kill, pound him until he is physically incapable of threat, but instead I punch the wall and kick a kitchen chair till it breaks.

Charlotte, oh-so-predictably, is now nursing his bloody face with a kitchen towel and is all sympathy and "does it hurt?"

Oh, how I hate the politics of aggression. It brings it all back to me, all those wasted, wasted years. Maybe if I'd met Stefan when I was eleven instead of fifteen I would have taken a different course. But instead I lived this double life, seeing Stefan and talking about films and books and sex, absorbing it all like a sponge; then he'd see his girlfriend and I'd go out with the lads chasing birds, booze and fights. Eleven fights in all. By the age of seventeen I hadn't kissed that many girls or read that many books. I wasn't a mindless thug, I was a thug with a mind, but had no idea what to do with it.

But I am in fight mode now and can't get out of it. My main preoccupation is absurd for someone of my age, but I really want to survey the damage. I need to know if I got Brian's lip or his nose, and if the slight graze on my knuckle came from his teeth. I nurse my knuckles, which now begin to hurt from thumping the wall. The graze came from Brian's teeth I think. I've lost my touch.

Good.

As aggression wanes, houseguest anxiety waxes. I had wanted so much not to offend, to cause no embarrassment to my hosts—to the point where I dared not disagree with anything they said. I have not only disagreed with them, but I have smashed a chair, wrecked their relationship, and punched the host so hard he's on his fourth kitchen towel.

My exit is long overdue.

My hosts busy themselves with first aid.

"Sorry," I say, uselessly, with a touch of winner's remorse. As often happens in nightclub scraps, the loser is surrounded by sympathetic female faces, the winner is bounced out, with music and punches still ringing in his ear, wondering where his friends are.

I slip into the hall and up the two flights of stairs. I gather my things into the plastic garbage bags. One of them splits so I am down to one. I am elated, hyped up and ashamed. I go down the stairs. I wonder if I should bid my hosts good-bye but I can hear a heart-to-heart going on and bridges are being built. I don't want to stop the work. I slip out into the morning air.

They are digging up the road and the pneumatic drill is hyper-loud, and I need to run from it, and to use up the spare adrenaline in my system.

I wish I had let Brian punch me. I should have let him do his worst. Then Charlotte would be dabbing the blood from my nose, I would be being loved now, and Brian would be walking the streets.

As I turn the corner at the end of the road I slow down and walk. Mr. Blame-your-parents taps me on the shoulder for a quiet word. If only I had had two parents who gave me books to read and were interested in posh things like poetry and theater. Then I wouldn't have been a troublemaker and would have worked hard at school and not got into fights and would not have been labeled no-good and got an arts degree and a career like Stefan's and I'd feel comfortable about being with Victoria and would not be so in awe of Stefan and I would not just have punched my best friend's boyfriend and wouldn't be walking along the road with a tear in my eye blaming my mum and dad for feeling all alone.

Boo-hoo, boo-hoo, boo-hoo.

* * *

There's no answer at Gerard's house and his mobile is still on divert. Maybe he's found himself a job. Maybe he's moved out. Maybe he wouldn't want me to stay with him anyway—what did I ever do for him except tell him his ideas were crap?

So it looks like I won't be staying at Gerard's tonight. And I certainly can't stay at Charlotte's. Or Victoria's. This is how people end up homeless. All it takes is for a relationship to break up, a friend or two to let you down and an empty bank account. It's a wonder the homeless don't outnumber everyone else. Next time I'm accosted by four different beggars in the same morning I will say to myself how amazing it is that there aren't many more of them.

I do not have anywhere to stay tonight. I should be panic-stricken. *I do not have anywhere to stay tonight.* I actually *want* panic to take over and galvanize me into action. Come on, Panic, this is serious, I need you.

Oh, I could go back to Taunton and stay with Dad. Yup, that is certainly an option. So when I next see Victoria I will have some exciting news to tell her. "Guess what? I've moved. Back to Dad's in Taunton. My room hasn't changed a bit. I still recognise the Blu-Tack stains from my poster of Soft Cell and my football books are still on the shelf. Got into some good fights too. Oh, I can still hack it." That will impress her no end. She'll want me back, all right.

I wander down to Kentish Town Library—with half a notion that Gerard might have got his old job back, or gone there to use the toilet. In any case I don't have anywhere else to go and think it might be a good place to work on my idea. Crazy, really—I have no money and no home, but I think a reasonable way of spending my time is to work on an idea that has about a one in ten thousand chance of making me a millionaire. I know that this isn't rational—part of it is addiction, an escape from my problems and into the glitzy world of showbiz. When I work on a game format I see the show in front of me and hear the music and feel the heat from the lights. I can see the host walk on and greet the audience. It's all real to me. I'm in this world of questions and answers, winners and losers, decision time, success and failure. I am in the world I've created and everything is perfect. Not unlike getting drunk or coked.

But I call my escapism "work."

By late afternoon I have put the idea onto a page of typing paper. A page is all you need to get a producer's attention. Any more than that and they won't bother reading it. Maybe it's worth a million pounds, maybe it's not worth the cost of going on line. It's all or nothing. Hit or miss. Money in the bank, or I go home with nothing. I enjoy the fact that the game-show business is as ruthless as the shows it creates.

I pop into the new internet café opposite and start typing it up (no way am I going back to Print Stop). Now, normally you never send an idea off on the day you write it. That is reckless. Ideas need to be left to stand. But today I have nothing to lose and the nothing-to-lose mentality has worked quite well for me over the years.

Also, this idea is different. Yeah, yeah, I thought that about some of the others, but I really, *really* think this one is different. I mean I think this one is different in a different way than I thought the others were different.

To:———
From: James Hole
Subject: I Hate Game Shows

Hi ———,
I hope you don't mind me contacting you directly but I thought the following idea might be right up your alley. I have a number of

projects in development with other companies but this particular one is so very *you*.

It does for the game show what *The Young Ones* did for sitcom.

It's bonkers. And only someone with real vision would touch it.

(I've always believed that flattery gets you everywhere.)

You can e-mail me, or if you prefer to express your enthusiasm personally then give me a call on my mobile (0789339203) and we could meet up. I have some time next week.

Best wishes,

James

Off it goes to every producer and development executive in my little green book, a valuable contact list compiled by combing *Broadcast* every week, phoning round production companies, and visiting every website that includes the word "television."

Each e-mail is individually addressed and any scintilla of knowledge I have about the addressee is utilised (congratulations on the BAFTA, loved your last series of *Blah*, glad to hear *Blah* is moving to peak time). The whole process takes an hour.

Time to pay the online fee and snap back into the real world. The sunlight is harsh and punitive. This must be how gamblers feel when they walk out of the casino into crushingly hard, natural light that overexposes them. But when the pupils adjust, the world is duller then ever.

The dank blankness of the high street makes me want to waft back into colorful game-show land forever. I would love a man in a glittering suit to come up beside me, put a paternal arm on my shoulder and say, "Now James, you *had* Victoria, then you lost her, *maybe* you can win her back, maybe not. It's your decision. The clock starts now." In that world the answer would be clear.

So much clearer than spending months in therapy or seeing a priest. We should all have personal quizmasters who arrive in moments of confusion. "Mrs. Carter, your mother is on life support, and is probably brain-damaged. You *could* bring her back or let her die. It's your decision, the clock starts now." Thirty seconds later our lives might not be perfect but we'd have made a decision and moved on.

A moment ago I was winning. I had a million-pound idea. I was sure of it. It was happening before my eyes. But now, as I begin to acclimatize to the Real World, I feel like the one they say good-bye to. *Time to say good-bye to James. Thanks for being on the show. You were unlucky but you take with you 20 pounds in cash plus this souvenir goblet.*

I must have left half a dozen messages with Gerard. Maybe his mobile's fallen in the river or something. I've got about 240 pounds in the bank saved up from Print Stop days (was it really two years?) and the money Gerard and I were paid for the *Natural Selection* format. Two hundred won't even make up a deposit on a flat-share. I am now beginning to get a little panicky. I really can see myself phoning Dad and telling him that his son is on his way home having failed to get a career, a relationship or friends.

James, you go home with nothing.

I stop to buy an *Evening Standard;* it's time I started looking through the flat-share section.

I have nowhere to sleep tonight.

I park myself on a bus-stop bench to flick through it. On the opposite side of the road is one of those rather nice double-fronted Victorian houses. All the lights are on in the hall, blazing away, and it's not even dark yet. There's a grand piano in the bay. A woman is arranging flowers on it. A man walks past her and carrying some papers. The woman bursts out laughing at something and walks out of vision. I have no idea why this sticks in my mind, but I include it in case its significance is realized by readers cleverer than me.

On page four of the *Standard* there's a piece about hate mail. Millionaire Sir Tim Rice has been receiving loony letters. What motivates these people? " 'I don't deserve this,' says the millionaire song writer, 59, 'British people hate success. They build you up and knock you down.' A top psychiatrist explains . . ."

What to do if YOU get hate mail. The do's and don'ts . . .

What loon would systematically send hate letters to Sir Tim Rice?

No wonder Gerard is lying low.

I fold up the *Standard* and call Dad on the mobile. It's crises like this that bring dads into their own. I will tell him I have nowhere to sleep tonight. He'll put me up for a few days and might even be pleased if I stayed a week or two.

"Hi James. Any . . . news?"

He means about Victoria.

"No."

"Oh. Oh well. Are you ok?"

"Yes. I'm fine."

"Sure? Just a minute." He calls out. "It's Jamie."

"Is that Catherine?"

"Yes. Hang on a sec."

I can hear muttering.

"James, we've got some news."

More muttering. But I know what's coming. It's the word *we've* that gives it away, doesn't it? When *we've* got news it generally means *we're* getting married or *we're* pregnant. It's never *we've* got some news, *we're* splitting up. It's never *we've* got some news, *we're* being charged with embezzlement.

"We're getting married."

"That's great, Dad. Do you mean to each other or to two other people?"

Dad likes that kind of joke.

"Ha, ha. Ha. Catherine is moving in next week."

Catherine is Dad's girlfriend of two years. I had thought I might go home tonight for the traditional catch-all reason "until I can get myself sorted." But with Catherine moving in, I think I'd better let them do whatever it is that people of that age do together (I wouldn't want to walk in on a game of whist, if you get my meaning). Besides, I would be a houseguest in "my own" house. Dad and his fiancée would be host and hostess. The thought of it sends a tremble down my legs. I'm really going to have to see someone about this.

Despite the fact that this nuptial news thwarts my plans for a bed tonight, I express delight, which I do with aplomb. I even use the words *marvelous* and *thrilled* and *overjoyed,* to which my lips are unaccustomed.

And at any other time I *would* be thrilled. Dad's been wanting to get married for years, and I like to think that if I was still safely with Victoria I would have nothing but warm feelings about Dad starting a new life which didn't involve me. But now I am getting a little desperate. I'd like to tell him that it wasn't my decision to grow up, it just happened. I would like to be treated like a child again now, please. But I guess when your home, your *old* home where your dad lives, isn't your *home* anymore, even in a crisis, is when you're all grown up. And to be frank, it's not entirely nice.

But, hey, I'm not exactly the only person it's happened to.

I ask the usual questions about who proposed to whom and during the answers I'm thinking, now, can I ask Dad for a loan? No. That would remind him that I haven't repaid the last one.

I say that I have to go in a sec, the bus is coming. There's a pause.

"You're a good boy, Jamie."

I know why he says this. He says it a lot and it always affects me. He says I'm a good boy because he told me I was a bad boy so many times. He's trying to make up for it. But I *was* a bad boy, Dad. You were right, and someone had to tell me.

"You're a good kid, son. I always thought so."

I know what this means, too. It means that he's forgiven me. For not utilizing all the knowledge about animals, plants and bees that he poured into me for a decade. For smoking. For taking his Norton motorbike without permission (or license) and forgetting where I parked it so he had to report it stolen. For getting into fights. For getting brought home by the police, twice. For blaming him for the divorce. For calling his girlfriend a bitch. For being embarrassed about his yokel accent in front of Stefan. For not getting my hair cut for Gran's funeral like he begged me to. For moving to London. For wishing I had a dad like Stefan's. For forgetting his birthday more often than not. For saying I'd never marry Victoria. For phoning him the day before a camping holiday-for-two in Scotland to tell him I wasn't going. For hating Taunton. For hating bees. For hating rugby. For hating his antique prints of British birds. For not loving the Beatles. For not loving him as much as he loved me.

The bus comes and we say good-bye.

One of my comfort phrases is: You've been in worse scrapes than this, Jamie boy. I repeat it to myself when things look bleak. But *have* I been in worse scrapes than this?

I have nowhere to stay tonight.

I really can't understand how someone like me has found

himself without a home, job, partner or money. I look at my reflection in the bus window. I don't *look* like the sort who would end up like that.

Did you see it coming? Was it bound to have happened in some way I couldn't see?

It's now 6:20. If Gerard hasn't called me by seven I'll find a B & B for a day or two. Yes, one of those cheap places for homeless people. Four to a room. Nice.

The reason I'm not panicking is because it won't happen, it can't happen. I just can't *see* it happening.

But I have nowhere to stay tonight.

Me, homeless? This only happens to other people, and other clichés. Should I spend my money on a hotel? But then what would I use for a deposit on a flat-share? How will I get a flat-share without a job? Who wants someone loafing round the house all day getting depressed?

Excellent, impossible questions are coming thick and fast—the first sign of panic.

Who Wants to Be a Millionaire?

I do.

SEVENTEEN

We're walking along Brecknock Road to her parents' house. Victoria has only had two spritzers (the maximum recommended for a pregnant woman) and I am fairly sober too.

She says, "I'm tired and feeling queasy."

The night is incredibly calm, and calmness isn't the kind of thing that is incredible very often. In fact this is the only time I've observed meteorological calm that in any way challenged credibility. There's a kind of rain in the air I have never seen before. It's really a mist of tiny droplets that don't fall, but float in the air, oscillating gently in minute currents. You can see them swirling in the glow of street lights. We both remark on this calm, strange rain that moistens rather than wets, for which an umbrella would be useless. We walk silently, arm in arm, observing it for several minutes, wondering how the evening will end, knowing that this is one of those turning points in life that actually has a sign saying "turning point." Most turning points have signs about a mile up the road saying "by the way, there was a turning point back there—didn't you see it?"

I try to give myself a progress report on the evening.

1. *I have told Victoria that I was in love with her. She was incredulous at first but has now taken it in.*

2. *I must find out if this love is reciprocated.*

3. *I must tell her that I am STILL in love with her and want her.*

I begin by ignoring the above points and going for this: "Well, do you love Teacher the teacher?"

She stops to look at the front garden. There's an unruly looking clematis in bloom. I try to be patient but I do want an answer to my question and not another observation about the strange, calm rain or the clematis. I take a long draw on my Silkie and exhale. The smoke mingles with the strange rain and floats and swirls just as gently as if we were indoors. Again I think to myself that this calm is incredible.

"Well, do you love him?"

I guess she has asked this question to herself a hundred times. She has a hundred different answers—she's not trying to form a sentence, she is trying to remember which of the many pre-prepared sentences is most apposite for the occasion.

"I'm not in love with him. But I love him." That old chestnut. "I respect him, I get on with him, he's kind and . . . I can see myself being quite happy with him. He's a really good friend, which is quite important."

"Is he funny?"

"Yes. Quite."

"Quite?"

"I love him."

"But you're in love with me, aren't you?" Such is the boldness of one who has nothing to lose.

"I was."

"Do you wish . . . do you wish . . ."

"It was your baby? How can you ask that?"

"I wasn't going to ask that!" You bloody liar, Hole. Think of a different question, fast. "I was going to ask if you wish we had started going out together back then. At university."

"It's kind of the same question."

"Well all right then. Do you wish it was our baby?"

"You shouldn't ask me that!"

"I know. But Victoria, you used the word quite three times about him."

"No I didn't."

"You did."

"I did not!"

"You said you could be quite happy with him, he's a good friend, which is quite important—"

"It's very important, then!"

"Too late! And he's quite funny."

"You and your 'funny.' Funny's not very important, it's only quite important."

"Touché."

Neither of us wants to go inside, such is the beauty of the strange rain. We linger in the garden, observing its gentleness and trying to hear if it makes a noise. It doesn't. I suggest we hold our dry hands out to see how long it takes them to moisten.

"I wonder if they'll moisten as quickly on the palm as on the back. Look, they do. The droplets are going upward as much as they're going downward. They seem to be weightless."

We watch the heavenly droplets whirl madly in the light from the bay window. We stand over the birdbath on the crazy paving to see if we can detect pinpricks on the surface of the water but there's nothing.

We walk up the front steps of Victoria's Victorian house.

I hope Mr. and Mrs. Maginot aren't up. I really do.

We go up the steps to the house and in. My heart drops a few inches in my chest when I discover that Dad Maginot is indeed in and up, drinking red wine and watching Newsnight. *Although I am not strictly a houseguest, I feel that old overwhelming stifling need to please and not offend.*

"The trouble is the presenters are so thick these days. Even Paxman's losing it. He used to be smart. He's thick now," *he says after we've done the formal greetings.*

A man who thinks Paxman is thick. Maybe he's saying it on purpose. Maybe he's saying: Listen, I am Victoria's dad and I'm telling you Jeremy Paxman is too thick for her. Now, how clever are you?

I would like to argue with him like I do with my own dad. But when your beloved girl's dad speaks, you have to agree. He knows that. Those are the rules.

"Good news, isn't it? About the baby."

"Yes." *He knows I'm lying, I'm sure of it.*

"Do you know what I think? There are too many women in TV. They haven't got the bite, the aggression. What do you think?"

Oh God. I am tired, I am drunk, I am probably not as clever as him and now he wants to prove it in front of his daughter. (His daughter is pregnant by another man—you'd think he'd give me a break.) I know this is a trap. I know if I agree he'll twist it in some way and accuse me of being sexist. If I don't agree then I'll be stupid in some other way. I can't ignore it because the remark is intended to provoke. Ignoring it would be weak. He's got me over a barrel.

He's done this trick before: he mulls over an argument in his mind, collects a few facts, and then makes a statement that is so provocative people have to take him on. Then he ambushes them with all the facts and logic he's prepared earlier.

So, let the humiliation commence.

"I'm not sure I would agree. Women are quite good on TV, I think." *How utterly feeble. Usually I am better than that, I really am. Luckily Victoria comes to the rescue.*

"Come on James, let's make some coffee." *We leave Dad Maginot to argue with himself.*

There is a mirror over the toilet and I can see myself as I urinate. I tell myself not to let that bastard get to me. I am good enough for his daughter. I think. No, I am. Ok, I'll never have her now, but I am not a piece of shit and how dare he make me feel like one. Come on, James, you have nothing to lose now. (Having nothing to lose is a state that's getting more and more common these days.) Victoria is pregnant, she's with another man, she's out of my reach. Therefore rejection's no longer personal—anyone and everyone would be rejected under these circumstances. The thought of this safety in numbers makes me strong again. I leave the bathroom as spotless as I found it.

As she pours the coffee in the modern Victorian cosmopolitan farmhouse kitchen, I can say anything I like, because nothing can reduce my chances.

"Victoria, ditch the Teacher and come and live with me." She looks at me for a second, then picks up the phone on the wall.

"John? Hi. Just been thinking, you know that baby that I'm having? I've decided that someone else is going to father it. Yes. I know I said I wanted to have a family with you but that was yesterday. Thanks for being so understanding. I'll come and collect my hairdryer and those tights I left in your bedroom tomorrow." She puts the phone down. I always find Victoria's flights of piss-taking funny. But I also want to pursue my line of thought.

"It's your life." I shrug. I think I have just made the assumption that somehow, deep down, Victoria would rather be with me. Gosh, that's really presumptuous of me, but I like it.

"I've got his baby, I love him, and I don't want an abortion, thank you."

"I didn't say that. You can . . . well . . . I mean . . ." I hadn't thought this through but I meant well. "If you go with me, I won't mind if you have the baby." Yeah, that is what I said, verbatim. It is one of those lines that stay with you. "I won't mind if you have the baby." It's such a "young-man" thing to say. And I actually thought it was supportive, that it would win me a brownie point or two. Victoria picks it up and plays with it, of course.

"You won't mind? Well thank you so much. Can I clear a few other things with you? Let's see. Eating? Do you mind if I do that?"

"I won't mind."

"Are you sure? What about breathing?"

"I won't mind that, either."

"Thinking? No, that's pushing my luck. How about punching you in the face?"

"Now and again would be fine."

"Really, really, really hard? So that you're disfigured for life?"

"I do love you, you know."

Who said that?

Guess.

It was her, not me. Hoorah! (Sorry, but recalling this moment is making me so happy.)

We face each other and I hold her hands to my chest. God, just holding her hands and caressing them after all this time feels like nothing else. It's just beautiful.

"I know you think I'm too young to start a family." Of course I think she's too young.

"I don't think you're too young. But I am surprised. You've never given any indication that that's what you wanted."

"Maybe I've changed. Look, I haven't got a job. But I have got a nice man who has, and I happen to be pregnant. Why on earth shouldn't I start a family now? Mum's over the moon. My nephew will have a little cousin to play with, I'll finally be able to get you out of my system."

Wow.

"The reasons are piling up! Want me to go on?"

"Go on then."

"It'll take the pressure off trying to find a job in the stupidest profession in the world."

There's nothing I can do. I've never had a pregnant friend before, but something tells me that you can't argue with them. You can tell a friend "you're mad— don't do it—resign," when they say they've become a mercenary or an accountant or a traffic warden. But you can't tell a pregnant woman what to do. "You're mad—don't do it—get an abortion," is not on. Almost any other decision we make is open to friendly debate, but pregnancy puts up its own firewall against logic. She's having a baby and that has to be a good thing because she's having a baby. So I toe the line. Open the box of clichés.

"Right, well, it's great. You've found what you want to do." We sit in silence for a while. The rain, if it's there at all, is invisible from inside. I decide that I am definitely going to let her speak next. Eventually she does.

"So that's the end of us, I suppose."

This is weird. We'd just told each other we were in love (kind of) and now she wants to split up.

I say, "I don't want it to be the end. I want . . . I want . . . well, you."

"But you know that's impossible."

"I am saying that I would like to give it a go."

"If I wasn't pregnant."

"I am saying that pregnant or not, I want you."

"But you know you——"

"I don't know anything!" That was a bit of a shout. "I can't see what's so hard about understanding me. I want you. That's it. I want you. Baby and all."

She is silent, and I am relieved, because maybe this means the message has sunk in.

"But——"

"There aren't any buts. Not from my end. Will you . . . be my girlfriend?"

"It's been four years! Most men say they want to go out with me after four hours."

"I'm a slow worker."

"You're glacial."

Before the evening is finished I want Victoria to understand, without any confusion whatever, that I want her. This must be achieved. Not because I think it'll make her want me in return, but because I know I can't move on until I have made this point, and known that she has understood it. After about twenty minutes of to-ing and fro-ing I reckon the point has finally struck home.

"So you understand, and you believe me."

"Yes, yes, yes, yes. I understand that you want a relationship with me, you love me, you have done for a long time, you want me, no buts."

"At bloody last. Now, we can move on to the next bit."

"The next bit?"

"Your response?"

"You sound like a lawyer or something."

"I want to know what you think."

"I think . . . We can't."

"Ok."

"I'm with . . . Teacher." She smiles at her use of his surname. "And much as I adore you and have done, I think he is the man for me and I'm having his baby."

"Ok. Thank you."

"Do we have closure?" she says, American-style.

"We have a result."

Dad Maginot walks in with an empty wine glass which he puts into the dishwasher.

"I'm off to bed now, darlings."

"Night, Dad."

"Night," I say.

"Can you believe I'm going to be a granddad?"

Victoria and I smile but we don't want to encourage The Parent to linger. On his way out he puts his hand on my arm, looks me in the eye, and squeezes firmly.

"Don't worry, son, you'll find someone else." I am genuinely touched. But then he says, "You're too boring for her."

I have been punched many times and kicked on the head, kidneys, and spine, but nothing has knocked the sense out of me quite like this. Maybe that's because it came at the end of an evening of revelation, after a day's preparation, after four years' procrastination. Maybe because, like the best insults, it was credible.

Not necessarily truthful, but credible.

My knees give way and I have to take a firm grip on the sideboard. I can't believe that a few words can have such physical effect. Not for the last time it occurs to me that the hyperbolic phrases about being "knocked sideways," "floored," "struck down," are all rooted in something literal.

"Dad, that was extremely rude and not true at all. Are you drunk?"

Victoria's immediate defensive reaction inspires an equally defensive one from The Parent. He holds his palms out, all innocent.

"Can't a dad give his daughter's male friends a hard time anymore? I thought that's what dads were for."

Ha, ha.

"You're drunk, Dad. Now can you please just GO?" He pauses for a moment. I suppose he realizes that he is indeed drunk. Drunk, and angry that he hadn't tasted victory with me in a polemic about TV presenters, furious that I had given him the slip. Angry that he's going to be called "Granddad" and he's not sixty. And he's not fifty, and he's not forty, and he's not thirty, and he's not twenty and he never will be again.

"I'm off to bed. Night-night, Mother."

He goes. We say nothing until we hear the opening and closing of an upstairs door. A door into a drunken sleep in a sexless bed, one long since done with conception.

"I am really, really sorry. I am speechless. Speechless with anger. I don't know why he said that. I have never ever said anything like that about you to him and I don't think you're boring at all. You're anything but boring."

Victoria's voice has a tremble in it.

"It's Teacher I feel sorry for," I say. "That's his father-in-law."

Some insults flatten you in an instant. Some don't hurt much at the time but work on you like a slow poison. Dad Maginot's remark was both of the above. I wish I'd been so drunk that I couldn't remember it.

Victoria and I both know that this is the last time we'll see each other for a while and we don't want the remark to spoil it so we try to move on. We talk about kids and families and childhoods instead. But I still want to get things straight between us. I blow the smoke from my Silkie up towards an open bit of window.

"Do you think we should see each other as friends?"

Victoria shrugs. "It might be difficult. Difficult for both of us. I might want to jump on your bones, which wouldn't be the best thing for a young mother to do."

I nod. Message understood. We are going to get on with our lives.

"But in time . . ."

"Sure. Maybe when you have a kid of your own."

"That would be great."

I think about having a child quickly.

I decide I will go at exactly 12:30. (I often pick on a specific time to leave Victoria. I do this because if I didn't choose a time in advance I would linger for the rest of my life. There is never a time when I've had enough of her, or feel that I "must be heading off," so the leaving must be contrived.) I have six minutes left with the woman I have loved for four years and may never see again. Six minutes to leave a lasting impression. Six minutes of wit, engaging conversation, impressive insight. Six minutes to be anything but boring.

"Are those halogen lights?"

"Yes."

"I like the kind of light they give off."

Boring? Me? Nah.

"They're good."

"But you need a special dimmer switch for them."

I'm fascinating, me.

"Dad keeps saying he's going to get one."

"Where's the transformer? They need a transformer. Perhaps it's concealed."

"Got me there."

Pause.

"Are the bulbs expensive?"

"I don't know. I know you can't touch them."

"Oh yes, like theatre lights. You're not supposed to touch the bulbs because the grease on your fingers makes them burn out or something."

Pause. We're probably both thinking about how we first met—lighting Giles's silly film.

"I'll be going in a minute."

"Ok. Shall I call a cab?"

"I'll walk for a bit. Catch a bus. I like buses. And I like the strange rain."

"God, it is strange isn't it?"

"The rain?"

"Yes. And everything."

We're in the hall and the door is open. I decide to go for it. Nothing to lose. I pull her gently toward me and kiss her softly on the lips. She responds tenderly. Actually, not so tenderly now. There's a bit of hunger in this tongue; perhaps this is going to lead somewhere after all. Perhaps passion is going to overrule the decisions made by the Sensible Committee. I pull her close and feel her breasts against my chest, my cock against her—

And she smiles as she straightens her hair. I understand. Of course, of course. It wouldn't be . . .

I squeeze her tightly again, my tightest ever. I could stop the tears if I wanted, oh I could easily. But why? Why not show her how I feel for once? I want her to see them. Nothing to lose. We look at each other. We smile. We squeeze each other's hands and . . .

" 'Bye then."

" 'Bye."

. . . it's over.

Over and out.

I walk from Kentish Town to Hornsey, about four miles. I stop at a petrol station to buy twenty Silkies and three chocolate bars: Twix, Mars and Flake. I feel like doing something interesting—or rather, something that would make me appear interesting to others. I imagine scaling Nelson's Column in protest that my girl has chosen another. Get in the newspapers. "Spurned Romeo risks life for love." At least Dad Maginot couldn't refer to me as "the boring one" anymore. "The mad idiot," perhaps, but that would be preferable. (And more accurate, I like to think.)

Maybe if I went round there and beat the crap out of him he would reconsider his judgement. How boring is a punch in the face?

But maybe I am boring. What have I ever done that's interesting? I don't even say very interesting things. Let alone think them. In fact, the most interesting thing about me is that for four years I've been in love with someone, who's in love with me, and somehow I managed to get nowhere.

Now stop it. I mustn't let this fester. Victoria doesn't think I'm boring. I will keep saying that till I reach my front door.

Victoria doesn't think I'm boring.

Besides, Victoria and her dad are now part of the past for sure. I really have to let go. Isn't that what all sensible people would advise?

Victoria doesn't think I'm boring.

I finish the last chocolate bar: a Twix. Is eating three chocolate bars in a row interesting?

Stop it.

Gobbling one more would make me really rather eccentric.

Stop.

I approach my front door. The rain is still calm, still strange. It is the strangest, calmest rain I've ever seen.

EIGHTEEN

"The Brotherhood of God is just five pounds per night."

"Very good."

That's about a fifth of what I was expecting to pay.

"You have to stay for three days minimum."

I nod.

"And you have beds available?"

The boy at the desk looks about twenty. He scans a desk diary and nods.

"Yes. Where did you hear about us?"

"There's a poster on the thirty-one bus."

It had a picture of four smiling young people in clothes that were all the rage three years ago. The female was Asian-looking, the three young men were white, black and Asian respectively with the white guy sitting in a wheelchair. It looked like each of these young smilers had been cut out of a magazine to form part of a junior school mural on equal rights.

The poster offered help, advice and accommodation for

homeless people. It didn't say anything about being almost free but I figured that a place that takes political correctness so seriously can't be a capitalist rip-off. Even if it's pretty naff, it will at least afford me some interesting anecdotes. I will save them for Victoria. Except that she's now my ex, I remind myself.

I am homeless.

Yes, I know that sounds dramatic. But to say anything else would be euphemistic. I could tell myself that "I haven't got anywhere to stay at the moment" or that "I'm between homes" but why not use the proper term? I could tell myself that I'm not *really* homeless because I could use my last couple of hundred on a hotel but that would completely blow the possibility of putting any money down on a flat-share. I *could* go to my dad's. I *could* beg Victoria to lend me money. I *could* beg Stefan. Yes, I still have some lifelines left, but you can't just look at things logically. You have to put things like pride, embarrassment and shame into the equation. Let's say I put money, need, fear, embarrassment, pride and shame into a big pot, gave it a good long stir, and this is the result: the decision to make my way to The Brotherhood and put myself in the hands of God. The poster helped me to acknowledge the true depth to which I had sunk. I am, in truth, without accommodation. I have no entitlement to even a square inch of space anywhere on this planet.

I am up shit creek. I know that. But I do have a paddle. I know that I will soon be a game-show millionaire.

"What is your name?"

"James Hole."

The boy looks at me with such interest that I guess his name must be Hole too.

"Really? Your name is Hole? That is amazing."

"You get used to it."

"Room thirteen. Are you superstitious?"

"No."

It's going to be the biggest, fastest rags-to-riches story ever told. You wait.

"You need to fill in a form and this—the conditions—and come to our gathering."

"I'm not religious."

"We welcome people of all faiths and no faiths at all."

"Good."

"But attendance at the gathering is necessary to keep our charitable status."

"I understand."

"You'll be sharing with one other."

"Yes of course."

I calculate that this Edwardian building has about twenty rooms. It's slightly seedy and it was until recently the headquarters of a travel company called gocheap.com. How much would you say? Given that it's in King's Cross? Three million? In a year's time I'll be able to *buy* this place. And maybe I *will* buy it, as a little souvenir of a terrible year.

"The conditions are no drugs, no drink, no smoking, no guests, no loud music, no shaving in the showers, no mobile phones at night and all valuables must be kept in the safe."

Boy, this place is going to be a scream.

"Otherwise, think of this as our home. And you are our guest."

The feeling of being a guest in someone else's home. Just what I need. He takes my passport, credit card, Switch card and banknotes, and puts them in an envelope. He puts the envelope into a wall safe behind a picture of a besuited man smiling in a sunny rose garden. He looks like he has been given the world for his birthday.

I place my garbage bag on my bed. The fossils clunk together heavily at the bottom of the bag. I survey the room I am to share with Otto, a painfully skinny Lithuanian boy of about eighteen. The room clearly used to be a small office and the walls are barely more than portable partitions.

We quickly establish that Otto speaks no English, and I, strangely, no Lithuanian. In my pockets I have five bars of chocolate: Twix, Snickers, Mars and two KitKats. I offer Otto one of the KitKats. His eyes widen at the prize and he looks at me for more assurance that I really am giving it to him.

The idea of sleeping here stone-cold sober is out of the question. I will have to get plastered in a pub first. I make up my mind to slip out on my own after the gathering or whatever and drink myself happy—or at least tired.

I point to my watch at 8:30 and Otto nods. It is time.

Tea and elderflower squash are served by a large black girl called Florence. I elect tea and I am given a very sympathetic smile. Florence was perhaps homeless, but has made this place her domicile. She probably does some cleaning and helping out and the Brotherhood let her stay for free. Something like that. And she, this homeless cleaner and dogsbody, has sympathy for *me*. I can see how low I have sunk in her smile. I think that if ever I should become disfigured, I would not look in the mirror but go to church and mark the horror of my injuries in the smiles of well-meaning strangers.

I am the second-oldest "guest" at the gathering. But I am not really a guest, you see. Because I am a millionaire. No, I am. Virtually.

I'm sitting in a room that had, until six months ago, been the engine room of gocheap.com. There is a logo stuck to the wall next to me and in the corner are some labels and posters. The company went bust when people began to realize that "dot com" really meant "mail order" and "website" really meant "catalogue" and "hi-tech" really meant "telephone line." This was a ship full of people wanting to drown in money and then it sank.

"Yesterday Tina was asking why God allows us to suffer if he loves us so much," says Pierre, who greeted us all on the way in with the hug equivalent of a limp-wristed handshake.

"Tina, are you talking about your own suffering?" says a bloke who looks like his brain had been removed, used to mop up whiskey stains for ten years, then replaced.

" 'Coz, like you bring it on yourself, yeah? I mean God doesn't punish us, we bring suffering by being selfish, yeah? Or ignoring Jesus, right? I'm not going to blame anyone for what I am, who I am, ok? You make your own chances, you make your own luck, yeah?"

"What about people who get ill and that?" says a young Scouse kid with a boy-beard who looks exactly like a homeless person *should* look—gaunt and dirty.

"AIDS. What about that?"

"Are you saying that's like God's fault?" says Sponge-brain.

"What about Jesus?"

"What?"

"He suffered, innit. It wasn't his fault."

"That's different, Mike."

"What about the starving? The people who were killed on September the eleventh?" pipes up a girl of about seventeen.

These kids have excuses for being here. They are young,

deprived, unlucky. I am old, I've got a degree, and only yesterday I lived in a nice place with the woman of my dreams.

"The people in New York are in heaven now, nuffin' to worry about."

"But they were capitalists, yeah? They were not blameless, yeah?"

"What's that got to do with it?"

"Let's not get into that," says Pierre.

"I still say you make your own luck, yeah?"

"What if you ask the audience and then the audience gets it wrong? That's unlucky," says the third-oldest person in the room. There is some laughter but only about as much as I expected. And so the discussion goes round and round and I say nothing. I am not part of this, remember, I am a game-show millionaire.

Pierre begins talking about Job. (Job is a big hit with people who feel sorry for themselves.) He also talks about how money doesn't make people happy. The richest people in the world are the most miserable, apparently. Then comes some weird stuff. The world is full of holes.

"Holes are used for eating food, and also ejecting it. They are also used for reproduction."

There are a few good-natured sniggers. But Sponge-brain looks mesmerized. Pierre continues.

"What else are holes used for?"

Various suggestions are put forward: egg-cups, plugholes, mineshafts, man-made lakes, screw holes, holes for animals to sleep in. No suggestion is rejected—they are all interesting and utterly valid contributions—even holes in Polo mints is greeted with warmth and amusement. The young Scouse says that lunch hours are holes in the working day. Perfectly permissible. Now that everyone has suggested every kind of hole they could imagine (I had suggested, prosaically, black holes) our teacher resumes the lesson.

"Frederick Sheen, our founder, believes that there are more invisible holes on our bodies and in the universe than anyone has thought possible. Some holes lead to happiness, some to suffering."

This gives a new meaning to the word holistic. Come to think of it, it gives new meaning to the name James Hole.

Apparently, only Frederick Sheen (the smiling face guarding the wall safe) knows where these holes are, and one day he will reveal all, and his followers will go through these invisible holes into life everlasting.

Pierre builds up to a flourishing finish: "Never has there been a greater need for the holes. There is a war in the world—materialism verses spirituality, there is a hole between them. It's the hole of truth. Or should that be the *whole truth,* and it leads to eternal bliss."

Here endeth the lesson. There's a pause and I find the faces of my fellow disciples difficult to read. Do they think there's something in it? Strange the way desperate, vulnerable people, people with no self-esteem, can kid themselves that bliss is just round the corner. Still, it doesn't affect me, because I'm going to be a millionaire in a couple of days.

Nine-thirty. I ask to get my money out of the safe and the smiling Frederick Sheen makes way for the removal of my envelope. I head for the nearest pub. Six bottles of Newkie should make me happy.

And I'm right. Six bottles later and I am even more certain that I'm going to be a game-show millionaire than before. I am in my own happy hole. I practically sing on the way home. I am on the verge of mega-success. *I Hate Game Shows* exists in the computers of four dozen TV movers and shakers. They'll love it. Truthfully, it is my best yet.

And given this certainty, why bother to go flat-hunting tomorrow? In three days I will collect my replies at the local Internet café. In a week I'll have a letter of intent from a production company on the strength of which I can get a loan and take any flat I fancy.

And somewhere over the Milky Way there's an arch between Victoria and me and it's always going to be there. We finished when it was still good. She's happy. Stefan and Victoria are where they belong. They are in their happy hole.

I finish my last Silkie of the night and stamp it out before stumbling into the Hostel Hole.

Three days later. Not only have I survived the hostel, but I am rather chuffed with myself for having started writing a book—this one. All it needs is a decent ending. Frankly, if I don't ever sell a game show, or see Victoria again, then the end is going to be vaguely disappointing. Then again, it could end tragically (with my suicide, or Otto killing me for my chocolate, or Victoria killing herself because she thought I didn't love her, and I was the one she wanted after all). All those might be satisfying denouements from a commercial perspective, but speaking personally I am looking for something a little more feel-good.

I key in my user name and password. In a few moments I will discover what the world thinks of *I Hate Game Shows.*

I feel optimistic. Too damn optimistic. I need to lower my expectations *big time.* I have been trying to do this but my sense that glory is almost with me is hard to shake off. In my experience optimism and in-boxes don't go together.

So, this is my routine to banish optimism, the conversation I have with myself to avoid crushing disappointment:

James, there are NOT going to be dozens of e-mails saying "I loved your idea, here is a million pounds." A good five of the addresses are going to be obsolete. Some of the people will be away filming or on holiday. Some never read unsolicited mail on principle; some will not have the power to do anything without the say-so of ten committees.

And what about those who simply don't like the idea?

So, realistically, worst-case scenario?

Just twenty replies out of the fifty-one.

Worst case, James. WORST case.

Ok, fifteen. Fifteen replies.

How many straight rejections?

Four.

Worst case. *Worst.*

Six. Six rejections and another three or four saying "promising, let's talk."

So five positive responses? That's the *worst* case?

Worst case. Honest. It can't be worse than that. If I predicted anything worse it would be a mind-fuck, a trick. Just five positives is a *realistic* worst case.

And the other matter?

Victoria?

Do you really expect to find a love letter from her saying Stefan is rubbish, come back, come back?

Maybe a little friendly note?

Worst case?

Just a quick note about something practical but ending with a little kiss by her name?

Worst case!

Nothing. Nothing from Victoria at all.

Prepare for it.

I heave a sigh, maybe like a stunt-diver preparing for a plunge down a sheer cliff. Exhilaration and danger, what an intoxicating concoction. I open the in-box with a click. There are nine replies. Worse than my worst case, but only just. Four of the replies are automatic—so-and-so is not in the office.

Five left. I try not to be optimistic about these, I try. I think it's called steeling oneself. *Click.*

To: James Hole

From: ———

Subject: I Hate Game Shows

Hi. Thanks for this. Not really for us. In future please address material to the development unit.

This could be a rogue. One rogue response is only to be expected. Click.

To: James Hole

From: ———

Subject: I Hate Game Shows

James, I read your proposal with interest, but I do not feel sufficiently enthusiastic to want to develop it. I wish you success in placing it elsewhere.

I always thought this was going to be a hard sell. *Click.*

To: James Hole
From: ———
Subject: I Hate Game Shows

James
Thanks for the idea but I am not looking for game-show ideas at the moment. In any case, I really didn't go for this, isn't it a tad puerile? Definitely not for us.

It's an idea you either love or hate, no in-betweens. *Click.*

To: James Hole
From: ———
Subject: I Hate Game Shows

Thanks for sending the above drama script to_____. It has been forwarded to me. I will be in touch when I have had a chance to assess it, which usually takes eight to ten weeks.

Administrative error, not my fault. The next one has got to be positive. It really has to be. *Click.*

To: James Hole
From: ———
Subject: I Hate Game Shows

Dear James Hole,
I'm afraid it doesn't leap out at me, although there are some funny bits and you have talent.
Keep it up.

Nothing from Victoria. Fair enough. Fair enough. Fair enough. No, fair enough, Victoria, really, fair enough.

Fair enough.

I ask the guy if there's been a problem with the e-mail. Are you sure? Are any servers down? Any reports of technical problems? Are you certain?

He asks if I'm ok.

I make my way slowly back to Hole Hilton. They think I'm a confused, homeless, lonely young person with a feeble, vulnerable mind. Ha.

I stop by at a bridge over King's Cross Station. No, I'm not *that* depressed. (If I did have a weak, vulnerable mind I might be tempted. But not me.) I just need one more Silkie before going back to the smoke-free zone. I look down at the tracks below to get an idea of what it feels like to suffer so much that you want to end it all. To suffer, and to lose the capacity for hope. To write yourself off totally, and to write off the possibility that something good is just round the corner. But if you're Brian, another corner means another disappointment. You might fall down a manhole. And if you're from the Brotherhood of God a manhole might be just what you're looking for.

Perhaps all I need to do is adjust my expectations. I now expect to light a Silkie (having rejected Camels already) and kill the dread that's crawling around my lungs like an immured insect. But the book of matches I find tucked away in my inside pocket only has the one match. The book is from the Moon and Sixpence, where this tale began. There's a fair breeze blowing, and the strike pad on the book has worn thin. I'd say I have a 40 percent chance of lighting up.

For no reason I can think of, I decide, perhaps hypothetically, perhaps not, that I will take the ultimate closure, fall from the bridge, if I fail to light my cigarette. Perhaps it's just a mind fuck, a game of pretend. I will only know how serious I am if the cigarette doesn't light.

Any last requests?

The best games have elements of chance, as well as skill. They have unfairness built into them, because sometimes we want the dummies to win and the clever bastards to lose.

What is it like to have that sinking feeling as you submit yourself to gravity? I twist the match from the book. I turn my body away from the wind and huddle against an extended wall of the bridge. There are so many variables here. The match, the wind speed and direction, my manual dexterity and timing, and the amount of friction left on the strike pad.

Why would a person prefer the cradle of darkness to anything that light might show? I won't do it, but I want to know what it feels like. Jumping off a bridge would give a whole new meaning to the phrase hitting rock bottom.

Ladies and gentlemen, a joke. Unintended, and not a *good* joke by any means. Quite feeble when you think about it, merely a fusion of literal and figurative. You are wondering why this lowly bon mot deserves a place in a book otherwise devoted to wit only of the highest order.

YOU: I'm not.

It's because it made me laugh. I mean really, really laugh. I don't think it was a mad, hysterical laugh, or a demonic laugh, or even a hopeless laugh. It was a plain old funny laugh. A funny, funny, laugh.

When my laughter fades into spasmodic reflexes, I strike, and the match fails. That's funny too. I'm about to strike again when my phone rings. It is the first time it has rung for a couple of days. I will see who it is.

After all, I'm not busy.

It's her.

"Hi."

"It's me. The Royal Free Hospital rang. They've got Gerard. He's in a bad way—some kind of accident."

"Victoria . . ."

"What is it? James, did you hear me? *Gerard has had some kind of accident!* Just get there as quick as you can. It's the Steeple Ward."

I put the cigarette, match and book in my pocket and flag down a cab. I get inside and there's a sign saying thank you for not smoking. That's funny, I think.

NINETEEN

We're lying in bed, after coffee, toast and sex. We're in a postcoital dozy haze. No radio, no television and definitely no newspapers. How can a morning be content with the pain of millions spread on your carpet, table or bed? And if you avoid the news, you are surrounded by people richer, cleverer, fitter, prettier and better at cooking than yourself which is even worse. Commit the Sunday papers to flames, I say, and give your soul a break.

Morning shadows shorten, and the dawn begins in my head. Time had been trying to creep past without my noticing, but this autumn day can't be wasted on sleep—it may be the last before the trees are bare. I want to walk under boughs with someone I love. Get up, lazybones.

But it is so nice in bed, too. The skin on her back is soft and smells of lemon. I put my lips to it, and try to drink it; it tickles, she laughs, then inches away. She has her own waking thoughts of unsolvable problems. Her skull is a rioting prison of inmates trying to force their way out. But there is nowhere for them to go, all alternatives are worse.

We doze again and the morning steals towards noon. Nothing accomplished, nothing done.

The phone rings and we let it ring. Then it's picked up.

"Hello? Yeah, just a minute. It's for you."

I take the phone sleepily.

"Hello?"

"Is that you, James? Did I wake you up?"

"My God. Victoria?"

We scream excitedly at one another. It's been four years, or is it five, far too long, and other clichés. Everything is fine, fine, fine.

Yes, of course I would like to see her and catch up with her news and she'll tell me everything. You're free today? Why not? Let's meet round Primrose Hill somewhere for a late lunch. You don't mind, do you, Sandra?

Sandra, raven-haired Sandra, sad Sandra, for whom nothing is going right, doesn't mind.

It's on then. Great. Let's meet in the park at the top of the hill. (Do I choose that spot because it is romantic? Don't be silly, James.) Here's my mobile number in case we miss each other.

Sandra turns over lazily. In her briefcase she has some school books to mark so it would actually be handy to have the afternoon to herself. How she hates the school. How she hates her life. I am all she's got. I stroke her hair and her back to make her feel wanted and not abandoned. It's a big job, being all someone else has got. But I want to get up and doing. I wonder how many strokes of her hair and back buy me an easy morning. I would advise any man in this situation to simply do what feels right—trust your instinct. Then treble it. This is what I do but, even so, by the time I'm in the shower I feel guilty. A dozen more soft, slow downward strokes on her back would have done the trick for sure.

It will be nice to see Victoria as a friend. The four years of separation were necessary, of course. The first two years I missed her a lot and wrote a couple of letters that I didn't send. One of the letters was angry. It went something like, you fool, you live with someone you don't really love, you took the coward's way out, what you're doing isn't fair on you and it isn't fair on Teacher. I gave you the chance to change your mind and you didn't.

Of course I didn't send it. But I did feel the anger, and in a way I liked the anger. I suppose I had to do either anger or grief and I do anger better. I just wanted to shake her and tell her that she had to love me and live with me. Sometimes it's impossible to believe that someone's gotten over you. They've moved on, you're history. You are dead in their mind. You don't live there anymore. And I suppose in the same way that people need to believe that their departed loved ones are alive in heaven, you want to believe their love for you lives on in some way that they aren't quite aware of. They love you but they don't know it. (I'd make someone a great stalker.)

Last year I received Victoria's e-mail address from a mutual friend but somehow I thought contacting her would lead to either seeing her, or not seeing her and wanting to. Also, I thought maybe I'd write something angry or ridiculously romantic after a few beers and I'd punch "send" and immediately regret it. I didn't even put it into my PC's address book.

So much to talk about, so much to hear. But making my last four years sound interesting is going to be hard. Print Stop isn't the kind of place where interesting things happen. Except that Jonathan Ross is a regular customer. Can't stretch that very far, though. Never mind, I've done loads of other crap jobs I can talk about. A few good stories to tell. I'm not too worried about my completely failed film career, to tell you the truth, Victoria. I am jealous that my old friend Stefan seems to have wrangled his way into films, of course, but I will find other outlets for my creativity, I'm sure. Ah, how nice to have this wonderful person as a friend that I no longer need to impress. I don't need to make the last four years sound interesting. She is a friend in whom I can now confide. Victoria, my career started in the toilet and it's still in there——I thump on the door as loud as I can but it won't come out. (Not bad, might try to remember that one.) Will I mention Sandra? Sure, why not?

I don't even feel the need to shave. Or put on a clean pair of jeans. No, ok,

I will put on a clean pair of jeans but I won't shave. No special treatment for Victoria from now on. Ok, I will shave.

I kiss Sandra good-bye; I'll be back around six I should think. Have a good day, now. But I know her day will be like all the others.

The morning has matured into a windy afternoon and I wonder how blowy it'll be on top of Primrose Hill. Just on a point of information, I wonder if Victoria has missed me. Oh, and I wonder if she'll think meeting actually on Primrose Hill is me trying to be romantic. I hope she split up with Teacher. No I don't. Why would I want that? No, actually I hope she's still with him, it'll make things even easier between us.

I love the view on top of the hill. And being windy, it's particularly sharp. The houses at the bottom of the hill are home to writer Alan Bennett and game-show stalwart Les Dennis. I wonder what they chat about over the garden gate.

I have no idea from which direction Victoria will come so I stroll round in circles keeping an eye out. A Scottie dog yaps at my heels and a pretty young girl beckons "Blacky" back to her with the obligatory "He won't hurt you." No, but he does irritate *me.*

She pushes a pram and I guess she's a nanny rather than a mummy. No young family could afford to live round here. I suppose that's why Victoria moved out of London. Graham, a vaguely mutual friend-of-a-mutual-friend heard that she and Teacher bought one-third of a converted barn or something in Kent. So, your daughter became a country bumpkin after all, Mr. Maginot.

I wonder what I will think or feel when we meet. The big question, I suppose, is will I be in love with her? How can I not know the answer to this question? Surely her mere physical presence, lovely though it is, can't decide that one way or another. No, I feel certain that it'll be fine.

I keep thinking I see her in the distance but it's not her. When I do make her out at the Zoo side of the hill she is unmistakable. It's that walk, forthright and determined, but not especially straight, that makes me smile. It makes me smile even more because gusts of wind make her look like she might suddenly be blown away into the Zoo.

I wave and she waves back. Perhaps I should start running toward her with my arms wide open and then lift her up and spin her round.

Oh, why the hell not.

I start running with my arms wide open. An arms-wide-open run is something you can't do by halves. You can't start it and then decide, on balance, that it's a bit tacky. And you can't stop simply because the other person has decided not to follow suit. It's a do-or-die thing. And if the other person doesn't reciprocate, then it's just a die thing. You begin to wonder what you're going to do when you eventually meet up with the person. You can't do the whole running shebang only to give them a little peck on the cheek. So I am relieved to see Victoria start running toward me with arms wide, and she is smiling—no, I think she's laughing. As we get closer I am running faster because the hill's gravity is being a little over-helpful. A gust of wind practically sends me for a burton. I begin to slow down for the great hug when Blacky (I'll always remember you, Blacky) appears from nowhere barking like mad. "Fuck right off!" I shout, without looking down. He makes a beeline for my right foot. "Fuck OFF!" I shout again. The next thing I know I tread on his paw, there's another gust of wind, and Victoria and I come together.

Then we go down together.

We're lying on the grass, Victoria is practically sitting on top of me, laughing. We laugh and kiss each other and try to hug. We are both giddy with laughter despite various pains in our bodies. Victoria buries her head in my neck and our jerking bodies are entwined. All I can see are clouds, that seem so near I could reach up and grab one. I'm in some kind of dizzy, giddy heaven.

Victoria is not laughing now but crying. She's holding her left hand and tears are streaming down her face. And I think to myself what a galumphing great nincompoop of a man I am.

We are in a taxi heading for the Royal Free Hospital.

"It was that bloody stupid dog. Blacky his name is. I met him earlier—I knew he was up to no good."

"You can't blame a little dog."

"Why not? Animal lovers want us to treat them more like humans so let's

blame them for doing stupid things like biting people's feet. Any human being would be done for assault. Foot-biting might even be considered a sex attack. That dog should be put in the perverts' wing."

"Do you think the sentence should be in human years or dog years?"

"Whatever's longer. In fact, hang him."

Victoria is laughing again.

I once heard a "dating expert" say that if you're on a date and something goes wrong—such as you pour wine down someone's front, or vomit on them, or make them fall over so they hurt their hand, you shouldn't spoil the rest of the date by apologizing over and over again. Apologize once and move on. But what if you damage someone's legs so badly it causes permanent loss of mobility? Just saying, "I'm very sorry your life is ruined, how about some dessert?" doesn't seem proportionate.

Not of course that this is a date. But I am anxious to do the right amount of apologizing, not more or less. I stop at around fourteen, when Victoria says, "James, please, please, please stop apologizing. It really is ok and it really wasn't your fault. It's just one of those things. I do hate you for it, but apologizing won't redeem you."

"What will?"

"I will think of something and tell you when I've seen the doctor and you're buying me dinner."

"Ok."

We wait in casualty for four hours, but it seems less. I learn that Victoria is not with Teacher anymore.

"You heard I had a miscarriage?"

"Yes. Sorry. I was going to . . . I didn't hear about it till long after."

"Teacher wanted to try again, and I thought it seemed only fair."

"Only fair?"

"He was so devastated by it all. But we couldn't. Or didn't. Or something. He wanted to see doctors and all that but I knew in my heart of hearts that I didn't want to have kids anymore. Not yet, anyway, and not with him. So it was all very sad and I felt incredibly guilty for giving him all that hope and then not going through with it."

"You didn't get married, did you?"

"No. He wanted to, but I couldn't. I told him I didn't like the idea of mar- riage, which is true but not the whole truth. I think sometimes having kids is a ca- reer substitute. Like cats can be kid substitutes. And careers can be love substitutes. Is everything a substitute for something else?"

"God knows. No, even God is a substitute for something, I'm sure."

"I was terrified of not having a career, a purpose in life. A child would have given me a job and security and . . . God, I'm glad it didn't happen, which is a ter- rible thing to say but I am glad. I want kids eventually but it would have to be with you, I think."

Keep cool, you didn't hear that.

"I put my energies into getting a career instead. I'm enjoying TV production now. Not really graduate kind of work but you know how it works—you either know someone and go in at the top or you start at the bottom."

"And so you split up?"

"In the summer. He's such a nice bloke. I've ruined his life."

"Of course you haven't! He'll find someone else."

"Not like me. I've never felt so loved."

"Well, it's very nice to see you. A lovely surprise." Meaning, why did you phone out of the blue?

"I got your number from Graham ages ago. Always meaning to phone but just . . . well . . ."

"I know. I had your e-mail address but . . ."

"I smashed a plate last night."

"At a plate-spinning class?"

"That's what I thought of straight away. 'Stop clowning around!'"

"'They cost twenty pence a throw!'"

"I thought about you a lot in the night. Well, I think a lot about you anyway."

"Maginot?"

"Over here."

"That way please. Booth four."

And off she went behind a curtain. I offered to go with her but she said she'd rather I went and bought us both a cup of tea and some chips.

I know. I heard what she said, too.

She said "I want kids eventually but it would have to be with you, I think." That is what she said, isn't it? Or did I mishear? She can't have said that. She can't have just casually said that in mid-paragraph, and then moved on to talk about her career. And what did I do when she said it? Nothing. I just continued my "listening nod" as if she had said nothing out of the ordinary at all.

I need to mentally regroup, and I welcome a few moments to myself as I attempt to procure two cups of tea and a packet of cheese & onion. Easier said than done. Doing anything at all in a hospital is tricky, I find. How surgeons manage to perform intricate brain surgery in hospitals is impressive because finding an exit, or a place to park, or a toilet, or somewhere to buy chips is pretty testing for most people. On Sundays it's harder still. The main café is shut and the other one round the back somewhere is apparently closed for refurbishment. I am eventually directed to a café on Red Zone, which is on Level Five, of North Building—Annex. I am now in Green Zone, Level Two, East Building—Main.

Trying to work out where my life should go from here on a macrolevel, while also working out where my body should go from here on an immediate microlevel is a bad combination. Should I take a lift to Blue Zone Level Two so that I am at least on the right Level but the wrong Zone, and should I consider starting a family with someone I haven't spoken to for nearly five years? Am I in the Annex section now? Is my current relationship worth holding on to? Is Blue Zone after Green? Is Victoria after me?

I am now panicking—and I think I am more frustrated by getting lost in the hospital than my romantic dilemma. I sprained Victoria's lovely wrist and now I can't even get her a hot beverage. Please, someone, show me a sign. Look! That porter is holding two cups! I will ask where he bought them. No, I will offer to buy them at cost price plus a finder's fee.

"Are they both teas?"

"One tea, one coffee."

"That's fine. I'll give you a fiver for them."

"What?"

"Come on. Please. I am lost, I have no tea. Someone urgently needs tea. Fiver just for the tea."

He looks at the fiver in my hand and I reckon he's thinking to himself that he is doesn't want to exploit someone in their hour of need. On the other hand, a fiver is a fiver.

"Please."

"Ok."

Thank goodness for appalling NHS pay. I would be able to deliver. I had hunted down the tea and, bloodied from the fray, I am taking my kill back to the cave.

Easier said than done. I go through a myriad of Zones, Levels, lifts, stairwells and corridors. I begin to feel eerily panicked, like someone caught in some science-fiction nightmare where there are just corridors and signs all leading nowhere. Where is everyone? Why are hospital dramas full of people running this way and that but real hospitals devoid of human life?

When I eventually return to casualty, Victoria is nowhere to be seen. Perhaps the condition was more than just a sprain. I ask a fierce nurse where she's gone.

"And you are . . .?"

"Er, boyfriend." She asks another nurse who asks another nurse who asks another nurse and I eventually ascertain that she has been given a splint and bandage. Then she went.

"Perhaps she's in the Ladies."

I look around trying to imagine where she possibly could have gone. I poke my head into the two ladies' loos and call out her name. Perhaps she thought I'd gone off, or is looking for me and has got lost. I decide to stay put for a while; she's bound to come back and find me.

I return to the casualty waiting area.

A broken plate, then, sparked the phone call. And now a mix-up and we've lost each other. Too much of this affair has been left to chance. If this were a game show I would want to beef up the skill factor.

TWENTY

My taxi pulls up at the Royal Free. I feel assured that Gerard is fine. If he wasn't fine he'd be in intensive care or casualty or in surgery. That's where people die, not ordinary medical wards. That's what I tell myself.

Victoria and I are meeting here again, two years later. Funny, that. (Oh, I think most people have funny, inconsequential thoughts even at times of life and death. For me, it seems they all go together.) I also notice that the front café is open for tea. But I still expect hospitals to be as frantic and bustling as they are on *ER*. Instead it is quiet as a library.

I take time to look at the map. I am *here*. Steeple Ward is *there*. Good, they have dropped the color-coded Zone and Level system so I might be in with a chance.

I approach the ward, and see Victoria sitting in a waiting area by the yellow double doors.

"Can I get you a cup of tea?"

Gallows humor, I know. My way of coping? Hiding the pain?

No, I'm just sick. I don't know, I just say it, make of it what you will. I think Victoria gets the reference but there's no laugh or smile. But then she knows the situation is more serious than I realized.

"He fell on some tracks, that's all I know."

"Oh Jesus Christ. He'll be ok, though?"

"I have no idea." She says this like she's been talking to doctors and nurses and not getting far. "This fourteen-year-old girl in a white coat told me he's 'very poorly'—they're going to take him back into intensive care as soon as a bed's available."

"Jesus. What do you mean, *back*?"

"He was there early this morning. They thought he was all right and then . . ."

"Poor old . . ." Throughout my journey to the hospital I had reassured myself that since Gerard was not in casualty or intensive care, he was fine. So, he's been here since this morning.

So, Gerard. Are you going to live or die? The decision is yours. Take your time. The clock starts now.

For some reason this stupid thought makes me laugh. Gerard would have enjoyed it. He's probably the only person in the world who would, and now we may never share it. (I think he would have enjoyed the tea gag too.) Victoria puts her arm round me when I sit down.

"Sorry about the other night. I was writing you a letter about it when this happened."

"It's ok."

"I'm really sorry. I mean about Gerard. Such a nice, mad man."

"He was ok." I say *ok* in a way that means *great, one of the best, I'll miss him if he goes.*

"How are you?"

"Ok. I thought of a game-show idea."

"Good."

"I want to tell Gerard about it. Might cheer him up."

"Yes. Tell him about it when he wakes up."

"Yes. He'll be pleased." I think about his face for a moment. I'm sure he'll be pleased about the idea. We can get back in the saddle. He can be bonkers again. Normality wasn't for him.

"What do they mean—*when a bed becomes available?*" For some reason this had not sunk in till now.

"There are no beds available in ICU at the moment, said the child doctor."

"Right. I want to see the consultant."

I get up and make for reception. I will see the consultant and get Gerard a bed if it kills me. First I speak to a nurse or sister or someone.

"What do you mean—no beds available?"

"We're doing everything we can."

"Where is he?"

"I'll take you to him." Victoria follows me.

"James, there's no point in getting angry."

"Oh there's a point. There's a point all right. I agree there's no point in getting *personal,* but angry, yes."

Victoria gives me a look. I think she decides that on this occasion it would be best to let me get on with whatever I have to do.

Gerard is asleep. He's got tubes all around him and a couple of monitoring machines. It's odd to see him like this. Is that really my mate Gerard? This looks too much like television.

"Where's the consultant?"

"He'll be coming round in the morning."

"I want to speak to him now."

"Mr. Stanly can see you. He's the registrar."

"I want Gerard in intensive care *now*. Not when a bed becomes available."

"He's not due to go into intensive care."

"Yes he is."

"Who told you that?"

"The doctor. Steeple," says Victoria as she approaches.

"That's the *ward* name," I say in a moment of total recall.

"I mean Stanly. Dr. Stanly. Young woman."

"Just a minute."

The nurse/sister/matron, or whatever, goes and checks something. A couple of the others are talking to her about something and looking at a clipboard. I have a definite sense that a cock-up has occurred.

"We are going to send him to ICU straightaway."

Then another nurse arrives. "There are no beds in intensive care available."

"Right." No point in saying I told you so, I feel. "Does anyone here know what is going on?"

And now a woman appears in a white overall. "I am Dr. Pearson. Can I help you?"

I am now getting very upset, kind of half angry, half grieving. It's beginning to show in my voice.

"No one seems to know what's going on."

Dr. Pearson looks at some notes. Then looks at Gerard and has a quiet word with the nurse.

"I'll make sure he gets into the IC unit in the next two hours."

"Why two hours?"

"Bed shortage."

Again I have the feeling of being on TV. Not a game show but a hospital drama. I am the bolshy relative. I seem to be imitating art.

"What's wrong with this bed here? It's got wheels, let's roll it down to intensive care." Then I know who I remind myself of. It's Gerard. I'm saying what I think Gerard would say. Coming up with daft ideas. Not giving up, just charging along not caring about whether it's awfully sensible or not.

I demand to see the consultant. I have no idea what I'm talking about of course but I stand there simply disagreeing with everything Dr. Pearson says. I tell her that I am making a note of everything that happens. "This just isn't good enough, my friend might die at any minute. I want to know who to sue."

I don't think this strategy would always work and I'm not sure I could do it again, but half an hour later Gerard is in the IC unit. I am aware of Victoria through all this but only vaguely. Not until he's safely in the care of about five nurses and doctors do I relax slightly.

Victoria and I stand by Gerard's bed and hold a hand each.

I say "He's a man with nothing but a stinking old house, a pair of wellies and a thousand crap ideas for game shows."

"And us."

"Why did the hospital phone you, Victoria?"

"They got his parents' number first. But his mum told them to phone our number. She said you were Gerard's closest friend."

So I am Gerard's closest friend. Not just closest friend but next of kin, too. That hit me in the solar plexus. I know he's not a man with a lot of friends and his family had pretty much bought him off with the house, but . . . well, it just hit me, that's all.

We stand by his bed for a while then move into the small

anteroom reserved for relatives of the condemned. There's a water fountain and a coffee table on which there are several boxes of NHS regulation tissues to mop up the grief. On a wall hangs a print of trees in autumn. How symbolic.

Crowded into the far side of the room is a family of Muslims. The mother is praying. Presumably asking Allah to spare her loved one from death. Or to deliver him to a life of eternal bliss.

I have no God. Only explanations.

We are the only living creatures which commit suicide. There is no obvious evolutionary reason for it. Young suicides can't pass on their suicidal genes. One might think that older suicides, who have already produced, might have more successful offspring because, by dying, those offspring have one less elderly parent to feed. But natural history studies have shown that grandparents (especially female ones) are biologically beneficial to the family, which is why women survive long, long after their ability to reproduce has faded. They pass on skills and nurture grandchildren. But young suicides are up an evolutionary cul-de-sac, which is why more than 99 percent of us avoid it.

But then again, one could argue that a group's strength might be augmented if the mentally weak, instead of sitting in the corner of a cave saying life is shit, eliminated themselves. Which is going to be healthier for the group? A quick, clean death, or someone lingering on, not pulling their weight, just sitting in the cave telling everyone that life is meaningless and listening to The Smiths?

But how would I explain mass suicide? Why am I trying to explain everything in terms of evolution, anyway? Some things are anomalous.

Why am I, sitting here with my friend clinging on to life, asking myself these questions? I watch the Muslim woman pray for a second. She has her own habits, rituals and procedures. I wonder if my evolutionary explanations are any less of a ritual, a habit, a crutch. I've got my Evolution and everything must be explained by it. She has Allah. Frederick Sheen has his holes.

But what do I really believe in? An explanation isn't a belief. It's not a guide to live your life by. Evolution won't tell me how to live, or bring comfort in hours of doubt. Nor will God or Allah or Frederick Sheen.

The Muslim woman gets up to leave as Victoria enters holding two cups of tea.

"Did you find it ok?"

"No problem. But I nipped outside for some fresh air."

We are sitting on Parker Knoll chairs. Between the boxes of tissues on the coffee table there is a assortment of magazines—*OK!*, *Hello!*, *Celebrity Secrets* and several copies of *True Stories.* I wonder if someone has worked out that this is what the relatives of the dying like to read.

"You were very good, Jamie. You probably saved Gerard's life."

"Let's hope so."

"When did you last see him?"

"Four days ago. We split up. Things weren't going well." I didn't want to say they weren't going well because I was so depressed about her. It might feel like I was blaming her. "Maybe you were right about him being a manic depressive. But Gerard has always been blindly confident. Until that day. He said all he had in the world was a pair of wellies and a thousand crap ideas for game shows. If that wasn't a cry for help . . ."

"He wasn't far wrong, though. He didn't have a lot going for him. I mean he *doesn't.*"

"I should have said something like, you've got *me.* I'm your mate. But I didn't really think it at the time. But of course we were more than just colleagues. But going from being colleagues to friends is, you know . . . blokes don't find it that easy."

Victoria holds my hand. "It's at these moments when my head just fills up with clichés and I know how you hate them. I wanted to say you mustn't blame yourself."

"You know, I think he was sending hate mail to Tim Rice."

"Good."

We chuckle for a moment.

"I'd like to read the letters. I'm sure they weren't vicious or threatening. Just a bit bonkers and funny, I expect."

"James . . ." I feel my hand being squeezed more tightly.

"What?"

"Are you going to be ok?"

"Yes."

"Stefan and I were planning to go to Edinburgh tonight."

"Then you should."

"No, I can't now. I want to be here with you and Gerard. We can go tomorrow or the next day, whenever we hear that Gerard's going to be all right."

"He's a nice guy."

"Yes. He is."

A smart-looking man in his thirties enters the room.

"Are you the friends of Gerard?"

"Yes."

"I am Mr. Rogers, I'm the new consultant. I am in charge of Gerald's care—no, Gerard, isn't it, do excuse me, long day." I am amazed by his smart, almost dandyish clothes. A gold clip holds his tie in place. An ironed white handkerchief nestles proudly in his breast pocket and both sleeves display jeweled cufflinks. I wonder if he would ever be tempted to sell a cup of tea for a fiver.

"I just wanted to have a little chat with you and go over a few things."

He sits down and smiles at us.

TWENTY-ONE

The 5 pound cup of tea is still in my hand, getting cold. I stubbornly refuse to drink it or throw it away. Well, when you pay ten times over the odds for something you want to hold on to it. Victoria is probably looking for me now or trying to phone and then I remember that my phone's off because I'm in a hospital. I'll go outside and check my voicemail.

"James, it's me. Where are you? I've got a splint on my wrist. Look, I understand if you don't particularly want to see me after what I said. I know you've got a girlfriend and everything." Ah yes, she did speak to Sandra on the phone before she spoke to me. "But running off is a really crap thing to do. Ok, I assume you just got lost or something. I'm going to go to the nearest pub, wherever the sodding hell that is. Join me if you want and be prepared to grovel."

So I did hear right. She said, and I remember the words exactly, "I do want kids eventually but it would have to be with you, I think." She not only says it but she remembers saying it, and she regards it as significant.

There's another message. It's Sandra, whose lemon-scented back I kissed five hours ago.

"I hope you're having a nice time with Victoria." This is so neatly balanced *between arch and sincere that I can only admire it.* "I finished all my marking. There's nothing in your fridge. Look, I feel low, how about seeing a film tonight? Betty Blue's on. Why is your phone off? Anyway, give me a call."

I dial my flat. I look round for the nearest pub and start walking. Sandra picks up and I tell her there was an accident—Victoria fell over, no, nothing serious, I'll be back at around seven.

But I won't be back till around eight. I will explain what happened but leave out a lot. I will say Victoria tripped on a stick. We will see the film, Betty Blue, late showing. She will want to go to Pizza Hut afterward.

I know this is not the right time to leave. The builders took her money and didn't fix her roof, her skin condition has not been diagnosed, she hates her work to the point of it making her a nervous wreck, her mother is being evicted and they can't rehouse her. But I can't stay with Sandra out of pity.

I will bring the conversation round to my day and Victoria's fall. I won't say that I was running to embrace her and that she landed on top of me and that her laughter turned to tears. I will not tell her that when Victoria landed on top of me and laughed and cried I called myself a total great, galumphing nincompoop. Not because I had hurt her hand, but because I had told myself I would not feel the same after all these years. I won't tell Sandra that the moment brought back all those years of playing footsie with love.

At Pizza Hut I will tell Sandra that I'm sorry. Genuinely sorry. She is a wonderful person but things are not quite right between us. Yes, we're good in bed, and we get on "really well."

"What more do you want?"

"I don't know." But I do.

I'll tell her that when I woke up this morning I knew something needed to change. (I will not say that I wanted to walk under trees with someone I love, but that someone wasn't Sandra, but I didn't know who it was, just someone.)

I'll tell her I've known things haven't been right for a month or two. No, that's a lie, they've never been quite right. I'll tell her I just haven't been able to find the right time to leave. I wanted to leave when something good was happening for her; but nothing good has. She will suggest trying to work at it, and other clichés. I will say that I suspect the whole notion of "working at it." We're not building a cathedral, or starting a family or even living together. We're just going out—why should that require hard work? And six months is long enough to discover what we really feel for each other. (I will not tell Sandra that I knew how I felt about Victoria in one moment—no, six seconds. Ok, you're not going to plan your life on the basis of a six-second reaction but sometimes, just sometimes, those six seconds can be flukishly prophetic.) I will tell Sandra that I will miss her a lot, that she's beautiful and will find someone else who—but I will not be able to get my words out before she interrupts with a contemptuous remark such as, "Don't patronize me. This is about Victoria."

"No it isn't."

I will tell her that I had a drink with Victoria and that we told each other that it would be hard for either of us to really love anyone else if there was a possibility we might get together. Sandra will say that I should have told her all about Victoria ages ago. I have deceived her, she'll say. I will wonder if that's true. I will wonder if all relationships have an element of deceit. I will think of a phrase "deceit management" and wonder how long it will be before some agony aunt or self-help book uses the phrase in earnest.

Sandra will feel hurt, destroyed. I am the one thing in her life that's ok. She'll cry and not mind if people notice. But she won't storm out quite yet. She will want the whole story first. People always want the whole story. She will ask questions.

"Is this really the first time you've seen her in four years?"

I will assure her that I have not been seeing Victoria on the quiet.

She will pour scorn on the whole notion.

"You haven't seen or spoken in four years! What does that say about your commitment to each other? She's probably just on the rebound. She's probably working through her address book, seeing all the men from her past who fancied her. Girls do that at her age."

I will try not to let these questions shake my resolve. Perhaps she is right, *perhaps what we're doing is folly. But I'll say that sometimes we need to do folly. We need to go into the circus ring with our clown make-up on, and fall flat on our asses. She'll be annoyed that in the middle of an emotional crisis I can find space to make a supposedly witty observation about the human condition that sounds rehearsed.*

Although I should be thinking about Sandra and how she feels, my mind will stray to Victoria and my new life with her that will begin in a matter of hours. (Ten? Twelve? Fifteen?) Victoria will be waiting for me tomorrow morning, in her new flat, as planned. I will go to her when the chucking is over. Whatever happens, in a few hours I will be in Victoria's arms. Without this thought, my resolve might weaken and I would let this thing with Sandra trudge its weary way through more of my life.

Sandra will cry. She'll cry and cry and cry. But I must go. I must finish. I will deliver a blow to the solar plexus.

"I don't want you. Sorry. I am really very sorry."

That will be the end of it. But I won't leave her in a state. I will stay up till the small hours talking, repeating, repeating. At four o'clock, with eyelids fighting the light, I'll say that I'll only go on talking if we stick to saying things we haven't said already. But it's not possible. The same things will go round and round and round the washing machine.

In the morning I'll take her and her bits and pieces—two pairs of tights, a couple of hairpins and a make-up bag—to her flat in a taxi. Her head will rest on my shoulder as we go past Highbury and through Islington to King's Cross. I'll think: a lot of people settle for what we had. They smile and make homes together, and have kids and pack their hearts with trivia, and it works ok. You can fake your own happiness if you try hard enough. Sorry, Sandra, but if we had found any happiness it would have come from the outside in.

I go straight to Victoria's flat after dropping Sandra off. Yes, it feels indecent. Climbing up the ladder of Sandra's pain to get to my pleasure. It's eleven in the morning but I feel this is a champagne moment. Sadly, most of the champagne moments in my life are not accompanied by the bubbly nectar itself. Having spent nearly thirty quid on a taxi I just don't have any cash left and I'm regularly having my card retained. (Sorry to burden you with this, dear reader, but I never promised you a romance. This isn't that kind of book. The irritations of life keep bubbling away. True, there's a bit of love and romance coming up but that doesn't mean I don't still have athlete's foot, an overdraft, damp walls, a noisy neighbor and no career.) So with a bottle of Cava and a large packet of corn chips I board the bus.

I call Victoria from the top deck.

"Victoria?"

"Is it all over?"

"Between us? No!"

"I mean Sandra!"

"Yes."

"Thank God. Poor girl. But I'm relieved. I thought you might change your mind and say, oops sorry, I thought you were someone else."

"You are Jane Thomkinson, aren't you?"

"Excuse me while I split my sides."

"You haven't changed your mind, have you?"

"No."

"How's your wrist?"

"Annoying."

"Do you have any doubts? I mean, is this crazy? After four years of no contact?"

"Ah, you're having doubts now."

"I'm not, but I think you are."

"You're trying to put the doubt onto me."

"I'm not, but if you want to call it off tell me now."

"Are you trying to get out of this?"

"I'm not! I thought you might be, though."

This kind of questioning goes on for quite a while. I will spare you from it because it's quite repetitive and it's making me a little red in the cheeks. Young love, huh?

"It's all so exciting," says Victoria.

"Scary. Let's call it off."

"What?"

"Joking. Victoria? We didn't kiss yesterday. I mean in the pub. We didn't make out when we said good-bye."

"You suddenly had to go."

"I would have kissed you!"

"I thought you were too anxious about Sandra and . . ."

"Victoria? I want you to promise me that within ten minutes of entering your flat we'll be writhing on the sofa. No ifs or buts."

"It'll be my pleasure."

"I refuse to spend the whole evening wondering if I should make a move or not, you know? Ten minutes and that's it."

"Cool. Let's make it five."

"Ok. I just keep thinking something will happen to stop it."

"That's because something always did happen in the past. Neither of us can believe that it is finally going to happen. Let's make it four. No ifs, no buts, no doubts, no insecurities are going to stop us. We're going to go at it like rabbits."

The traffic is horrendous, but hey, it's slowly, slowly getting me nearer to her, the girl I love. It is like a dream and I keep pinching myself and other clichés.

Twenty-six minutes later the bus arrives at the stop and I get up to leave. "Good luck on the sofa, mate," says the young man behind me.

"Thanks."

I walk up the path to Victoria's door. This is it then, James, you old luckster. In four minutes you'll be writhing on the sofa with the girl you have loved for seven years. It's twenty to twelve. Nothing will go wrong. Not this time. No. Not this time. I won't let it. Nothing is going to stop me. No doubts. No circumstances. No daft goings-on in the shower. No boyfriends suddenly appearing. I am Victoria's man. I think I need a subheading (well, the others got one).

VICTORIA'S MAN—JAMES HOLE

I ring the doorbell and after a few moments it opens. Victoria looks . . . well, picture your own perfect human. I put the Cava down on a shelf by the front door and we kiss briefly on the lips. I know we both want it to be perfect, whatever happens. I feel ready now, and press Victoria to me. Her bottom feels just as great as I always imagined. She smiles cheekily—I guess she can feel just how ready I am. We kiss with full passion once again, and I take her hand—the one without the lint.

"James . . ."

"What?"

"The writhing on the sofa thing . . . Don't get upset."

This is her little game. I knew she would wind me up about this.

"You're winding me up."

"I'm not."

"I am taking you on the sofa. Get your knickers off."

"I really couldn't do anything about it. I really, really tried."

"Yeah, sure." *This so has to be a joke.*

Her voice goes into a whisper.

"Don't get upset. I want you to calm down first. We'll be writhing on the sofa tonight, I promise. But not now. Just take a few deep breaths."

I walk into the sitting room, dragging Victoria behind me, confident that this is a little joke. There, reading the paper on the sofa, is . . . oh, Christ-on-a-bus.

Dad Maginot. My nemesis. Or one of my many nemeses. And on the other chair is Victoria's mother.

"Ah, James."

"Dad's come to London—buying wine."

We all shake hands. I'm not sure if I smile or not. I can see a vision of myself punching him. I just want to punch everyone. In fact I would like to take a chainsaw to both of them.

"Nice to see you again. You're a bit of a face from the past," *says the female one.*

"Bought ten cases of red," says the male.

"Gosh, that's a lot of wine, ha," I say reflexively. There's "gosh" where there would normally be "fuck" or "blimey" or "shit."

"A lot? I've never bought in such small quantities before. Have I, Margaret?"

You see what he did? He said, in a boastful manner, that he had bought ten cases of red. He didn't say "only ten cases." He said ten cases. So naturally I want to sound vaguely impressed: it's only polite. Then he takes the rug from under me and makes me look very slightly foolish. Fine, no problem, I don't want to make a big deal of it, but that's what he does fifty sodding times an hour, every hour of his miserable stuck-up life. Sorry, and I know this isn't very articulate, but ERRRRRRRRRGGGGH!

I persevere.

"Right. Still, it must be pretty nice stuff. You're an expert."

"Not at all, I pay other people to be expert. I just do the drinking."

"Excellent, ha. That's the right idea. Excellent." God, talk about putting on airs, I sound like Hugh Grant's posh cousin. Still trying to fit in, still trying to make them like me.

"Victoria tells me you're still photocopying." He imitates the noise of a photocopier and whooshes his hand along like a piece of paper in a machine.

"Actually we do a lot of other things. Print, e-mail, Internet, photography, graphics—"

He cuts across me. "But you're trying to get into game shows or something."

"Game shows, not 'or something.'" Pretty bold for me but I think he misses it.

"So James, answer me this. Aren't a lot of game shows prurient these days? I find them very mindless. Mastermind, University Challenge, fair enough. But some of them! Are they for idiots? Or are they just made by idiots?"

Seven years on from the melon and Parma ham, and I am still utterly intimidated. What trap has he laid for me?

"I'd love to answer that but . . ." I am at a loss. "But I have a prior engagement." I hear the formality of my tone bouncing back at me.

"Oh Victoria, I couldn't have a glass of water, could I?"

"Sure. James——"

"My mouth's dry."

"Ok."

"Are you off somewhere, then? For this prior engagement?" inquires Maginot.

Victoria goes toward the kitchen but, before she does, she gives my arm a little squeeze. That makes the difference. (Looking back, that small gesture is what did it. I have never thanked you for that, Victoria, so thank you, it was needed.) I am not drunk, but suddenly I feel a surge of courage that feels quite Dutch.

"No, the prior engagement is here. In about two minutes."

"Pray tell," he says, with contempt in his voice. Is he irritated by the fact that I, the boring one, have managed to arouse his curiosity? "Pray tell what this mysterious activity might entail."

"Best you don't ask."

"Are you affecting some mysterious side to your personality?" He says this with another chuckle, trying to pretend this is mere friendly banter. Margaret is smiling inanely at me for some reason. Perhaps she feels that Victoria has reached the age where anyone will do. Even me. Her husband continues.

"I don't think you'll ever make it as the enigmatic type." He laughs quite loudly now because this insult requires a thicker cloak of fake badinage.

"I'm really not trying to——"

"Well then, tell us what you're about to do."

"Mr. and Mrs. Maginot, in a couple of minutes I'm going to have sex with your daughter. Tell a lie, in exactly one minute. It'll be our first time, so we're both rather excited."

Now, Dad Maginot did not spill his wine out into his glass. But I suppose if anyone is ever rash enough to make a film of this book then he probably will. The shock on his face is a joy. I will never forget it. (Thank you again, Victoria.) I do not look at Margaret. I daren't.

"The plan was to start on the sofa, and then progress to the bedroom. But, as you're here, we'll skip the sofa and start on the bed. Unless you really do want to watch."

Dad Maginot isn't quite lost for words.

"Right. Well . . . Margaret?"

I now dare to look at Margaret. Oh my. My oh my oh my. What a picture. I have never, before or since, seen a mouth that actually gaped. It is the result of a jaw literally dropping. Gosh, she is frozen, too. Scared rigid. These phrases (jaw dropping, mouth gaping, scared rigid) really are rooted in reality. Her face is like a still from a corny old horror movie, where the girl victim is captured in mid-scream. I wonder if her hair will now stand on end.

My God, they're psychiatrists, how can they be so shocked? Shocked by the crude description of sex? Or shocked by an outburst of anger? Either way, you'd think they'd be pretty unshockable in their line of work.

Dad Maginot puts his glass down and gathers himself.

"Margaret, don't sit there gaping, that's what he wants."

"No need to rush off. We'll be finished in half an hour or so. Mind you, I do like a lot of oral."

Both parents are now in the hall and I have followed them out. Sometimes retreat provokes the aggressor. This isn't a fight, but by God it feels like it.

"Are you really off? Not boring you, am I?"

Victoria enters the scene with some mineral water.

"Are you off?"

"Yes, we only popped in briefly. Hope your wrist gets better."

I guess Victoria senses that it might be best to help them get out of the door with as little fuss as possible.

A moment later they are gone. As soon as the door closes, Victoria turns and opens her mouth to speak, but in true Hollywood fashion I stop her with a kiss. A moment later Victoria and I are in each other's arms and in five seconds we are on the sofa.

Writhing.

My arm is wrapped round her shoulders and I notice the time: seven minutes past. A minute late, but who's counting? Victoria strokes my hair.

"They left in a hurry. What did you tell them?"

"I told them we were going to have sex."

The notion is dismissed with a raised eyebrow and tiny slap on my face. (If you're honest enough, no one will believe you.)

Victoria's body and mine fit perfectly. I wonder at the beauty of it—not simply her body—but the way anatomy and love come together. It feels like a final acceptance of our love for each other, an exchange of gifts.

I unwrap her.

We make love, we fuck, we make love.

My imaginary Victoria, the one who has been with me so many years, flitters in my eyes when I close them. But she is joined by this real Victoria, this flesh, this warmth, this hand.

TWENTY-TWO

I scrutinize this doctor's appearance. For clues perhaps. Clues that might indicate his level of competence. His hands are as immaculate as his clothes. His nails aren't simply clean, as you would expect, but manicured. Each nail is rounded perfectly and a ring shines from his little finger. I guess he is a man who overlooks nothing. Everything in the operating theater must be just so. But can he think on his feet in the chaos of an emergency? Sometimes very organized people go to pot when chaos reigns—they fear it so much.

As he sits I look down at his shoes, which look just as neat and polished as everything else. His socks have tiny colored dots. I wonder that a man who sees so much death can be so devoted to the minutiae of life. He smiles perfunctorily at the Muslim family, who are sitting in quiet contemplation.

"Electrocution isn't always fatal, obviously," he begins, as he places some papers neatly on his lap. He's preparing us for the worst. "I've had a look at his records and it appears that Gerard was on medication. Perhaps he stopped taking it. He's clearly confused about what happened. Now, we've done some tests for kidney failure and those were positive."

So. That's it then?

"So what's the prognosis?" Victoria asks.

"Not great. We are trying everything, of course, but he is very poorly."

"How long do you think . . ."

"It's very difficult. These things are never as simple as they seem on TV. He has a strong constitution, but the full effects are sometimes slow to work through, especially if the kidneys are already a little weak, which Gerard's are. We're doing everything we can. I'd say a week at the very most."

I wonder that he can give this kind of news in front of another family. Perhaps he assumes, like I do, that they don't understand English.

I will have to tell Gerard's parents. How do you tell a mother, even an estranged one, that her child is dying?

"Would you like to see him? He's still asleep."

"Does he know?"

"He knows it's fairly serious."

Fairly serious.

"Well, when you're ready. Remember, even if he appears to be asleep he may well still be able to hear you."

We stand on either side of the bed. This is no time for weakness but a time to appear strong.

"Gerard?"

"Yes?"

His eyes remain closed.

"It's me, James. And Victoria's here too. We came straight away."

"I tried being normal. I got up this morning, put on a suit and went to the train station with the other commuters. I wanted to blend in. I thought I was getting on a train like all the others, but there was no train there apparently. Either that or someone is playing a trick. Maybe someone took the train away just as I was getting on it. I really did think I was doing a normal thing for once."

"How are you feeling?" asks Victoria.

"Never better. These drugs are great. Am I in heaven? I can't be, my crap-detector is here. But there's no crap in heaven, is there? My wellington boots and my thousand crap ideas for game shows I leave to you, Mr. Hole."

We try to engage Gerard in normal conversation—well, normal conversation under the circumstances. Have the nurses been nice, does he want us to call anyone, is there anything he needs. But it all goes nowhere. I decide to talk game shows. If I know Gerard, that's what'll perk him up.

"Gerard, I went through some old ideas of yours."

"Yes? And did they stink the place out?"

Victoria encourages me to continue.

"There's one called *I Hate Game Shows.*"

"I don't remember that one. It was probably just a statement of fact."

"I think it's good."

"Wow. Are you sure *you're* not the sick one?"

"It's basically a piss-take of game shows. Each round is some kind of send-up. It's only a germ of an idea. We'll need your daft ideas to flesh it out. The dafter the better. *Climb Christopher Biggins, Shark Survivor, Whose Lung Is It, Anyway?* We could do them all. Not with real people getting eaten but, you know, the whole thing is postmodern and ironic."

"You mean you actually have a use for my crap ideas?"

"Yes. Even *Name That Decomposing Corpse*. Well, maybe that's pushing it a bit."

"Who would have thought it? There is finally a demand for what I do best—think of unworkable ideas."

"Obviously they don't have to be real lungs and stuff but the idea is that it's a spoof."

"It's good. I knew I had a good idea somewhere."

"And someone at the BBC is dead keen. But Channel Four is even more keen. Jack Dee's up for it." A benign lie.

"Fan-bloody-tastic." His eyes are closed. There's a moment of quiet, and Victoria and I exchange weak smiles. Stupidly I begin to wonder what Gerard's last words will be. I'd think he'd want them to be memorable.

"Sir Tim fucking Rice! He nicked my fucking train!"

Victoria indicates that she wants a word with me in private.

"We'll be back in half a tick, Gerard."

We walk down to the other end of the ward by the wash basin.

"I want my friend to die with some hope in his heart," I rasp.

"Gerard isn't going to die. I don't care what the doctor said. He looks perkier than Carol Smillie. That's what I wanted to tell you."

At that moment the dapper consultant comes over.

"I've got a question for you both. Do you know where Gerard will go after here?"

"What?"

"He needs to be in good hands."

I shrug. I hadn't given a thought to the funeral. So much to think about and organize. I'm sure Gerard would want something irreverent. "You are gathered here today in memory of

Gerard. Look at the three caskets. Which one is he in? Fingers on buzzers. Remember this is for tonight's star prize . . ."

"James," says Victoria, bringing me back.

"I don't know where he should go from here, doctor. A local undertakers?"

"Um, no, I don't think you've understood. When he leaves in a week's time, he needs someone to look after him for a bit at home while he gets well again—mentally and physically. He will of course be seeing a psychiatrist."

"What's the point in delving into his psyche a week before he dies?"

"Die? He's not going to die."

"You said a week."

"A week in hospital."

"But the tests for kidney failure . . ."

"Very positive."

"But you said the outlook was *fairly* serious."

"It is *fairly* serious."

"But I thought that was doctor-speak for fatal."

"He's done himself some real harm, though luckily not permanent."

I know it's probably wrong to shout in an intensive care unit but . . . "YOU HAVE SERIOUSLY MESSED US ABOUT!"

"What?" He goes slightly white with shock at my outburst but I continue. "You need a course in communication skills! I'm not joking!"

I turn to address the whole unit: nurses, patients and relations. "Hear that, everyone? This doctor's a disaster. My mate's going to *live!*"

Our dapper little friend walks neatly over to the nurse at the desk who has already picked up a phone—presumably to call security. The ceremonial handkerchief that stood to attention in his breast pocket is now reduced to mopping up perspiration.

Victoria has tears in her eyes. I don't think the intensive care ward has ever seen the like before. She presses her fist into her mouth. Her laughter runs, but it can't hide.

"You've got to admit, it's funny."

"*You* thought he was going to die, too."

"That doctor's got even worse communication skills than *you*."

"I'm just glad it was this way round. Imagine if we thought he was coming *home* in a week and then they said—no, you misunderstood—he's going to *die* in a week. Sorry."

We've finished our coffee. Something about the strip lighting in the hospital café reminds me of that first time we met, nine years ago in the University coffee bar. Pulling faces and falling in love, but not really believing it.

"You saved his life, didn't you?"

I shrug.

"By getting him into intensive care."

"He's going to want to kill me when he finds out Jack Dee hasn't even *seen* his idea."

"*Your* idea."

"Whatever."

We're holding hands. I'm beginning to think I could be friends with Victoria. I could get used to it. I mean, look at Gerard—a friend. If he was an ex-lover I doubt I'd even be here. Friendships last. If you want to know someone forever, don't go to bed with them, and other clichés. Yes, I think as long as we can hold hands now and again, and we don't become physically estranged, this will work out ok. You know, I'm beginning to feel a bit better about myself. I may be virtually penniless, jobless, careerless and homeless but Victoria is always going to be a friend.

"Sorry again about the other night."

"What?"

"When I asked you to come to bed with me."

"Oh, that."

"It was mean. I would suggest going for a drink or something but . . ."

"Stefan."

"Yes. I just rang him to say that Gerard's going to be ok so we're going to drive up to Edinburgh after all. Quite exciting. I've never been on a long car journey at night. Sorry. I shouldn't . . ."

"I told you Stefan was great. He is right for you, isn't he?"

She looks a little sheepish.

"Come on, I can take it. He's perfect."

"You really want me to tell you?"

"Yes. I think I can take it."

"He's a very nice, intelligent, thoughtful guy."

Guy. I grab the one crumb of comfort that she didn't say "sexy."

"And sexy."

"Better than Giles?"

"Giles? What made you think of him?"

"I don't know. And what about Supercock?"

"Oh, him. Too busy to rescue me from a fate worse than death. Ugh."

"Is Stefan better than Danny? Plimsoll Man?"

"Ah, I know where this is heading."

"Better than Teacher the teacher?"

"Go on."

"Better than James the . . ."

"The man who set his girlfriend up with his oldest friend." She shrugs. I shrug. We've been doing a lot of shrugging.

A rotund West Indian lady asks if we've finished with our cups before she takes them. I'm reminded of my only two visits to the BBC. All the smartly dressed people are white and the ones in overalls or uniforms are black.

"Stefan is perfect for you. I knew he would be. I just feel bad . . . I am actually feeling bad about not introducing you sooner."

"I think the timing was right. You needed to do what you did. But what really made me angry is that you never explained. Why didn't you tell me *why* you had to leave? That's all I ever asked."

"I didn't really know myself."

"That sounds corny."

"The truth usually does."

"Do you know now?"

"Not really."

"I do."

"How come?"

"I read that note you left on my kitchen table."

"The illegible one?"

"It took me an hour to decipher. But I think I got a pretty good idea of what you were thinking."

"Could you tell *me* why I left? It seems only fair. And I'm as keen to know as you are."

She smiles.

"I'll post it to you."

"God, I hate hospitals. I think they should put a bit of dirt in hospitals to make them feel more homey."

"Plus a few rugs, some socks hanging up to dry, a few empty wine bottles by the bins."

"An old pair of pants on the floor, condoms, needles, you know, things people have at home."

"What are you going to do now?"

I had told her about the Brotherhood of Holes. I'm not going to play the sympathy card, but nor am I going to make things out to be better than they are.

"Go back to the hostel."

"Oh Jamie. Don't be daft. Come and—"

"I can't stay with you and Stefan!"

"But you could stay while we're in Edinburgh."

"Thanks, really, but I have to move on. It's important for me."

"You'd rather stay in a loony hostel?"

"Until I can find a flat-share, that is basically my situation. But it is temporary. It's my fault for not having more friends."

I am being totally straight, you notice. Not trying to put any spin on my life. Not making out that things are going better than they are. I am admitting that I have no friends, money or career and I am going to a hostel. I suppose a near-death experience (by that I mean a friend nearly dying) takes the edge off one's pretensions a bit, even mine.

"You know something?"

"Not much."

"I would have married you."

I am stunned.

"But you blew it."

"Just as well you didn't marry me or you might never have gone out with Stefan. Where is he, by the way?"

"He's coming to pick me up. I don't suppose you want to say hello."

"Let's see. Do I, or don't I, want to say hello to the man who's won the heart of the woman I love, and is rich and successful and has a place to live? Erm . . . *no.* I'd best be getting the bus to King's Cross."

"You and your buses."

"I'm a buses kind of guy."

We get up and make our way to the stop.

"Do you know what really annoys me?"

"What?"

"Your dad. Mr. Maginot. Have you told him yet? That we're finished?"

She nods. "I thought you'd developed a grudging respect for each other." She smiles, knowing this isn't true.

"I would have married you, too. I would have loved to see his face at the wedding."

"Is that the only reason you would have married me?"

"The main one."

"Ha, ha. I thought you didn't believe in marriage, anyway."

"I do now. All that stuff about not making a commitment and people changing and all that. It's guff."

I stop for a moment. Victoria does too. We're just at the end of a little pathway leading up to the bus stop on the high street. I just want to look in her eyes.

"I think getting married is a kind of . . . well, it's a statement of hope, I suppose. I hope to be with you forever. I hope to love you forever, I hope to be loved by you forever."

"Should that be *hoped*—past tense?"

"I suppose it should. Oh, fuck it. No, it shouldn't."

We reach the bus stop and now I just hope the bus doesn't come. Ever.

I say, "Let's always be friends. I think we always will be."

"I think so too."

I put my arm round her, as a friend, you understand.

"That's Stefan's car."

The old blue Saab turns a corner yonder and stops. I want this to be over quickly. We kiss perfunctorily and that's it.

Then she says, "Don't get this bus. Get the next one."

"Why?"

"Please?"

"Ok."

And off she goes. Stefan, nice guy to the last, keeps away and I suppose tactfully pretends not to see me. Off they go into the night, into each other's arms, into the rest of their lives. I don't feel too bad. This feels all right. In the end things have come right.

Maybe for all of us.

I'm not too jealous, not too mixed up. I have been good today. I haven't been a prat for four hours and that is good going for me.

The first bus comes and it goes. I stay put. I know Victoria, and I know she's off to get me some chocolates or a bunch of flowers to make me feel better. Maybe something for Gerard too. She wouldn't disappear without making a gesture of that kind.

So, back to holes.

You've been in worse scrapes than this, Jamie lad.

Keep thinking about the game show. In a week I could get the call—come in for a chat. This is going to be big, big, big. I still believe in it. I also believe I'm a fool for doing so. Like I was a fool to think I fell in love with someone in six seconds.

I think about what'll happen if I run out of money before

I can get a flat-share. Five minutes later another bus comes. This one has my name on it.

Maybe Victoria had trouble finding a present, or Stefan felt they had to get a move on. Maybe the shops were shut or something. Anyway, Victoria, I appreciate the thought.

It's quite full and someone else is sitting in the front seat so I take the back. The bus moves about two feet and stops at the lights.

There's a blonde girl on the bus who looks a little like Victoria. This is the start of my new life so I . . . well, I'm not sure what I do. I think I *try* to fancy her. I mean, I glance at her a couple of times and imagine that she is my girlfriend. But I also imagine that she acts and moves and laughs just like Victoria. That's no good, I tell myself, that's cheating. I can't go through the rest of my life looking for someone just like Victoria.

I look down on the pavement. Just as the bus pulls away I see a blonde girl about twenty yards away running like mad, trying to catch the bus. *Victoria!* But I'm going to see Victoria everywhere, and in every girl. I will keep hoping she is around every corner. But it will fade with time. I know that love is not unique, you do get other chances, and Victoria will be a friend if I want her to be. I hope that one day I will be glad things turned out as they did.

The blonde girl not only looks like Victoria but she runs like her too. That determined but slightly off-balance run, like when she ran into my arms on Primrose Hill. This is going to be tough. Even her clothes seem . . . *just one cotton-picking minute.*

Just one damn, cotton-picking, fucking minute.

"You'll never make it!" I say out loud, though I know she can't hear. There's a Rastafarian sitting behind me.

"She'll make it, man," he says.

Late at night, a well-dressed blonde girl running like the wind gets quite a lot of attention.

"She'd be better off waiting for the next one," says a curmudgeonly white-haired lady.

"No, she'll get this one all right," I say, having changed my mind.

"She a friend of yours, man?" asks the Rasta.

A tweedy man and the Rasta start cheering her on but the curmudgeonly lady seems to want her to fall on her ass.

"She'll never make it. Silly girl."

"If she gets on this bus, I'll ask her to marry me."

And suddenly the grumpy lady lights up like an angel.

"Go, girl! Go!"

This gets the attention of most of the passengers. They gather at the rear window and begin cheering her on. I can hardly get a view myself. I go downstairs only to be followed by half the bus.

Downstairs the conductor isn't having any of it.

"Do not stand in the conductor's area, please."

"He's going to ask her to marry him." This changes his mind in an instant.

"Shall I stop the bus?"

"No. Let's see her run for it."

She runs like mad. Her face is contorted—that wonderful rubberized face is grimacing like a demented clown. I start to laugh between cheers.

"Come on, Victoria!"

The others on the bus start calling her name.

"Victoria! Victoria!"

Just as she seems about to make it the bus speeds up and all seems lost, she slows down.

"Don't give up!"

The cheering from the crowd inspires her to give it one last ounce of effort. I reach out. She clasps my hands and I pull with all my might and she collapses onto the deck. She gets a loud cheer for her efforts, but she's so exhausted she can hardly stand.

"Go on then, mate. Ask her."

"Ok. Victoria? Will you marry me?"

Victoria is too breathless to speak. She is doubled up and clinging onto my arm.

"Victoria?"

She's about to collapse.

"The girl's ill."

"Will you?"

Still no answer. Just grotesque wheezing and coughing.

"Marry me!"

She nods and mouths the word yes. Another cheer goes up and she resumes her doubled-up position. I lift her head and try to kiss her. Unfortunately she pushes me off almost violently as she is so short of breath.

"What about Stefan?"

"Stefan?" says the Rasta. The name *Stefan* reverberates around the bus. "Stefan? Stefan?"

Victoria shakes her head. She is trying to gather enough breath to speak. "Perfection . . ." She stops. "Perfection . . ." She stops again. "Perfection . . . isn't . . . all . . . I can't." She stops and takes four or five deep breaths. "Perfection . . . isn't all . . . it's cracked up to be. Besides . . . *shoes.*" She gives a thumbs-down.

"Shoes?"

She nods.

"Shoes?" I say again. "You don't like his shoes?"

She nods again.

"Plimsolls, were they?"

"Tassled . . . tassled . . . tassled loafers."

Fuck me. I have been saved by footwear. Even Stefan Catchiside has an Achilles heel.

"I love you, Victoria."

Victoria nods her head vigorously, points to her heart, then to mine, then back to hers.

TWENTY-THREE

That was three weeks ago. It took two weeks for Victoria to get her breath back. She's fine now, singing away in the kitchen, and I hear the chopping of knife on breadboard. There are few sweeter sounds than that of someone you love chopping an onion.

Gerard is watching TV in the other room. He's going to be staying with us for a while. In his quest for normality, he had stopped taking the pills that kept him from going under. Extraordinary that one tablet a day can so affect the human soul. Biology rides again.

The other night we shared a bottle or two of Newkie and I had a serious word about the Tim Rice letters. Now, I don't want to implicate Gerard in criminal misconduct, but let's just say Sir Tim can stop having his letters vetted.

Gerard's nuclear-strength optimism has returned, only this time with good reason. The day after I proposed to Victoria I opened my in-box and amongst a cluster of replies was this:

To: James Hole
From: Giles
Subject: I Hate Game Shows

James!

Our paths cross once more! From hit student film to (I hope) monster game-show hit. I trust this finds you well, and still drinking stout and lounging around looking lost.

What a tremendously exciting idea! It deconstructs the whole genre! Always thought you were a dark horse. Have already thought of sets. How about something Richard Rogers-ish? Hand-held cameras, methinks.

I have a big wad of cash to spend on account of being head of development (get me!) here in Cardiff. (BBC keen to be seen squandering cash on its deserted outposts, hence MONEY APLENTY and naught to spend it on.)

One snag—you will have come to meetings and pretend to be Welsh. It's NOT hard. I have been here a year and no one's sussed. (Suspect my boss is at same game, though.)

Also would need Welsh host. Gareth Jones?

Let's have lunch.

Giles (for it is I)

P.S. Not sure about the comedy element. Is that crucial?

P.P.S. Haven't given up on films.

YOU: Who's Gareth Jones?
ME: Precisely.

Now, you might think someone in my position might leap at the chance of being bunged a tidy sum to have an idea destroyed— happens all the time. And from my experience, in television, you don't sell your soul to a devil, you sell your soul to an idiot. Yes, I would have been quite happy to sell mine to that idiot were it not for this:

To: James Hole
From: Frances Farra
Subject: I Hate Game Shows

James—thanks for this—it made us all laugh. A lot. I think it would work well on Channel Two or Choice. It needs development and a good supply of totally bonkers ideas. Would we hire some writers or do you have someone in mind? Do you have any other (straighter) ideas? We are expanding our operation here and are on the look-out.

Please phone Zoë and arrange a meeting. I want to take out an option asap. And thanks for brightening our day.

Frances

An option isn't a great wedge, but it's money.

Victoria was delighted for me. She did what she always does when she's really happy—she shouted and swore. "You fucking, fucking, fucking deserve it. Hoo-fucking-ray. You are fucking brilliant." She was especially delighted to have been the inspiration for the idea (it was her exclamation about hating game shows that got the ball rolling). I bought her a massive bunch of lilies (her favourite) and took her out to dinner for the first time in far too long. And, wait for it, I ordered champagne. A small step for a man, but a giant leap for a bloke.

Later that week, Frances and I had a very nice lunch. I dipped bread in the olive oil, did NOT ask for a Newkie Brown, and remembered to use the fork on the outside first. I reassured her that I had someone who would supply enough bonkers ideas. I also went through some of our less mad notions and she took to a couple. A few meetings later I felt Gerard was well enough to bring with me. We were ushered into the managing director's office and asked if we wanted to join the company on a full-time, exclusive basis, working on original ideas and shaping their existing slate.

We tried not to look like overjoyed schoolboys but we failed utterly.

Gerard and I aren't millionaires, we're not even very well paid. But we are now professional full-time game-show writers. Really. Ask anyone.

It's funny how success has come when I stopped being desperate for it. I've come to the conclusion that one of my own little adages, "you can achieve anything with a little desperation," is just about as wrong as anything can be.

I can hear the gentle percussion that presages one of Victoria's special meals. In a few moments I will come up beside her, enfold her in my arms and say something very nice. I don't know what it is yet, but it'll make her smile.

Victoria is still working with Stefan on his film. I am ok about it. No, I am. I can stand it. I don't even wait in every night counting the minutes before Victoria comes home. Stefan is a great guy. Did you think some awful flaw would be revealed at the last minute? I thought so too, but no, he's still unassailable. But Victoria explained that love has nothing to do with how perfect someone is. If we only ever loved people who were right for us, the world would be a happier place, but it's not. "We love people who do us no good at all." I didn't like the slightly arch tone of this remark but she was smiling. I think. And believe it or not, Victoria and I are good for each other. I think.

St. Stefan e-mailed saying that we were both lucky people and that it was never meant to happen between Victoria and him. He had "always suspected she was a bit on the rebound." (I don't know if they slept together and will never ask.) I can't tell you how angry Victoria was with me, and I don't blame her. I have been, according to her, "almost unbearably contrite."

So Stefan, admirable though he is, was not selected. A weaker, less successful, less mature, less everything male has triumphed. (I'm sorry that this has become a bit of a nice-guys-finish-last story but Stefan does have everything *but* the girl.)

Charlotte and Brian. Now, I really should tell you whether they are still together but I can't. I did of course drop them an e-mail thanking them for putting me up. Also one to Charlotte saying I really valued her friendship and would be sorry if she didn't get in touch. I then left a voice message saying pretty much the same thing and I think that's about as far as I can go. No response. I know it makes this book a little unsatisfactory ending-wise, but I don't want to intrude just so that I can tie up a loose end in the book. Charlotte, I miss you. I do. But if you weren't happy, then I suppose you were in the wrong-shaped hole.

Speaking of which.

The Brotherhood of God mysteriously mislaid my Switch card and a hundred quid has gone missing from my current account. How they did this I don't know, and when I complained I was given a load of excuses. I reported it to my bank and then the local constabulary, who said that I was not the first to do so, but it's a civil matter. I still have no Switch card. I can only assume that the safe on the wall, guarded by the picture of Frederick Sheen, must have had a hole in it.

And what of Mr. and Mrs. Maginot? It's been two years since they left, red-faced and horrified, as I told them I was about to shag their daughter. In those two years I've been civil and so have they. But it seems they were relieved to discover that Victoria and I had split. "He was never going to amount to much."

Well, Mr. Maginot, I agree with you. I don't *want* to spend my life *amounting to something*. Not any more. I love your daughter. And I've amounted to someone that she loves back. And that's a gift that I can now accept comes free, with no strings. (But just for good measure, Victoria made it perfectly clear to Maginot on the phone that my new job was a spectacular achievement. He was surprised and Victoria sensed a humble pie being prepared.)

What I can't figure out is why Maginot kept putting me down. Victoria says it might be because I'm the only man she loves more than him, and being a psychiatrist he knew that from the start. A lovely thought, Victoria, but I'm not buying it.

And as for weddings and marriage, Victoria and I have talked about it a lot. We both agreed we didn't want God involved, that was easy. Then Victoria mentioned that she didn't really want the law involved. She didn't feel the state had a place in her love life, and just the idea of signing a contract that appertains to rules devised by strangers (most of whom are dead) is about the least romantic thing you can do. I don't feel strongly about the piece of paper so I said fine, no formal marriage contract.

I then added that I wasn't that keen on getting a load of people round. For one, I didn't think I had enough mates for a decent stag party, and two, I don't feel the need to declare my love to all and sundry. If anything, I said, that smacks of insecurity. A whisper in my lover's ear is good enough for me.

She said fine, no crowds.

So what does that leave us? I said, what about promises? We went through a few ideas but couldn't agree on anything except that the more certain you are of love, the less you need to promise. (You only ask the persistently late for promises to be on time.)

So we put that whole wedding/marriage thing on hold.

A couple of days later, while removing something unpleasant from my shoe, it dawned on me that if we had a wedding Dad Maginot would be there. And he'd see me marrying his daughter, giving the bride a kiss, and he'd *have* to say nice things about me in his speech. I mentioned this to Victoria, who said that that was a really daft reason to get married.

But then she said that if she was going to get married, she would quite like it to be for a daft reason.

I said what about doing it so we can invite Giles to see if he's still scrounging fags and fondling bottoms.

And that pretty much decided it. Plus the fact that I wanted to know what Gerard's best-man speech would be like.

I rang Dad to tell him the news and he said it was the best thing I'd ever said to him. "The best thing, the very best thing, well, well, the best thing, you're a good kid, son, I always knew you were."

And now he has the proof.

Meanwhile, Victoria and I are two people who hope to love each other for the rest of our lives. That, we reckon, is as much as anyone can say.

We're not "settling" down, oh no. If any of my friends (all three of them) ever say, "It's so nice to see James settled," then you have my permission to come and shoot me.

YOU: You said this book wouldn't end with a wedding.

ME: I wasn't to know, and we might change our minds—again.

YOU: Or you could rewrite the beginning.

ME: Easy. But with few exceptions I have written without the benefit of hindsight. It's a legitimate narrative method.
YOU: Oh, really?
ME: I asked Stefan.

Yes, I did say this book wouldn't end with a wedding but it has, more or less. I don't like it, but obviously I am not going to change my life to suit a book. (Hey, it does happen.) I don't like ending with a wedding, not because it's a bit fairy-tale, but because weddings and marriage kind of mean the end of a story, and I don't want our story to end. I love my story with Victoria—living it, I mean.

But just thinking about it, maybe our wedding won't be the end of our story. There's bound to be some pain, some joy, some sheer lunacy, more appalling behavior (and not just from me), some success, many failures, and above all, some tales to tell.

So let's not say this is the end of the story. But books have to end, and this is as good a place as any. Besides, Victoria is calling me, the dinner smells good and I have thought of something nice to say.

THE END
(OF THE BOOK, NOT THE STORY.)

Bill Dare is a writer and comedy producer. He created *Dead Ringers*, was the originating producer of *The Mary Whitehouse Experience*, and produced eight series of *Spitting Image*. He has produced many radio shows such as *The Now Show* and *The News Quiz*, wrote *Life, Death and Sex with Mike & Sue* and writes for *The Sunday Format*. Bill welcomes feedback from readers. Email him at billdare2@blueyonder.co.uk.